SUSAN, YOU'RE THE CHOSEN ONE

WELCOME TO MIDLIFE MAGIC

LAURETTA HIGNETT

Copyright © 2024 by Lauretta Hignett

All rights reserved.

No part of this publication may be reproduced, distributed, or transmitted in any form or by any means, including photocopying, recording, or other electronic or mechanical methods, without the prior written permission of the publisher, except as permitted by U.S. copyright law. For permission requests, contact Lauretta Hignett info@laurettahignett.com

The story, all names, characters, and incidents portrayed in this production are fictitious. No identification with actual persons (living or deceased), places, buildings, and products is intended or should be inferred.

No generative AI used at any time in the story and artworks of this book.

Editing by Cissell Ink

Book Cover by Covers By Christian

Character Art by AtraLuna Graphic Design

First Edition 2024

SUSAN

CHAPTER ONE

"Hey!" I hissed, keeping my voice low. I didn't want to startle the people who'd interrupted my dinner party by setting off fireworks and making a racket on the communal rooftop garden. All four of them were balanced precariously on the wall, facing away from me, looking out over the city—and, weirdly enough, wearing what looked like Lord of the Rings elf cosplay.

Models, of course. Three jaw-droppingly handsome men, and one stunning young woman. All of them stood on the wall, posing perfectly, surveying the skyline of San Francisco like superheroes.

My heart thudded; one little slip, one stray gust of wind, and they would plunge fifty floors and hit the pavement like a Renfaire tote bag filled with minestrone.

"Get down from there," I stage-whispered, mindful that they were probably filming. "Do you have any idea how high up we are?"

One of the men had already turned slightly; his eyes flicked towards me, one hand on his dagger.

I almost snorted. Method actors. Young people these

days were so dramatic. "Listen, I don't want to ruin your shoot, but get off the wall," I told them. "It's dangerous. Someone might get hurt. This has got to be an OSHA violation."

It was safe to assume there was a producer or director hiding somewhere. They clearly had a massive budget, with the actors wearing impressively realistic battle leathers and loaded with prop weapons—gleaming long swords strapped to their backs and jeweled daggers at their hips.

They were obviously using our apartment's communal rooftop garden to do a photoshoot—possibly illegally and without permission, since it was the tallest privately-owned apartment building in Lower Nob Hill, but that was none of my business. I just wanted them to *not* fall to their deaths. And be a little quieter, if possible.

I knew they didn't live in the building; I'd definitely remember them if I'd seen them before. Two of the men looked to be in their mid-twenties, one with dark skin, a shaved head, and the muscles of a bodybuilder, and the other one more lithe, with shoulder-length tousled blond hair.

The last one was slightly older, I thought, and taller. He was blessed with the most perfect warrior proportions, with long dark hair pulled up into a messy topknot.

The woman was younger than the others—a raven-haired beauty, barely out of her teens, with the longest legs and tightest butt I'd ever seen in my life. She quickly turned her head and glanced towards me. Her glass-green eyes were shockingly bright, and they widened in surprise when they fell on me.

I stifled my groan and waited for the rest of them to turn around and call me a "Karen" for ruining their shoot.

One of the worst parts of getting older as a woman these days was being dismissed as a "Karen" if you complained about anything. It was so unfair. Sure, there were lots of entitled women who needed to mind their own damn business, except the name was thrown around like confetti and used as a pejorative to dismiss and belittle any woman who complained about *anything*.

It wouldn't bother me so much if there was a male equivalent to a Karen, but there wasn't.

Well, there was. He wasn't called a Karen, though. He was called an "active shooter."

The tallest model—the one with the insanely beautiful proportions—shifted on his feet, turning slowly to face me, so graceful for such a big man. He moved as smoothly as oil on water, effortlessly, like it was nothing, but his movements hinted at an explosive power coiled inside him, simmering just beneath the surface of his smooth tanned skin. I felt like I was watching a huge, terrifying predatory cat turn to size up his prey.

I caught a glimpse of his profile and swallowed roughly, totally unprepared for how shockingly, brutally handsome he was. High cheekbones, the darkest emerald eyes, a carved, masculine jaw with a hint of rough stubble, perfect curved lips...

Get a grip, Susan. You're a strong, confident, mature woman.

I pointed at him sternly. "Get down from there. Someone will get hurt."

The younger two men and the woman immediately jumped off the wall and stood in a line facing me. The shockingly handsome one didn't move. He stood, staring with an inscrutable expression, looking at me like he was trying to crack my skull open with those sparkling dark emerald eyes.

Well, three of them were off the wall and safe now; I would chalk that up as a win. I backed away, opened the roof access door behind me, and scuttled backwards into the hallway. "Stay off the ledge. And keep it down, okay?"

I shut the roof access door, turned ninety degrees left, opened my own door, and walked back inside my apartment.

"Sorry about that." I bristled slightly, trying to shake off the strange, unsettled feeling the tall model provoked in me.

Bart Montgomery-Litchenstien, my work colleague, best friend, and my only guest for dinner, nodded graciously from the table, saluting me with his wine glass. "No problem, Susan. I know it can get a little loud up here." He beckoned me to sit down again. "So, what were you saying about that weasel, Richie Curran? I knew he'd applied for the same promotion as you, but I assumed you'd get it easily."

"Oh, that's what I was talking about. Okay. So." I took a deep breath. "Richie Curran threatened to expose me."

In retrospect, it might have been better to wait until Bart swallowed the sip of red wine in his mouth before I dropped this particular bombshell. He coughed, spluttered, gulped, and turned a little red himself.

"I'm sorry," he finally choked out, wiping his lips with the napkin. "He threatened to *what?*"

I crossed my legs under the tiny dining room table, bumping my knees against the air conditioning unit awkwardly. I'd given Bart the bigger side of the table. He needed it; he was a huge man, over six feet tall and very solid, with the rounded chest and belly of one of those guys who liked to do strongman competitions on the weekends. But paired with a razor-sharp dapper short-back-and-sides haircut, a manicured beard, and his purple silk dinner jacket and crisp white shirt, he looked like a giant, well-groomed teddy bear.

"It's true," I said. "Richie Curran told me to withdraw my name from the candidate pool, or he'd tell all the department managers my dirty secret."

"No." Bart stared at me from across the tiny table, his mouth open, aghast. "Richie said that to your face?"

"Uh huh."

"No beating around the bush? No subtle hints, no veiled threats?"

I sighed and picked up my own wine glass, extracting it carefully from where it was wedged between the wall, my main course dinner plate, and the vase holding a lovely arrangement of cherry blossom branches I'd stolen on the way home from work. I took a little sip, savoring it.

My tiny apartment wasn't built for dinner parties. In fact, it wasn't even built to have more than one person standing in it at a time.

In an apartment building filled with studios for single people, the only one I could afford was a half-studio; an afterthought apartment built on the very top floor of a very tall building. Most of the space on this level had been appropriated for the communal rooftop garden and lounge —some of which I could see right outside my window right now. The result was an apartment the size of a shoe box, right next to a busy communal area.

I'd been desperate for company tonight, so I folded my bed away, put my armchair in the shower, set up a tiny dining table under the one window, and invited Bart up for dinner.

Bart lived three floors below me. I adored him beyond reason. He was the only person from my former life who didn't spit on me in the street, the only person from my social circle who didn't turn their back on me when the Bad Thing happened. He was my only friend in the world.

I reached behind my back, grabbed the bottle of wine from the kitchenette counter, and splashed more into Bart's glass. He deserved much better than a seven-dollar bottle of Lindonne '22 Merlot, but it was the best I could afford, and he was gracious enough to drink it without grimacing.

"Yes, Richie said exactly that, straight to my face," I said. "While I know for a fact Richie Curran has the ability to be slimier than a snake when he wants to be, he also understands that right now, time is of the essence. He wants the promotion, and I'm standing in his way. So, he made it very clear. Withdraw, or he'd tell both Human Resources and the other department managers all about what happened. Not only will I *not* get the promotion, but it will also ruin my reputation in the office completely. Even if I don't get fired, nobody will ever take me seriously, and I'll never be able to work my way up *anywhere*. And," I added,

"Human Resources will be pissed that we fudged the details on that little gap in my resume."

When my interviewer at Base Budget Insurance had asked about the two-year-long gap in my employment, I fluttered my eyelashes demurely and told them I couldn't elaborate; there was a non-disclosure agreement in place.

Bart made a gruff noise. "You didn't lie."

"No, technically I didn't." There *was* an NDA. It had nothing to do with the gap in employment, though. "But I didn't tell them the truth, and those monstrous trolls in HR will be furious about it. Nobody in the world would be fool enough to employ me if they knew the truth."

Bart didn't disagree. He knew how important it was for me to keep the last two years of my life a secret, especially if I wanted to climb back up the corporate ladder. He frowned, glaring into his wine glass. "This does not bode well," he rumbled in his teddy-bear growl. "How did Richie find out?"

I sighed and hitched my shoulders, taking care not to bump anything. "I don't know. I'm assuming Richie did a deep dive on me after I rejected him."

Bart tipped his wine glass towards me. "I told you to report him when he did that."

"I couldn't, Bart! Imagine running off to HR on my *first day* to tell them that one of the Customer Experience and Support Team Leaders... uh... propositioned me."

It was a nice way of putting it. Richie Curran looked like a Loki cosplayer dipped in grease with his skinny, weaselly face, long black hair, and pronounced widow's peak. He'd slimed up to me at the sinks in the communal kitchen on my first day at the call center, only six months ago. He explained that it was Base Budget Insurance company culture to sleep with your co-workers, invited me into a stall to blow him, then blew it off as a joke when I very frostily declined.

"If I ran off to Human Resources to complain on my very first day," I explained. "They'd flag me as a problem. I'd be seen as a weak idiot who couldn't handle herself."

And I could definitely handle myself. I'd gotten used to it over the years. I was cursed—or blessed, depending on how you looked at it—with a very curvy figure, big boobs, a small waist, and long shapely thighs. No matter how many masculine power suits and giant nerd glasses and sensible loafers I wore, I somehow ended up looking like a poor man's Jessica Rabbit.

Even now that I was in my mid-forties and a tiny bit overweight, with sparkles of silver sprinkled through my thick, wavy dark hair, I still attracted the assholes—sleazy men who stared at my breasts and busybodies who demanded to know my ethnicity, wanting to know where I got my "exotic" coloring from. Because apparently, having light-green eyes and tanned skin was "exotic."

I used to be able to put people in their place with an arch of my eyebrow. I'd lost that ability in the last couple of years.

Along with everything else.

"I understand," Bart said. "Still, you should have reported him."

I inhaled and sighed it all out, trying not to let my deep breath bump the table. "Yes, in retrospect, I should have."

I was still pissed about being outmaneuvered on my first day. I'd been out of the game for too long; I'd lost my edge. I didn't see Richie moving his chess pieces, arranging his pawns around him to protect himself in case I did complain to Human Resources about his sleazy proposition.

"I didn't realize until it was too late," I said. "That afternoon, three other men asked me to go for a drink with them after work. When the last one approached me, I realized Richie had made sure I couldn't report *any* of them. Human Resources wouldn't believe that four men separately propositioned me on my first day in the office." I grimaced. "Richie outsmarted me."

"Hmm. You know..." Bart said, pursing his lips. "I always thought you were exaggerating about how complicated office politics are."

"Bart." I smiled at him fondly. "You're the head of the Base Budget Insurance *compliance* department. Nobody would dare mess with compliance. You know I love you, but your job is so boring I feel like my eyes are glazing over the second the elevator dings on the fourth floor. You wouldn't know office gossip if it walked up and punched you in the face."

He chuckled and examined his wine again, swirling the merlot around the big round goblet. Too late, I realized he was only holding the glass to be polite. My dinner plate had shifted forwards an inch, and there was no room on the table for him to put it down.

Smoothly, I tugged my plate forward into my chest and pushed the vase half an inch to the side, so he had a place to put his glass, which he did with a flourish.

"Could he be bluffing?" Bart said. "Are you sure he knows? Gordon and Delilah did a very good job wiping all traces of you from San Francisco society. Nobody even whispers your name anymore."

A stab of soul-crushing despair pierced my heart, penetrating through all my defenses. I inhaled sharply, still shocked at the pain it caused me. It took enormous effort to stop my hands from shaking, but I managed it, wordlessly repeating a mantra in my head, over and over. *I am a strong, confident woman. The past is the past. I forgive myself. I deserve a fresh start.*

"Richie Curran made it very clear." I swallowed, bracing myself. "He even dropped Vincent's name into the conversation."

Saying my ex-husband's name out loud hurt so much it felt like a dagger to the chest. I loved him so much. I mourned him like he was dead. The loss was so painful that I almost wished he *was* dead.

Instead, he was in my beautiful old house up in Pacific Heights, getting ready to marry his intern, a gorgeous, willowy stick-thin Irish beauty named Seraphina.

Seraphina was only twenty-four. She was nearly half my age.

I blinked. A flash of light had exploded outside the window, a sudden bright flare somewhere out in the communal rooftop garden. Someone was taking photos with a very bright camera flash, or something like that. I welcomed the distraction; it dragged me out of the painful past. And at least the models out there hadn't fallen off the edge of the building yet.

Bart peered outside the window for a second, but the light was gone. It was dark out there again. The twinkling lights of the cityscape shone merrily in the distance, leading down to oil-black water of the bay.

"Well. If he mentioned Vincent, then Richie definitely knows," he said gloomily.

I exhaled slowly, trying to keep a lid on the black fog that threatened to rise up and devour me again. "It's to be expected. Even with my surname changed, there's a lot of old photos of me at events floating around the internet. San Francisco is a big city, but I'm not naive enough to think that I'd become anonymous just because I changed my name." I swallowed. *You're a strong, mentally stable woman.* "Even with Vincent's parents trying to wipe all traces of me from the face of the earth."

A crash came from right outside. Both of us turned to look, but I could only see our reflections in the glass. I leaned closer, put my head on the glass, and peered out. From here, I could only see the fern wall on the left wall of the rooftop. Loud voices shouted furiously for a second, the young woman snapping, and one of the men arguing back in a sexy, low tone.

I stifled my groan. Apart from having half the floor space as all the other single apartments in the building, this was the worst part of living on the rooftop. Other residents could hold parties right outside my window, and there was no escaping the noise. It was the only apartment I could afford, though, and the leasing agent had only given it to me because he was a friend of Bart's.

Bart turned back to me, graciously ignoring the noise outside, and nodded thoughtfully. "Okay, so Richie knows. What are we going to do about it?"

Warmth bloomed in my chest. I smiled at him. "We?"

"Of course I'm going to help you."

"Bart..." My grin grew wider. "You are the best. I don't know what I'd do without you."

Another smash came from outside—the tell-tale tinkle of broken glass on concrete. Those damned gorgeous models were going to get broken glass all over the rooftop.

My lips thinned. "Excuse me for a second." I stood, carefully squeezing myself out from where I was jammed between the kitchen counter and the table, walked the four steps to my front door, opened it, and walked out into the hallway.

The door immediately to my left led out to the rooftop garden. I opened it with a bang and strode outside.

The cool night air breezed around me. It wasn't too cold tonight; we were still in the dying days of late summer and it wasn't as windy as usual, but goosebumps rose on my flesh anyway, just like they had before. The four stunning creatures were gathered around what appeared to be another special effects prop—a huge black circle ringed with blue fire, hovering in the air. For a second, I was fascinated, then, slightly concerned. I got my phone out of my pocket, brought up my camera app, then checked the scene in front of me through the screen.

Yes, they were really there. I wasn't hallucinating. The ring of blue fire must be a hologram.

Oh no. Too late, I realized they were all staring at me, and I was holding my phone up. It looked like I was filming them.

Karen mode activated. Goddamnit.

I whipped my phone away. I could hardly yell at them

for the broken glass now. I sighed deeply. "Just... just make sure you clean up after yourselves, okay?"

Before they could respond, I turned around and marched back to my apartment.

Bart stood in the middle of the room. He'd obviously very politely used my absence to remove himself from where he'd been wedged in between the wall and the dining room table. Now, standing up, all six-foot-two inches of enormous teddy bear almost filled my whole apartment.

"I'm so sorry, Bart," I said. "There's a group of models doing a photoshoot on the roof."

"Aha," he winked at me. "Let's go watch. Maybe we could make friends with them."

Like me, Bart loved beauty in all things—in art, in decor, in people, it didn't matter. If it was gorgeous, Bart would admire it.

"I'm afraid I might have Karen-ed myself out of making friends," I sighed.

"Understandable. Well, I should head off anyway," he said, draining his wine. "Bobby just texted me; he's on his way to come and shout at me again."

"What did you do this time?" Bart's on-again-off-again boyfriend was one of the best food critics on the West Coast.

"I was supposed to join him at Cloud this evening."

A warm feeling bloomed in my chest. Cloud was the hottest restaurant in the city. If you wanted to dine there, you had to make a reservation six months in advance and provide two years' worth of tax returns to prove you could afford it.

I smiled. "And you turned him down for my ham-fisted attempt at sheep's milk ricotta with sage and browned butter ravioli?" I hadn't eaten any of it myself; I was saving it for my lunch tomorrow. It was lucky that budgeting was in my blood because at the moment, I couldn't afford to eat more than twice a day.

He grinned at me. "Your company was much better." He inclined his head graciously. "Thank you for a lovely evening, Susan. And don't worry about Richie Curran. You'll figure out something. Nobody could ever get you down, so don't let that slimy creep be the first."

"Thanks, Bart." I hugged him and plastered myself up against the wall so he could exit my apartment.

It didn't really matter that my apartment was no bigger than a shoebox; as soon as Bart left, it felt big and empty. One of the hardest things about my new life was adjusting to being lonely. For fifteen years, Vincent had always been right there next to me; we were twin stars, peas in a pod, soulmates—Vincent, the gorgeous, blazingly talented painter who set the art world on fire, and me, the vice president at Orwan Bank, occasional board member, the corporate hotshot on her way to senior vice president status.

Vincent and I had everything. There was only one thing we didn't have. And I couldn't give it to him, so everything else crumbled into dust.

Now, I was barely the team leader at the call center of a shitty insurance company, and Vincent was in our bed, in our house, with his young, pregnant intern.

Stop it, Susan. I gave myself a stern talking to as I gathered up the dinner plates and washed them in my tiny sink, trying—and failing—to resist the temptation to chug the rest of the wine right out of the bottle. *You're a strong, capable woman. You can rebuild your life.*

Despair punched me in the chest for a second. Rebuilding would be a whole lot easier if I could have escaped San Francisco to start my life afresh where nobody knew me. I couldn't, though; it was a condition of my release that I stay in a familiar location.

The rooftop access door banged open; I exhaled, relieved. The models were leaving. Now, I could wallow in misery, in blessed silence.

There was a knock at my door.

CHAPTER

TWO

I frowned. What did they want? It was obviously the models from before; my afterthought apartment wasn't as carefully insulated as the others. I could hear them as clearly as if there was no door between us, arguing amongst themselves about whether or not this was necessary. One of the men spoke in a low, gruff tone—a too-sexy voice that sent shivers down my spine. "Waste your time if you wish, Cress. You have my permission."

Ah. The girl was coming to have it out with me for interrupting their shoot, and the men were still in character. Well, I was in the mood for a fight. Taking the three steps from my kitchenette towards the front door, I yanked it open.

All four of them stood in the hallway, taking up every inch of space, and my breath hitched in my throat. Maybe I was conditioned to appreciate beauty more than the average person, but these four were jaw-droppingly stunning. Their warrior-elf cosplay only made them seem more beautiful, more otherworldly. Or maybe it was their eyes, which were obviously some sort of new contact lenses that made their eyes glow.

The young woman stood in front; her eyes were the biggest and flashed light green. Good grief, she was beautiful, with smooth, dark tan skin, so bouncy and firm I itched to suck every little bit of collagen out of her like some sort of deranged vampire with a plastic surgery addiction. She had high cheekbones and a pointed chin, along with silky raven-colored hair framing her features perfectly. Long arms, even longer legs, both wrapped in what looked like alligator leather.

I eyed it carefully. It must be faux, although the variation in texture was impressive. I met her eye, resisting the urge to look at the men behind her. "Can I help you?" I asked sweetly.

The girl lifted her chin, meeting my gaze fearlessly. "Susan Moore?"

Oh, shit. They'd gotten into my mailbox. The last thing I

needed was to get hit by a lawsuit for interrupting an expensive photo shoot. My income was already being severely depleted by alimony and restitution payments. I shook my head and grinned at her. "Nope."

She frowned. "You are not Susan Moore?"

"No. Sorry."

She glanced into my tiny apartment, looking behind me. "Molinere is not with you?"

"I'm sorry?"

The girl met my eye again. "The instructor. Molinere."

Who the hell was Molinere? At least this time, I didn't have to lie. "I don't know anyone by that name."

"You are sure?" She leaned a little closer, lowering her voice. "You are *not* the chosen one?"

"What?" I reared back, confused. Then, finally, realization dawned.

They were still cosplaying. This was probably some sort of YouTube prank, one of those ones where the prankster approached people in the street, pretending to be on a quest, giving strange instructions, and waiting to see what the confused victim said or did.

I cleared my throat. "Oh, no, indeed not, my lady, I fear I am *not* the chosen one." I tossed my hair back dramatically for the benefit of the hidden cameras. "Nay, but if the chosen one you shall seek, you shall find her in her abode, yonder, directly across here." I pointed in the direction of my bathroom. "You must traverse down, step foot on the hallowed ground, and enter the domicile next door. Rise near to the sky, to, er, apartment forty-two, and seek the one which you call the 'chosen'—the Songbird of Nob Hill, the Fair Lady Audrina."

Audrina would get a kick out of this. She loved all those angsty teenage fantasy novels. I often saw her out on her balcony, reading something with a bare-chested pointy-eared man on the cover. And, if these beautiful idiots were cosplaying hard enough to follow my instructions and find Audrina's apartment, it would cheer her up a bit. Nobody deserved a pick-me-up more than my teenage neighbor.

The beautiful girl in front of me frowned with her whole face. "You are sure? It is not you, Susan, the chosen one?"

"Nay." I frowned just as deeply, shaking my head forlornly. "Go henceforth, young company, and find she who you seek."

"Cress," the tall man at the back growled. "I warned you this is a waste of time. Come." He strode off down the hallway, out of sight.

My eyes mourned the loss of him.

Then, immediately, I told my eyes to go fuck themselves. We did not spend time mooning over gorgeous men, no matter how good they looked in black battle leathers.

What the hell was wrong with me? Oh, yeah, that's right. Menopause-induced paranoid schizophrenia, intermittent explosive disorder, oppositional defiant disorder, acute psychosis, and rage.

The other three models followed him immediately, without another word.

CHAPTER
THREE

I shut the door, chuckling to myself, hoping that they'd keep doing their crazy cosplay and find Audrina in the building next door. She'd looked so sad this morning; she could use a little fun pick-me-up. Although, if her evil mother answered the door, the cosplayers' fun would end very quickly.

I moved around my apartment, doing the last of my tidying-up, putting my folding table away, making room for my armchair, and arranging the cherry blossoms on the windowsill. I walked into my miniature bathroom, took the armchair out of my shower, put it back underneath my window, and walked back into the bathroom to wash my face and do my skin routine.

Without even craning my head, I could see Audrina from the tiny bathroom window. As usual, she was sitting on the balcony, strumming her guitar, singing too softly for me to hear, sadness emanating from every pore.

My heart just about broke every time I saw her. I watched her for a while, listening as she worked on a beautiful new song, while I cleansed, toned, moisturized, retinol-ized, and waited to see if Audrina would be summoned inside.

After twenty minutes, I gave up. If the cosplayers had found the right place and knocked on her door, Audrina's mother, Jessica, wasn't letting them in to see her.

I opened my bathroom window wider, stuck my head out. "Good night, Audrina," I called out. "I love the new song."

She looked up. "Thanks, Sue." She brushed her bushy orange hair back and smiled a very crooked smile. "See you in the park tomorrow afternoon?"

I nodded. My heart clenched again. Audrina smiled like that because her top lip had a very pronounced bow, and her mother hated it. Jessica herself had lips that looked like car tires, over inflated with too much filler. And Audrina's hair was naturally a very light wavy brown, but in her yearly bid to try and mold Audrina into something that she would consider attractive, Jessica had taken her to a celebrity hairdresser, who had bleached it, aiming for a caramel-blonde balayage. But after just one shampoo the toner had washed out, leaving her with a wild mess of frizzy orange Koko the Clown hair. Jessica had gone back to ignoring her.

Audrina was only seventeen, and her self-confidence was already ruined. I was forty-five, and my own had only recently been destroyed. At least Audrina had time—and collagen—on her side.

I sighed into the mirror and told myself sternly I still looked great for my age. My face hadn't collapsed just yet. I was lucky to inherit my mother's complexion—an odd creamy-tan combination of her Greek, Portuguese, Danish, Malawi, Brazilian, and Japanese heritage—and not my Australian father's ruddy pale-and-pink freckled White-

Colonizer-turned-Convict skin. My lips had thinned slightly, which wasn't a bad thing; they'd been almost too full when I was younger. And thanks to a strict application of sunscreen twice a day, every day, for my entire life, I only had a light spider web of laugh lines at my temple and around my eyes.

I went back into my living room and changed, exchanging my dress for my nightgown, brushed the wall curtain aside and pulled down my bed, trying to keep the sadness at bay. This time—the moments before I took my meds and lay down to try and sleep—they were the worst for me.

I couldn't stop the loneliness. It ate into me, taking little bites out of all the things I'd done in the day to try and fill my cup, like a starving dog escaping a cage, desperate for happy mice to eat. Too late, I regretted finishing the bottle of wine; the alcohol dulled my mental armor.

I could feel the depression snapping at me. My beautiful dinner with Bart meant nothing when I was forced to hold it in a shoebox apartment where I had to suck in my tummy to get into my seat. My sexy black lacy nightgown was useless because I was all alone, with nobody else here to appreciate it. My clean, shiny skin meant nothing when it was likely going to collapse soon, like the dried-up old bag I was. Nobody would ever love me again. Not like Vincent used to love me.

Goddamnit, the memory of Vincent hit me like a gut punch—handsome, shambolic, helpless, talented, so warm, sexy, and so unintentionally funny. Vincent, who would forget to wear a shirt down to the corner store and wander in, covered in paint, blissfully unaware of the women gaping at his beautiful, lithe body and his messy, tousled dirty-blond Christ-like hair.

I'd lost him, and it was all my fault. I should have taken my mental health more seriously.

I'd hurt him. I'd almost *killed* him.

My front door banged; someone had snuck up the corridor outside and smacked on it with their fist. Sitting here on my bed, I was so close to my front door, and the knock was too loud. It scared me so much I jumped almost a foot in the air. Immediately, heat built in my stomach. I clenched my fists and counted to calm myself down to prevent my hormones from taking over. *I control my mind. My mental illness does not control me. I control my mind...*

The door banged again, and I jumped to my feet. Mantras weren't working. "Fuck off!"

"Susan Moore," a woman's voice called out. "We must speak with you."

I groaned. The hot models were back. "Go away!"

There was a pause, then, the sound of feet shifting on the hallway outside. The low, growling voice of a man drifted through my door. "Open this door now, or I will remove it."

"Is that a threat? Are you threatening me?"

His voice dropped so low it was almost a vibration, rolling over my skin, setting me to a tingle, and raising delicious goosebumps. "It's not a threat," he growled. "It's a promise. Open. This. Door."

I shook myself. *No, Susan. Down. Bad girl. Not sexy. No.* "Well," I called out. "I'm sure the superintendent will have something to say about—"

A bright green flash lit up the room, and suddenly, I was face-to-face with the tall, brutally handsome man. My door had disappeared.

CHAPTER
FOUR

I closed my eyes, breathing in through my nose and out through my mouth, repeating my mantras over and over. *I am in control. I am strong, and capable. I am firmly rooted in reality.* After a minute, I opened my eyes.

Goddamnit, they were still standing there. My door had not reappeared.

I scowled. It was a trick of some sort. "What did you just do?"

The man stepped forward. "I did what I told you I would." His voice was soft, but there was nothing gentle about it. He appeared to be having as much trouble with controlling his temper as me. "You didn't open the door as I ordered, so I removed it."

"How did you remove it?"

"I sent it elsewhere."

I cocked an eyebrow. "Elsewhere?"

"Somewhere in my own realm. Now that the way is clear, and we can enter your domain to speak to you, I will return it."

I stared at him for a full minute. The *audacity*.

An obvious thought occurred to me, and I groaned out loud. "Richie Curran put you up to this, didn't he?"

I let out a bitter huff of laughter. Richie wanted the promotion bad enough to hire models to make me think I'd gone insane again. Of course. "He hired you to mess with me, right? It's overkill, but I have to admit, it's creative. You guys must have cost him a fortune."

The beautiful man frowned, his brow furrowing deeply. "We are not in anyone's employ. Back up now, so we may enter."

"Fine, fine. Let's get this over with." I turned and lifted my bed up again so I had enough space to move away from the door, pirouetted, and gave them all a dazzling smile. "Come on in!"

The tall one—obviously the leader, he was truly owning his Alpha role—strode into the tiny space and stopped just over the threshold. The girl—who I assumed was his girlfriend, since they were obviously close and perfectly matched in beauty—glided in close behind him, her proud chin lifted, eyes taking in my whole tiny space in a fraction of a second, then, she frowned. "What is this place?"

"It's my apartment."

The two other men gave each other an awkward glance. There wasn't enough room in my apartment for them to come in.

The leader glowered down at me. "We must talk. Extend the wall, so we may all enter."

I shook my head, confused. "You want me to do *what* now?"

He stared at me. A muscle in his jaw ticked. Give that man an Oscar. "Extend it. We are wasting time."

I rolled my eyes. I hadn't blazed my way through the corporate jungle that was the San Francisco finance industry by rolling over every time an arrogant man ordered me to do something. "No, honey. *You're* wasting time. Don't get me wrong; if you haven't agreed on a billable set of hours for this job, feel free to milk that slimy bastard for whatever you can get. Otherwise, just get on with whatever speech you've got prepared, put my door back, and go home."

The leader's dark emerald eyes flashed; a deep, furious rage snarled at me from the depths of his iris. If I hadn't already danced on the edge of total oblivion, I would probably be quite scared right now.

When you laugh in the face of madness, you're not easily intimidated. Richie Curran didn't know who he was dealing with.

"Your Highness." The dark, overly muscly one in the hallway called out. "I will do it."

"Ooh." I winked up at him as he maneuvered his broad shoulders inside. "Your Highness. A prince, is he? That's a nice touch."

The muscled man faced my wall and clapped his hands once. Blue flames erupted from his palms.

I stumbled back as adrenaline surged through me. I couldn't even force out a scream. Speechless, I watched as he pushed the blue flames out from his palms, directing a surge of energy towards the wall closest to him. It shrank back. He pushed again, and it retreated with a subsonic rumble.

This isn't real. This is *not* real.

He pushed one more time; the flames pushed my apartment wall three more feet back. My whole living space was now double what it had been. Finally, he clapped his hands together and pulled them apart, creating a circle of flames in mid-air. The blond one strode in and reached inside the circle.

His hand disappeared. I gasped.

He pulled it out and tossed a little brown stick behind him. The stick stretched out as it flew through the air, expanding into my front door with a loud *pop*.

Both men arranged themselves behind the leader, armored muscular arms crossed over their chests, staring at me, while the beautiful girl lounged in the background, bright-green eyes flashing in the dim light of the room.

"Susan Moore," the leader rumbled, pulling my focus back to his perfect lips. "You are the Chosen One."

"Oh, no," I mumbled. My lips felt numb. "It's happening again."

CHAPTER
FIVE

I sat down in the armchair by the window, thumbing at my phone. Who should I call first? Not my psychiatrist; Dr. Byron was hard to get hold of even when I had an appointment. All he ever did was prescribe me pills, anyway, and judging by the hallucinations filling my apartment right now, the pills weren't working.

My therapist? I liked her a whole lot more. I had Bronwyn on speed-dial, but it was eleven at night, and she had a jiu jitsu tournament this weekend; she needed her rest. For a wild moment, I considered calling my parole officer.

No. Maybe I could just ride this out. Maybe it was just an episode brought on by a quick drop in estrogen. Maybe this time I really was going through menopause. That's what the official diagnosis had been two years ago, even though I continued to get my period like clockwork every month.

The leader loomed over me. The fury vibrating off him was almost visible, like a radioactive corona. "Woman. What are you doing?"

It's just an episode, I told myself. Just little hallucinations. You can ride it out. At least I hadn't tried to kill anyone yet.

A cold fear clutched me. Or had I?

I dialed Bart's number hastily and exhaled with relief when he answered. "Hello, Susan," he said. "Did you miss me already?"

"I was just making sure you got home okay."

He chuckled. "Yes, I managed to traverse the twelve steps downstairs safely. Thank you for a wonderful dinner."

"You're welcome," I managed.

"It was much nicer than sitting in a too-dark room eating dehydrated mushroom chips and listening to someone bitch about how hard it is to get a duck fat stain out of his eight-hundred-dollar chinos."

A voice hissed in the background.

Aha. Bobby was there already. "I won't keep you, Bart. Just making sure you're safe and sound."

"I am, Sue." His voice softened. "Goodnight."

"Goodnight." I hung up and breathed out slowly.

Bart wasn't just being kind. He'd always told me the truth. He was a loyal friend; I trusted him completely.

Bart's loyalty was, in part, because I'd stood up for him a few years ago, when his bitchy ex-boyfriend not only outed him to his very old, very conservative rich lobbyist parents, but also plastered near-naked photos of Bart, wearing a leather harness and assless chaps, all over his popular blog. His mother and father publicly disowned him, which in itself was awful, but Bart was independently wealthy and not very fond of his mean, crusty upper-class parents, anyway. The thing that had hurt him the most was how delighted some of our friends were about his humiliation.

At the time, I'd been shocked at the vitriol spewed against Bart from his friends. We were an arty crowd; we were supposed to be progressive, open-minded, and understanding. The mocking and teasing from our social circle had been relentless, and it had hurt even more since Bart was a very dignified and private person.

He didn't deserve that kind of torture, so I decided to do something about it. Back then, all I had to do was throw a dinner party in my enormous dining room, invite our wide circle of friends, and make subtle jabs about their cruel behavior until all of them felt quite ashamed of themselves.

Now, I had nothing. None of them would even make eye contact with me in the street. Not because I was dangerous—even though I obviously was, considering what I'd done to Vincent. They probably could have gotten over the fact I'd gone crazy during early menopause and tried to kill my husband. But I also had the audacity to let myself go and lose my entire fortune at the same time. Apparently, being both poor and a little overweight was unforgivable.

Luckily for me, Bart returned my tiny favor by sticking by me. He was the reason I had a job and an apartment in the first place.

"We cannot stay here while we are in this realm. This abode is *not* acceptable." The girl—Cress, they called her—was suddenly in front of me. "Chosen... Where is Molinere?"

I stared into her face and made a snap decision to play along with my hallucinations until my hormones stabilized enough—or, until I could get hold of Bronwyn. I could talk it out with her and come up with an action plan.

"Okay. I'll bite." I rose to my feet, lifted my chin, and put my shoulders back, facing the girl directly. "Who is Molinere?"

"The one sent to prepare you in case you were needed," she replied, her tone a shade testy. "The *múinteoir*. Where is he?"

I shrugged. It was only more evidence that I'd gone nuts. The name Molinere was strange, but I realized I'd heard it before. My scrambled-egg brain was just plucking things out of old memories and repurposing them.

"I honestly couldn't tell you," I replied. "I don't know where he is."

A man named Molinere had shown up at my house when I was eight years old, as part of a work crew that my mother had hired to landscape the garden one summer when it got too much for her to handle. I only remembered him because he was tiny and odd-looking—four feet tall with messy gray hair and a big, bulbous nose. I also remembered because my father happened to breeze back into my life that day. Dad brought a bottle of whiskey with him to celebrate his return and invited the work crew to join him for a welcome-back drink. Twelve hours later, my father and the work crew were all naked and dancing around a bonfire in the garden.

I smiled back at the beautiful hallucination glaring at me. "The last time I saw Molinere, I was eight years old, and he was butt-naked, trying to jump over our burning pergola without singeing the hair on his balls."

It was a good thing my father had taken off again that day. My mother would have skinned him alive. Every time she tried to bring a semblance of order to our life, my dad swanned back in with a bottle of bubbly and a charming wink and left with a trail of soot and destruction behind him.

Cress pinched her brow. "Molinere didn't stay with you? He didn't prepare you?"

"No."

The tall man let out a growl, deep in his chest, and turned towards the other two men. "Nate."

The dark one with the muscles snapped to attention and nodded. "Yes, my Prince."

"Go back, and see if you can get to the Under without bargaining anything. Ask for an audience with your aunt, and check the death roll for Molinere's name."

"Yes, my Prince."

"I mean it, Nate. Don't bargain anything, don't offer any favors. If Morganna's hounds won't let you into the Under without a favor, come straight back to me."

The dark man bowed. "I will, my Prince." He took a step back, weaving his hands around in a circle in a very dramatic manner. Silver sparkles flowed from his fingertips, creating a glittery frame in the air.

"Ooh." I nodded, impressed. I might have gone completely insane, but at least this time my hallucinations were pretty. Not like last time, when my brain vomited up the most horrific thing I could possibly imagine. "Well done," I told myself. "Very nice."

Suddenly, the hallucination I'd called Nate stuck his hands in the middle of the glitter circle and pushed out, widening the frame, before he jumped inside it and disappeared.

I clapped. Maybe this episode wouldn't be so bad after all.

Cress stared at me. "What is wrong with you?"

"You know what? They never really gave me an official diagnosis; they just provided a list of the most likely ones. Would you like the list?"

The beautiful prince grimaced. "I already regret sending Nate to check the death roll. There is no point. Cress, I told you that we do not need her."

She straightened up. "We do, Donovan. Of course we do. She is the Chosen One."

The prince—Donovan—grimaced. "She is not Chosen. She fell into the role by quirk of her birth."

"Then she is the Chosen. She is the only one in all the realms who can help us, Donovan."

He threw me a look of such blistering contempt, it almost scorched me. "She has no idea who she is. Molinere did not train her. She does not know what she is capable of. Even if she could help, she has no understanding of what she should do." He let out a dismissive, manly grunt. "I told you from the start we should focus on finding the spark stones first and hiding them before he could get to them."

Cress gave a delicate snort. "Even if we did, the danger remains. The stones need to be closed, or Connor will devour them and absorb their power. And the only person in all the realms that can do that is her."

"Ooh," I murmured. "Interesting. I should write this down."

Cress and Donovan turned to stare at me.

"No," I said. "Keep going, this is great stuff. Audrina's always talking about things like this in her crazy fantasy novels. If this episode has a good ending, I might see if I can pitch it to someone. Once I'm sane again, obviously."

After a long moment of silence, Cress cursed. "You do not know what you are."

"Nope," I said cheerfully. "I mean, apart from the fact that I'm the chosen one, obviously. Tell me. This should be good."

"You are the Chosen One because you are the only One of Every Blood." I could even hear her put capitals on the letters.

"Great, great," I nodded. "Now, what do you mean by 'every blood'?"

"You are the only creature in existence who carries the

blood of every species of every realm," Cress answered. "Your heritage includes everyone from the lower, middle, and upper Worlds. You are a mix of imp, demon, wraith, human, vampire, dragon, shifter, berserker, fae, elf, scribe, elemental…"

I snorted. "Okay. Here I am thinking I'm just a mostly white mixed-race girl, but it's nice that my brain wants me to feel super-special." I smiled up at her. "So, what are my powers?"

"You do not know." Cress looked horrified. "Even if you did not know what you are, you must know what you could do. There is no way you could suppress the power inside of you. To ignore it could lead to catastrophe. "

"Okayyy," I said, still smiling and nodding. "Is it like, the power of love? The power of heart? The power to make a delicious scallop linguine?"

"It means you can move between any of the realms without having to beg or borrow a Key. Your blood grants you access to all Worlds. Not only that, but you can also move the atoms in any realm. And that is where your destiny lies. You must—"

Donovan slammed his hand down on the counter, and I jumped. "Cress," he growled. "We are wasting time. The scribe stone is in this city, and he is hunting it now. We must find it before Connor does."

"We need her, my liege." The blond one finally piped up. "Now that he knows their power, nothing is safe until the stones are closed. The prophecy—"

"Damn the prophecy!" Donovan roared.

I jumped to my feet and clapped my hands twice. "Inside voices, please!" My hallucinations were getting a little testy; it was time to take control of them.

It was probably the best way to handle this episode, anyway. This bunch of colorful characters weren't much different from the team I managed at Base Budget Insurance. I had twelve staff underneath me, and they all had unique personalities and required careful handling. In fact, Cress's whole goth-warrior-badass aesthetic was quite similar to what Cora, one of the girls in my team, would gush over on Pinterest.

Silver sparkles erupted from nowhere, forming a circle, and Nate reappeared, straightening his enormous, muscled shoulders. "I'm sorry, my Prince. My aunt would not see me."

"Thank you for trying, Nate." Donovan let out a gruff sigh.

My curiosity pricked me. Nate's story must be a fun subplot; hopefully, I'd get to it. Follow the story to the conclusion, and they'd go away. And if they didn't, I'd ask Dr. Byron for the strongest antipsychotics he could prescribe.

"Okay, team." I clapped my hands again. "Let's focus. First, I'll open with an apology. I regret that I don't have the skillset that you were expecting, but it can be easily remedied. I am a very fast learner, and I promise you I will do my best to get up to speed." I turned my head, deliberately holding eye contact with each one of my hallucinations in the same way I'd do with the twelve lunatics I managed during our team meetings. *Build rapport. Get them on your side.* "But I need your full cooperation. In order to get up to speed, I need to know the details. We have a problem that needs to be solved, but I prefer to think positively. Problems are just goals to achieve. So. What is our goal?"

They all stared at me in silence. Finally, Cress blinked her big eyes. "To stop Connor from devouring the spark stones, absorbing the intrinsic power of every creature in every realm, and becoming an all-powerful tyrant?"

"Fantastic." I gave her a big smile. "Thanks, Cress! That's very helpful information." Positive reinforcement did wonders for every individual on the team. I just had to get the rest on board. Donovan would be the most unwilling; he reminded me of Thomas, the grumpy old bastard operator who'd worked in the call center for two decades. Thomas's tenure extended through five company name changes and at least two dozen team leaders, and he'd been a thorn in the side of every single one. Yvette, my department manager, had warned me about him when I started managing the team.

I had him eating out of my hand after a week. The trick was to knock his confidence first, then make him feel special. Right now, Donovan was disengaged—slumped over my kitchenette counter with his palm over his eyes—so I'd have to ignore him until he tried to get my attention, then ignore him some more to bring him down a peg or two.

I moved further into my kitchenette, pulled a whiteboard marker from a drawer, and popped the lid. "So, our goal is to stop Connor." In big letters, I wrote on my refrigerator *Goal = Stop Connor*. "Now, forgive me, you'll have to fill me in a bit more." Turning, I pointed with my marker at Nate, the dark muscly one. "Who is Connor?"

"He is Prince Donovan's younger brother," he answered immediately. "He is second-in-line to the throne of the Kingdom of the Crystal Gardens."

"Fantastic, thank you, Nate! Now..." I pointed at the blond one. "I'm so sorry, I didn't catch your name."

He stiffened. "I am Eryk." He bowed.

I gave him a warm smile. "It's lovely to meet you, Eryk."

Eryk's eyes widened very slightly.

Turning, I tapped the fridge. "Okay, so Eryk, please tell me if I've got this wrong, but I feel like I need to stop and summarize our goal. This Connor person is hunting these spark stones, correct? And these stones hold special powers?"

"Yes, my lady."

Ooh. That was a new one. Usually my team called me "boss" when I used my managerial rapport skills. "Fantastic," I said, writing down *spark stones* on my refrigerator. "Can you please elaborate on the spark stones a little bit? Tell me how they function."

"Uh, yes, my lady. The spark stones are primordial material from when the realms were brought into being. They are crystals that contain the essence of each realm. Each one is usually located at the center of their realm and is packed with the raw power and magic of that world."

"They are the first building block of every part of our universe," Cress butted in. "They—"

"Sorry, Cress." I held up a finger. "I understand you have something to share, but please wait until Eryk is finished."

Her eyes narrowed dangerously. I didn't flinch; instead, I gave her my "down, bitch" stare—a look I'd perfected during my stockbroker days. *I am in control here. Back off.*

After a long moment, I turned and wrote *spark stone = raw power magic crystal* on the refrigerator. "Eryk, please go on. Can you give me an example of a spark stone, and what it might do?"

He shifted on his feet uncomfortably for a second, watching Cress from the corner of his eye. "Yes, my lady. Every realm has their own stone, and that stone vibrates with magic. That magic seeps out to the rest of the realm, giving life to the world and the creatures in it."

"So, all those creatures you mentioned before," I said, tapping the marker against my chin. "The vampires, the shifters, the elves… they all have their own spark stones in their own realms?"

"Yes, my lady."

"And this Connor character—the Prince's little brother—wants to 'devour' these stones."

"Yes, my lady."

"Why?"

Nate tentatively put his hand up. Donovan, still slumped over the counter, let out a groan.

I ignored him. "Yes, Nate?"

"The stones are living things," he said. "They contain the essence of a realm's magic. You must understand, my lady—Connor may be brother to my liege, but they are opposites. My liege sacrifices everything for the safety and wellbeing of his people. Connor only serves himself."

I nodded. Nate, the kiss-ass, was trying to get me to like Donovan, the popular guy in the group. This was what happened when the team hierarchy was unsettled; the members tried to reestablish the status quo.

Donovan might be the popular one, but I was a boss. I turned my back on Donovan completely, subtly indicating with my body that he was not important to me at all. "So, Connor is trying to find all these spark stones, so he can eat them and take their magic."

Nate and Eryk both nodded.

"Where are the spark stones usually kept?" I pointed with my marker. "Cress?"

"Most are usually located deep under the earth, in the center of each realm," she replied automatically. "But as Connor began his evil quest, each realm began to take steps to hide them. In most cases, Elders have been entrusted with the stones."

"Okay. So, each realm has a stone, and most of them are hidden. Connor is trying to find them and eat them." I clicked the cap on my marker. "So... where do I come in?"

"As the Chosen, the One of Every Blood, only you have

the power to close the stones. To stop them vibrating and emanating magic," Cress explained patiently. "If you close them, their magic will condense and retreat to the center of the stone. The realm's magic will protect itself and hibernate beneath an impenetrable crystal crust."

"And what's the point of that?"

"If they are closed, they are worthless to the Devourer. Their magic cannot be absorbed. If he tries, the stone will pass right through without consequence."

I held back a snigger. My hallucinations wanted me to work some magic and get my imaginary villain to poop out a whole rock.

"If they are devoured while they are active," Cress went on. "The magic is drained from the stone and absorbed by the Devourer. He will take some of their unique power. And in time, *all* magic will fade from that realm. Forever."

"Right. That sounds serious. And Connor has done this before?"

"Yes." Cress nodded. "It started a long time ago, in our own Upper World. Connor entered another fae realm adjacent to ours—the Kingdom of the Creatives—with the view to court one of the princesses. In a bid to impress him, the princess showed him their spark stone. Connor was entranced, and for some reason, he was compelled to devour it."

"He saw something pretty, and he thought he should... eat it?" That was something a toddler would do.

"The stones vibrate with power." Donovan's low, rumbling voice echoed through the room. Damn, his voice really was something. "My brother has always craved power. He would have held the stone, and his instincts would have screamed at him to consume—"

"Right." I cut him off. "Tell me, Nate." I pointed at him

with my marker. "What happened to Connor when he devoured the Creative's spark stone?"

"He absorbed a core element of their magic."

"The magic of expression?"

"It is a great and powerful magic," Donovan's voice rumbled through the room again. "Do not underestimate—"

"I don't," I said icily, cutting him off again. "I know how powerful the magic of expression is. I know what a great power it is to make someone cry with a painting or a sculpture. To be able to imbue art with so much meaning so it provokes great emotion is truly magical." This was my hallucination, goddamnit. I knew what I was talking about. I didn't need someone to mansplain it to me, even if he was an imaginary man.

Donovan stared at me. I held his gaze, then tapped the fridge again, and wrote *creative stone = the power of expression.* "I'm guessing the magic made him better at manipulating people."

Nobody answered me. I turned around and raised an eyebrow. It was my "come on, people, please don't disappoint me" face.

"Uh, yes, my lady," Eryk said hastily. "That is exactly what it did."

"Great. What else has he devoured?"

"A handful of others. Most were from magically weak realms, because he found them easier to infiltrate and rob, but all the stones still gifted him with some magical power. The banshee stone, which gave him the power of knowing when someone will die, and the eovine stone, which helps him sense where someone's loyalties lie, and the *eeek eeek peonnak* stone, which—"

I held up my hand. I was obviously getting tired; my hallucinations were getting sloppy. "Okay. So, if I close a spark stone, that realm's magic will be protected, and the little brother won't be able to absorb the magic. Are there any other side effects from closing the stones?" I knew all about side effects. My medication had some fun side-effects where they made me forget what I'd opened my closet for, and they caused me to put on a ton of weight. Luckily, I was too poor to eat these days, so I was almost back to my usual figure. And there was barely anything left in my closet, anyway, so my options were already limited.

Eryk cleared his throat. "If the spark stones are closed by the Chosen One, then the realm will go on as normal. They will keep their powers, but the creatures of that realm will find their evolution paused. They will retain their magic and their world, but they will not grow any further."

"Hmm. Bummer." I clicked the cap on and off my marker. "So, that brings us to you guys. You've obviously been doing okay so far, stopping your brother from getting his hands on each stone. Why did you show up here now?"

"So far," Cress said. "Connor has mostly targeted spark stones from the realms in the Upper World. Of course, these stones are the most magically powerful, so he has focused on those."

"Of course," I murmured. "Because knowing when someone is going to die is a fabulous power to have."

Cress ignored me. "We have now ensured that all of the stones from the Upper World realms are safe and well-guarded. But recently, the Elonn Fae guardian of the scribe stone has gone rogue. This Elonn elder has come here, into the Middle World, with his realm's spark stone. We are afraid the weak magic of the Middle World will not be able to sustain his protections on the stone." She paused, grimacing. "And now we also know that Connor has entered the Middle World. He is here, somewhere in the human realm. So far, we have decided not to bring you, the

Chosen, the One of Every Blood, into this mess, because it was a problem for the Upper World. Now, it might be everyone's problem."

I shot a glance at Donovan. His expression told me everything I needed to know about how much worth I'd bring.

Maybe this episode—this hallucination—was my subconscious way of rebuilding my confidence. I'd find the stones, defeat the bad guy, and prove to this huge, brooding sexy asshole that I was worth something.

"Cress. This is futile."

She flinched.

"We do not need her," Donovan growled. "We must find the scribe stone ourselves and make sure it is guarded properly."

Cress lifted her chin. "We *do* need her. We have no experience in this human realm, and here magic is hidden by law, so our usual methods are forbidden. We can't find it without her, Donovan."

Donovan's eyes flashed dangerously. "She does not know what she is doing."

"She will learn. The scribe stone is too important. We must find it before Connor does."

I was losing control of this conversation. "Why is this one so important?"

"The scribe stone's power is unfathomable." Donovan didn't bother turning to face me; he spoke to the wall. "The Elonn are keepers of knowledge. Their magic is steeped in being able to assess information and find a drop of truth in an ocean of lies. If their spark stone is devoured, my brother could absorb any number of related powers. The ability to predict the outcome of any conflict, for starters."

"Right," I said, running my eyes over the notes on my refrigerator. "I'll make a deal with you, Donovan." Finally, I faced him directly, acknowledging him for the first time. Ignoring him wasn't going to work; he was far too arrogant to have his confidence dented in any way. Matching his energy might work better.

"If I can find this 'scribe stone' and close it," I said, doing the little air quotes with my fingers. "You guys will go home and leave me alone. This episode will be over, and I'll be free to go on with my life in peace. Deal?"

He stared back at me, his dark green eyes fathomless. "Since I have no desire to spend a second longer than necessary in this realm, in your presence, I take your deal."

Woah. I clearly had some unconscious self-loathing to work through. "So, this Elonn elder, the guy who has the stone. Who is he?"

"A venerable old fae. He is thousands of years old." Donovan grimaced. "I do not understand what possessed him to come here with his realm's spark stone."

"What's his name?"

"His name, in our Upper World, is Ahdeannowyn."

"Hmm," I said, tapping my phone. "No hits, but that's to be expected. He wouldn't be using that name in San Francisco. Maybe I should search for the stone itself." I had no doubt if I'd find something. This was my hallucination; my brain wouldn't give me something I didn't already know.

"None of us have the power to locate the stones themselves, Chosen," Cress said gloomily.

"You can call me Susan. It's not much of a stretch from Chosen." I chuckled to myself, tapping on my phone. "How were you planning on finding the elder?"

"We can try to sense a burst of fae magic, if Ahdeannowyn ever uses it." She turned and looked very dramatically out my tiny window. "But magic in this realm is hidden," she muttered. "It is a problem we cannot solve."

"Every problem has a solution, Cress," I told her. "You just have to find a new way to approach it." An idea hit me; I closed the web browser on my phone and opened one of my favorite apps. "What does the scribe stone look like?"

She turned back. "It is a light blue, clear, like your mortal sky on a cloudless day. Perfectly round, brilliant cut, with over two hundred naturally occurring facets, and measures exactly six thumbs across."

I tapped the information into the search bar. "Thumbs?"

"One and a half of your mortal inches."

"So... we're looking at nine inches in diameter. Okay."

"Enough." Donovan straightened up, squaring his massive shoulders. "I have indulged you enough, Cress. This is pointless. Eryk, Nate, open the portal; we will go back to our own realm and regroup."

"Wait." I waved my phone at him. "Is this it?"

On the screen was a picture of a crystal—a beautiful sparkling blue brilliant-cut stone.

Donovan froze. "Where did you find that image?"

"On eBay." I shrugged. "It's the best place to buy the most random stuff, like broken exercise bikes, or replacement remote controls for your discontinued air conditioner, or, you know, power-packed magical world-ending crystals." I was starting to feel quite giddy.

Donovan's expression grew thunderous. "It's for *sale?*"

"Of course?"

"Ahdeannowyn must have lost it. Take us to it. Now," he demanded.

"That's not how this works, Donovan," I told him, using my "patient kindergarten teacher" voice. "You have to buy it."

His eyes bulged. "*Buy* it?"

"You have to place a bid on it."

He leaned in closer to me, moving slowly, a panther stalking its prey. I caught his scent—a woodsy, clean, fresh river-leather-and-sandalwood. It was an overwhelmingly masculine scent, I almost swooned.

"Woman." His voice grew so low, so dangerous, goosebumps rose on my arms. "If you do not procure that spark stone right now—"

"Calm down, Donovan." I patted his arm, aiming to be patronizing, but I failed miserably. His forearm was strapped with thick, hard muscle; the feel of him under my palm sent an unwelcome tingle down into the core of my belly. My body refused to relax. I had to force my tone to remain casual. "I'll just see what the bids are... oh."

This pretty blue sapphire was well out of my price range.

"What is the issue now?"

I wasn't about to tell the sexy imaginary fae prince that I didn't have enough money to cover my bus fare to work tomorrow, let alone place a bid on a rock that had already gone over thousands of dollars. "The auction isn't due to end for another few weeks," I said breezily. "I'm sure we can find a work around... Oh!"

"What *now?*" he snarled.

Either this was a crazy coincidence, or I'd designed this whole thing in advance and just forgotten about it. Either way, it was fun to find a solution to every problem that came up. "I actually know the seller," I said happily. "I'd recognize that username anywhere. He uses the same one on all his socials." I pointed at my screen at the seller details. "ProfRizzardofOwen. He's an art collector, an old patron of my—"

Vincent.

It felt like a stab to the heart. I clamped my lips shut and slowly took a deep breath through my nose. In, out. In, out.

To give Donovan some credit, he waited patiently for me to get myself under control. As soon as my heart rate slowed down, I swallowed the lump in my throat and spoke as evenly as I could. "His name is Professor Dean Owen. He's a professor emeritus at Stanford, and he just happens to be a passionate art collector. He's a really kooky old rich guy, who lives in a big old Victorian manor house in Haight-Ashbury. I've been to a few of his dinner parties."

"Dean Owen?" Cress turned and met Donovan's eye. "Ahdeannowyn?"

He crossed those massive arms over his chest. "It couldn't be."

"Of course it could. This is my delusion; I'm not about to pluck a whole-ass personality out of nowhere," I said absently. A yawn escaped me; it felt good, so I inhaled deeply and yawned again. Donovan's eyes dropped to my chest, and he scowled.

I almost laughed. "I've even got his phone number. He's a night owl, from what I recall, so he'll be awake." I thumbed through my contacts and hit the dial icon.

The line buzzed. Cress turned and arched an eyebrow at Donovan. It was definitely an *I told you so* look.

A click sounded in my ear. "Ahoy-hoy!"

"Professor Owen?" I put my "charming deferential woman speaking to a crusty old man" voice on. "It's Susan Moore speaking. How are you this evening?"

His old, scratchy voice vibrated down the phone line. "Susan Moore?"

"Uh." My heart fluttered for a second. I turned my back on the four hallucinations, who were staring at me with their mouths open. "Susan... Andresano. Do you remember me?"

"Ha! Susan Andresano! Of course I remember you, my dear. You're cracking good company. How are you?"

"That *is* him," Cress breathed out from behind me, her voice filled with hushed awe. "She's done it. Donovan... she found Ahdeannowyn."

I'd managed to astonish my delusions. Go, me.

"I am fabulous, sir, thank you for asking," I said smoothly, smiling widely. People could always hear it in your voice when you smiled over the phone. They could also hear it in your voice if you were flipping them off while you were talking to them. I'd been trying to drum that into my team for weeks, but they kept doing it. "I was wondering if I could beg a favor from you."

"Of course, my dear, of course," he creaked. "What can I do for you, young Susan?"

"I just saw a beautiful gemstone on eBay; a beautiful blue brilliant-cut sapphire. I believe you are the seller?"

"Oh, yes, my dear. Why? Are you interested in purchasing it?"

I bit my lip. I couldn't afford to eat lunch tomorrow. But I didn't need to buy it; I just needed to satisfy my delusions enough that they would go away. "Oh, yes. Yes, I am."

He chuckled. "Liar."

I'd forgotten what a crafty old bastard he was. "You got me," I laughed with him. "It's already gone well above my price range. I would like to see it, though, sir, if I could. Before you sell it to the highest bidder."

"That can be arranged. Come to dinner tomorrow night, my dear. I'm having my usual Thursday night shindig. Gladioli is making her famous roasted cherry tomato and wagyu beef lasagna. And her peach and brown butter cobbler. Actually, maybe I can talk her into doing a tiramisu. I think we'll need it."

I hesitated. Dean Owen was a very rich old guy, and he moved in some of the same social circles as some of my former friends. Dinner at his manor house meant there would be a lot of other guests—some that I might recognize, maybe even some of those former friends who now hated me. The last thing I wanted to do was spend an evening listening to people whisper mean things about me behind their hands.

Professor Owen would have heard about what I'd done. In fact, I half-expected him to laugh and hang up on me when I called him. He was an academic, though, an odd character who didn't give a damn what anyone thought of him. He invited interesting people to dinner, regardless of social status.

Maybe this was the whole point of my psychotic break. I'd chosen to seek out the one man who didn't care about my downfall, knowing he would probably invite me for dinner. I was forcing myself to face my fears.

"I'd love to," I managed.

"Fabulous! Black tie dress code as usual, my dear. Eight on the dot." He hung up.

I stared down at the blank screen and checked my call log. Yep, I'd actually had a conversation with Professor Dean Owens. He'd really invited me for dinner.

"Okay, it's done," I said out loud. "I'll go to his house tomorrow night and get the stone."

"We must go to him now," Cress urged, her eyes very bright.

I shook my head curtly. "Nope. I mean, we could, but Professor Owen's house is wired up to the hilt with security, and he never answers his own door. If you ring his doorbell, he won't answer, and if you try to break in, Bonbon will eat you."

"What manner of beast is this... Bonbon?"

"She's the professor's rottweiler. A dog," I clarified when they all looked confused. "She's a monster. She never leaves his side."

"That confirms it." Donovan looked away and frowned. "This Bonbon is not a rotten wheel. Elonn fae have hellhound familiars. Elonn fae are cerebral creatures. They do not involve themselves in combat at all, so they evolved to bond with dangerous creatures who would protect them."

I nodded and stifled another yawn. "Cool." I clapped my hands cheerfully. "Okay, team, let's wrap this up. We've made some great progress today, so you can go home now."

All four gorgeous hallucinations stared at me.

I made a shoo motion. "Off you go. Go away, leave me alone so I can go to sleep."

Cress shook her head. "We are not leaving. We must stay in this realm until the scribe stone is secured."

Good grief. My subconscious obviously had a bit more to work through. "Listen, we can't do anything until dinner tomorrow night. You guys might as well disappear until then. Go on."

"We cannot leave now. There are other factors we must take into consideration." Donovan took a step towards me and crossed his arms across his huge chest, glaring down at me. "The most important one is that Connor may seek out other Middle World creatures and pursue their spark stones while he is here."

"Ugh, you gotta be kidding me," I muttered under my breath.

"And," Donovan said, his glare deepening, "less importantly, you may be in danger. You are the One of Every Blood. My brother is both ruthless and powerful, and he is more than aware of the prophecy. He may find cause to seek you out. We do not need you to save the realms from Connor, but it is in your best interests to accept our protection."

"Fine," I sighed. "Be my guest. I'm sure I'll be better at ignoring you in the morning. If I can get an urgent appointment with Bronwyn, she'll help me get rid of you. Move out of the way." I reached up and pulled my bed back down; all four jumped out of the way and sandwiched themselves against the wall. Even extended, there was barely any room. I turned off the lights, and got into bed, while the beautiful fae creatures posed against my wall, unable to move.

Now that the lights were off, I hoped they'd keep quiet and let me sleep. That hope was quickly dashed, though.

"Nate," Donovan said, his voice rumbling. "Go and get Cecil."

Nate gasped. "Cecil? You want me to get *Cecil?*"

Nope, I wasn't going to bite. I didn't care who the hell Cecil was.

"Yes. Bring him here."

"But... but the Queen..."

"Let me worry about the Queen, Nate. Go get him."

I didn't watch, but I saw a glowing green flame from the corner of my eye while I snuggled under my covers.

I'd be better in the morning. Everything would be better in the morning.

CHAPTER
SIX

A delicious smell of freshly roasted coffee filled my nostrils. I breathed it in, still half asleep, and moaned softly. It smelled like heaven—exactly like my lazy Saturday mornings with Vincent, in our gorgeous super-king size bed, wrapped up in crisp white Egyptian ten-thousand-thread count sheets. Vincent ran on coffee in the same way that cars run on gas; he always got up early, pulled a double shot of espresso, and brought it back to bed so he could talk to me about the coming day. Except now, he was bringing a tiny cup of espresso back to the beautiful, willowy young Seraphina, not me.

Heartache pierced the fog of my memory and reality set in. Vincent was gone. My old life was gone. And the only coffee I could afford was freeze-dried instant blend which tasted like old, boiled mung beans.

Keeping my eyes shut, I repeated my mantras over and over until the pain in my chest eased. *I am a strong, capable woman. I can rebuild my life. I deserve happiness. I am enough.*

The beautiful smell of fresh coffee lingered, though, and I cracked my eyes open, wondering if I'd forgotten to close a window or something.

There was a horse in my face.

I jolted and scrambled upright, backing up against the pillows behind me.

The horse sneered. "Well, look who *finally* decided to join the land of the living? I was beginning to think you were going to lie there and snore all morning."

I clutched my chest. "What... what..."

"Ooh. So eloquent." The little horse curled his lip, eying me bitchily. "It's nice to meet you too, Chosen."

My brain couldn't process what I was seeing. A tiny horse, smaller than a Shetland pony, was standing by my bedside, talking to me. His hide was a beautiful tan—no, a pure gold that sparkled in the morning light. He had a shiny black snout, and a long, shimmering bright-white mane of hair that tumbled off his crown and neck and down his back like he was a model in a haircare commercial.

I gaped. The horse was standing upright. On his back hooves. Looming over me, in fact, and somehow balancing a delicate blue china cup on one hoof.

I stammered. "W— Wh— Who are you?"

The little miniature horse clip-clopped backwards a little, still walking upright, and tossed his hair, revealing two stubby horns on his crown. "You do not know? You have not heard the deep sighs of longing when my name is spoken? You have not witnessed the frenzied bidding for my services?"

I pinched my eyes closed, then opened them again. Nope, he was still there.

"I am Cecil!" the horse boomed, striking a pose.

My lips felt numb. This was crazy. "What the fuck? What the actual *fuck?* You're a... you're a..."

His head whipped towards me, and his eyes narrowed. "Bitch, if you call me a horse, I will gore you. I don't care who you are. I will skewer you like a Thai chicken satay stick."

I closed my eyes again, breathing deeply. "I am firmly rooted in reality. I am a strong, capable woman. I am in control."

He let out a snort. "Ugh. You mortals and your delicate sensibilities. Here, drink this." I felt hot china nudge me sharply in my left boob. The horse was pushing a cup of espresso on me. "I forget how much your kind needs a jump-start in the morning. Maybe once you are suitably conscious, you will remember your manners."

I felt something crack inside me. All the progress I'd made, all the therapy, all the mantras, the medications... and I was seeing a... a...

"Unicorn?"

"*Please*." The horse curled his lip superciliously. "I am more than a mere unicorn. In fact, I am the only one who has evolved beyond the basic bitches in my herd."

I mouthed for a moment. No words came out.

He waved his hoof. "I'm sure the rest of my primitive brethren will catch up one day," he sighed dramatically. "Now, sip your single origin, and let's get on with the day. We have work to do!"

I stared at the little horse, realizing for the first time that there was something wrong with the wall behind him. It was far further back than it should be. A lot further back, and for some reason, instead of being painted stark white, it was now papered in vertical stripes of duck-egg blue and cream silk wallpaper.

I felt like I was falling. I'd really truly lost my mind, probably for good this time.

Just before I spiraled completely, a memory of my father suddenly popped up into my mind's eye—wild dirty-blond sticking out of his head like he'd been electrocuted, grinning at me with his huge banana-split smile that split his freckled white face in half. *Sweet baby girl, nothing is ever lost when you've still got a smile on your face. If you always look on the bright side, the darkness will never take hold.*

Dad, the eternal optimist. He was crazier than a bag full of snakes—the complete opposite to my prim, responsible, uptight mother, but he knew how to have a good time. I knew exactly what he'd say to me right now. *Roll with it, darl. Have some fun.*

He was right. I might have lost my marbles, but someone was bringing me a cup of coffee. It smelled delicious, too.

Fuck it. If I was going nuts, I might as well have fun with it.

"Oh, yes, of course." I nodded at the horse graciously. "Please forgive me. It's lovely to meet you, Cecil."

He put his hoof on his chest. "She speaks! And she has remembered her manners." Cecil bowed his long face. "Enchante, Chosen."

I took a sip of coffee; the smooth, delicious brew rolled over my tongue—rich, luscious, dark nutty with hints of cocoa and berry. I sighed with pleasure. "This is exquisite."

"I should hope so! I told them that only a double boiler three-group professional with no less than two steam wands would do." He wrinkled his nose. "And they kept coming back with those... those... pod machines." He shuddered. "What do they think we are? Savages?"

"Indeed," I murmured, taking another sip. Yesterday I would have given my right eyeball for one of those pod machines.

"Do you know how hard it was to get those two meatheads to follow instructions?" He huffed out a breath of exasperation. "I don't know how Prince Donovan puts up with them."

I peered at him. "You sent Eryk and Nate out to steal me a coffee machine?"

"Please," he sniffed. "They left gold coins. And it was the only thing I wanted for your new home that Violet couldn't manifest. On that note." He waved his hoof grandly. "What do you think of your new bedroom?"

I turned away from the sassy little pony and looked around, trying to keep my heart from thumping right out of my chest.

The room was *enormous*. The threadbare gray carpet was gone. Instead, beautiful old, bleached wood floorboards flowed seamlessly under a thick beige rug. The walls —that gorgeous cream and duck-egg blue paper—perfectly complemented the four black-framed arched windows that looked out on the flowing skyline of San Francisco, right down to the water. Delicate antique tables were placed by the windows, with tasteful vases filled with orchids.

The end of the room used to be less than four feet of space where my multi-storage closet sat; it was the place where I stacked my wardrobe, my cleaning products, and literally everything else I owned. The far wall was now twenty feet away, and the closet had disappeared. Now, there was an open door. Beyond the door, I could see a walk-in dressing room, with a French-style vanity, soft lighting, and a large gilt-framed mirror.

I glanced down, overwhelmed, and saw that my bed was different, too. It was almost a replica of my old bed, in my old house—a super-king, with crisp white sheets and a fluffy cream-colored goose down comforter.

A lump rose in my throat. "It's beautiful," I whispered.

"Of course it is!" Cecil clomped towards me. "This is my talent! My magic. I find space, and I make it beautiful, tailored perfectly to my client's desires." He pursed his lips. "I must admit, I was quite worried when that brawny idiot

Nate dragged me out of the castle. I wasn't sure what monster the Queen would be sending me to serve. But you, my dear..." He nodded graciously. "You have very good taste."

I swallowed, trying to get rid of the lump. "Thank you."

"Come." Cecil stomped his hoof, reached out, and plucked the empty china cup out of my hands. "Get up. You must see the absolute *glory* of the rest of the House."

"The house?"

"House. With a capital H, my dear. Violet House has established herself in place on top of this dwelling like a fruit tree grafted on a useless, ugly base. I have been working all night! I have spared no ounce of magic! I am simply exhausted!"

I had no idea what he was talking about. "Oh, you've done the rest of the house, too? Okay." I rolled out of bed, savoring the warm oak floorboards under my feet. A strange zing pulsed through me, rising from where my toes wiggled on the floor. It felt odd, but pleasant, like a perky little kid patting me, saying *good morning! Good morning!*

I stretched, pushing my arms up over my head. A silk robe dropped down from nowhere, slipping over my hands, draping over my shoulders, the cool fabric brushing my bare skin. "That's a nice touch."

"You're welcome. It wasn't for your benefit, though. Prince Donovan has urgently requested your presence, and there's no way anyone will be able to concentrate on anything with those enormous boobs thrust in their face."

Cecil clip-clopped on his hind legs, dumped the china cup unceremoniously on the delicate side table by the window, and stomped out in front of me. "I have arranged your space so that your sleeping quarters are at the furthest end of the west wing, for privacy and comfort. Your bedroom opens out to this morning room." He waved his arms as we passed a wide room filled with plush lilac chaise lounges. Another row of arched windows flowed along one wall. The space was breathtakingly beautiful. Outside, I could see early morning sunshine twinkling off the water.

I grimaced. No matter what kind of delusions I was having, I should probably get ready to go to work soon. "What time is it?"

"Just past dawn, my dear. Now here, through the morning room, we come to the portrait gallery, where I have taken the liberty of hanging some of the most admirable men and women from your childhood memories."

I looked up and saw dignified portraits of Tom Selleck as Magnum PI, Cher in a plunging gown, MacGyver holding a matchstick and a length of number eight wire, and the guy from Quantum Leap in his silver jumpsuit, ringed in blue flames.

I glanced out the window, desperate to ground myself in some sort of reality. Yep, I was still in San Francisco. In fact, I could see Audrina in the building next door, still on her balcony, strumming her guitar.

Worry pierced my personal doom spiral. That balcony was Audrina's refuge, as well as her cage. She hid there to avoid her family. Had she been out there all night, avoiding her mom, *again?*

I'd never officially met Audrina's parents in my former life, but they'd shown up at a lot of events I'd attended, so I knew who they were. Audrina's professional-athlete-turned-property-mogul father wouldn't be home; he barely came back before midnight each night, if he came back at all. Her mother was a former Miss America contender.

Offended by the fact that Audrina looked almost exactly like her father and was not blessed with her beauty-queen looks, Audrina's mom had completely ignored her since birth and made being a "mom-of-boys" her whole personality. Every time I saw them on the street she was piling all three teenage boys, hockey masks, basketballs, football pads, and all sorts of sports paraphernalia into an SUV, shouting at them good-naturedly or talking loudly about their talent, their dates, their D1 status.

Poor Audrina—seventeen, shy, clumsy, with frizzy orange hair, an upturned button nose and heavy brow—was not good at sports. It made everything much worse for her.

Every day, she retreated from the scornful glares of her family and hid out on the balcony to play her guitar. I was lucky enough to hear her; she had a voice sweeter than a nightingale.

Not that it did her any good. Stopping just short of outright abuse, her mom refused to let her do anything outside of school, telling her she was no good at sports or anything else, so there was no point forcing herself out of her shell. She laughed when Audrina tentatively asked if she could go to music school when she graduated, and outright refused to pay for it, saying it would be a waste of money. You're too shy, her mom said. There's no point. Go to a tech college, do some STEM subjects, go hide in a lab somewhere.

Before my downfall, I'd heard that Audrina's mom never admitted to having a daughter at all. Only her sons were ever mentioned in conversation. If her mom found out I'd been encouraging Audrina to busk down in Golden Gate Park, singing and playing her guitar in full view of the public, she'd track me down and kill me with her bare hands.

There was no chance I was going to let Audrina live her life all alone, a little bird in her balcony cage, so I always made a point to open my window and have a conversation with her whenever I could get away with it. I took her for hot chocolate in the square when her mother and brothers were out. I also helped her secretly apply for scholarships to performing arts schools, and thanks to her busking, she'd saved enough money to keep herself afloat if her mother refused to let her go. She was a sweet kid; she deserved so much more than the hellish family she was born into.

I watched her for a second to make sure she wasn't crying and made a mental note to check in on her the second I stabilized a little.

We walked through the portrait room, heading towards the dark-oak double doors at the end. Cecil kept up the monologue the whole way. "Through here, we have the drawing room, which will serve as a common space, as it is closest to the front door. Prince Donovan and Princess Cress will occupy the east wing." He pursed his lips. "Those two thugs, Nate and Eryk, I have thrown into a little hovel in the south rooms."

I stopped in my tracks, facing him. "They're still here?"

"Of course they're still here. Where else would they be? They must stay here with you until the danger has passed and the stones in the Middle World realms are closed and safe. They have accepted you as part of the company now. You're in it right up to your wrinkly neck, sweetheart."

I groaned out loud. "I was hoping I'd already worked through that delusion."

"Hmm. You are very odd," Cecil said, gazing at me through narrowed eyes. "I understand your education has been sorely lacking, but we don't have time for this. Please stop being so weird immediately."

I rubbed my temples. "The horse has already bolted from that particular stable, Cecil."

He whinnied loudly. "Was that a slur? Are you trying to insult me?"

"No, no," I said hastily. "Um, let's just get going. What are we doing, again?"

"I told you: the Prince has requested to speak to you urgently."

"But not too urgently, obviously, if you think that giving me a tour of my imaginary house is more important."

He popped me on the forehead with his hoof.

"Ouch!"

"Do *not* disrespect Violet House! You are her servant just as much as she is yours. I warn you—don't forget that, or you might find yourself buried beneath the floorboards."

"Sorry." I took a deep breath and sighed it out. "Listen, Cecil, this is all lovely, but it might be a bit... too grand. Can I just have another coffee in a nice kitchen, or something?"

He put his hoof on his chin, tapping thoughtfully. "Yes, I suppose I might have gone a bit overboard. I was trying to teach you to fly without first letting you walk. Nevertheless, the bare bones of the House have been established and my magic has carefully fed and watered and nourished her. Violet House is now awakened and functional, so the main part of my job is complete. You could fashion a kitchen to your own tastes if you like. Provided it is not too hideous," he muttered under his breath. "I retain the power of veto."

"What do you mean?"

He stared at me like I was an idiot. "Just ask Violet House to produce what you want."

"Right. Violet..." I turned and faced the door. "Please give me a replica of Martha Stewart's farmhouse kitchen. The Bedford estate, not the Hamptons one."

The floor beneath my feet vibrated enthusiastically.

"Good, good." Cecil nodded. "Do you want to include this Martha Stewart person, too? You can't do it yourself, but if you like, I could push with my magic a little and abduct her—"

Yeesh. "Oh, no. No, that's okay. Let's save that for when I'm back in the padded calming room and I need a little company." I turned and walked into the most gorgeous kitchen I could possibly imagine.

It was straight out of a design magazine—polished concrete floors, a long stone counter, pots and pans hanging from the island, a dazzling collection of sharp knives on a magnetic holder, four ovens and... *ohhhh*. The coffee machine.

All four of my gorgeous hallucinations were sitting at the long, scrubbed oak table. Nate and Eryk leapt to their feet and bowed. "As you were, gentlemen," I said silkily, walking over to the coffee machine. I didn't care if it wasn't real; my hands greedily caressed the grinder, stroking up and down the frother in a way that was probably obscene. I didn't care. I'd been living on freeze-dried instant for too long.

"Out of the way, you heathen." Cecil headbutted me aside. "I'll make you a cappuccino. Sit down. I believe the Prince has new developments to share with you."

I sighed and walked over to where Donovan sat, huge and brooding, at the kitchen table. I'd been trying not to look, but my stomach flipped at the sight of him. Let loose from the topknot from yesterday, his jet-black hair was long and tousled, flowing over his broad shoulders. He'd removed his weapons, and instead of black leather, he wore a white shirt and tan trousers. Enough buttons of his shirt were undone that I caught a glimpse of his hard, muscular chest. Even in stillness, I could sense the power in those muscles, the tightly coiled danger that could explode out of him at any moment.

I averted my eyes. They itched to swing back, so I turned around completely. "I don't mean to be rude, but do you think this could wait until after work? I've got a big day today; I have to stay sharp, and, er, as non-psychotic as possible."

Donovan's eyes bored into my back; I could feel him staring at me. "What could possibly be more important than securing the scribe stone?"

"My promotion," I said simply. "I don't want to go into details, but I'm trying to rebuild my life. There's a very long corporate ladder out there. I've climbed it once from the depths of the basement mailroom at a bank, so I know I can do it again." I clenched my fist. "And one greasy Loki wannabe named Richie Curran is standing in my way."

"Loki?" Cress gasped. "He is here? In the human realm?"

"Not the real one," I told her. "A fake one. Richie thinks he's cool like Loki."

"Loki is not *cool*. He is a mad god. He changed himself into a mare so he could mate with a giant stallion and gave birth to an eight-legged steed named Slepnir. Does this Richie transform and mate with horses, too?"

"Keep him away from me!" Cecil snorted from the coffee machine. "Until Thursday, when I get my laser hair removal done."

"Urgh. No," I sighed. "We have a watered-down version of the Loki story here, where he's just a cool-looking trickster type of guy. Richie Curran has the same kind of hair, and he thinks he's crafty, so he leans into the comparison."

"Oh. And this fake Loki is standing on a ladder?" Cress frowned deeply.

"The ladder was metaphorical," I told her. "Look, forget all the Loki stuff. What I'm trying to say is that I can't afford to miss work today. I can't give Richie any ammunition against me."

Cecil clopped over, tossed his beautiful mane over his shoulder, and thrust a cup into my hand. I inhaled the milky coffee aroma gratefully and took a sip. Perfection.

"Besides, there's not much we can do about the scribe stone until we go to Professor Owen's for dinner later tonight, anyway."

Cress, posing like a superhero by the window, turned around. "There are new developments, Chosen. Our Lower World informants have come to us with new information—we may not be able to trust it, but at this stage, it would be unwise to ignore what they are telling us. We have learned Connor intends to pursue the other Middle World realm's spark stones while he is here."

I sighed and held up a finger. "Wait. Wait, I need visual input to process this. Cecil, is my top kitchen drawer the same as it was before?"

"Of course not," he snorted.

"I need my whiteboard marker—"

There was a tiny bright-purple flash, and a marker appeared in mid-air, right in front of me. I caught it as it fell, and stared at it, lying in my hand. "Huh."

Roll with it.

Okay, then.

I strode over to my enormous new double-door refrigerator and uncapped the lid. "Let me just get my head around this World and realm stuff. You guys say you are from the Upper World, right?" I wrote *upper world* in big letters. "Which is a horrible display of class snobbery on my part, but I suppose I can hash that out with my therapist at some stage." That reminded me. I patted my pocket. Where was my phone? I should call Brownyn and make an appointment now.

"Upper does not refer to anything other than vibrational resonance," Cress explained. "Higher vibration is order—scribes, elementals, warriors, unicorns, brownies, sages, priests and priestesses. Lower vibration is chaos—imps, wraiths, pixies, demons, berserkers and the like."

"Oh, yeah?" I shot Donovan a smug look. "Which realm is your brother from, then?"

He stared back at me, fury simmering in his eyes. There was an uncomfortable silence.

Finally, Eryk cleared his throat. "There are many different realms in the Upper World."

"Like…. Like pockets on a jacket?"

"Yes," Cress said. "Donovan and I are High Fae from a kingdom in faerie, which is the biggest realm located inside the Upper World."

I wrote *fae realm* underneath *upper world*. "Are you all from the fae realm?"

"No," Eryk piped up. "I'm an Elemental from the Fire Realm. We're like…. close cousins of the High Fae. And Nate here is a Batalan, a race of combat mages, another cousin. We are all from the Upper World."

"Okay, I got it. From what I understand, I live in the Middle World." I wrote *middle world* on the refrigerator. "And there's a Lower World, with naughty little pixies and wraiths and whatnot. They live in their own little pocket realms inside the cargo pants of the Lower World, am I right?"

Donovan was staring sullenly out the window. That man could go in the dictionary as a photo illustration of the word "brooding."

After a long moment, Eryk answered me again. "Yes. The Upper World is a jacket, its realms are in the pockets. The Lower Realm is your cargo trousers."

Cecil piped up from the kitchen, where he was inspecting one of the four ovens. "And the Middle Realm is like a drug dealer's fanny pack right in between the hideous cargo pants and the jacket, with lots of different baggies inside, filled with uppers and downers."

Everyone turned and stared at him.

"What? I have to study pop culture in every realm as part of my studies. I did a whole paper on the human realm's heroin chic aesthetic."

"So, the Middle World is kind of a mix of order and chaos?

"Yes," Cress said. "A mixture of Upper and Lower. Mostly humanoid creatures that have both order and chaos within them... mer, vampire, shapeshifter, centaur, witch."

I chuckled to myself and wrote it down. "Okay, it's all coming together. So, Connor, a prince from the fae realm in the *Upper World*, has, out of nowhere, decided to devour each realm's spark stone."

Donovan let out a grunt. "You misunderstand. Upper does not mean good. It just means we crave order. There is nobody that demands order more than a tyrant." His voice lowered to a rough whisper, and he turned away. "Connor wishes to rule all. He will stop at nothing."

The pain in his eyes took me by surprise. Maybe I should cut him a break. "So... you've heard from some informants in the Lower World that Connor has decided to go for the spark stones in all the... what? The centaur realm?"

"Rumor has it he will go for the siren stone first. Mermaids are notorious for being vain and proud, and therefore, easily tricked."

I winked. "And nobody does tricks better than the fae, huh?" Audrina and I have had several window-to-balcony conversations about her fairy smut books.

For a moment, Donovan closed his eyes and breathed heavily through his nose. He seemed to be struggling with controlling his temper. "You have no idea how much danger you are in," he said softly. "You have *no* concept of what is at stake right now."

I took a sip of my cappuccino. Mmm. Delicious. "Look, this has all been very interesting, and of course I'm happy to help you lovely hallucina—I mean, people. Later on, I'll talk to the professor and take a look at that pretty blue crystal of his." I patted my pockets, checking for my phone. There was another flash, and it appeared on the counter in front of me.

I looked at it, my equilibrium wobbling. The atoms in the room quivered with nervous expectation, like the house was a little kid desperate to be praised for doing a good job.

Go with it.

"Thanks, Violet," I told her. "You are a truly fabulous imaginary sentient house." I picked up my phone and checked the time. "But sorry, Donovan. For now, I have got to get to work."

Donovan stood up abruptly. Good grief, he was tall. At five foot eight, I wasn't short myself, but this man had to be almost a head taller than me. "We will come with you."

I shook my head firmly, trying to remind my stomach that he wasn't real. "No, you will not."

"We must. You may be in danger."

"The call center of Base Budget Insurance is hardly a lion's den, Donovan. Besides, the building has security. We all have to wear ID passes to enter."

He crossed his arms and glared down at me. "You have no knowledge of your innate power, Chosen. If you did not have a teacher, you must not have any idea on how to control it. Your magic can be wild and destructive." His green eyes flashed dangerously. "Perhaps I am not concerned for your safety. Perhaps I am concerned for everyone else around you. That is why we must come with you."

I stared up at him. His words hurt, like a whip crack over bare flesh. For a brief second, fear clutched my heart in a cold fist and refused to let go. I squeezed my eyes shut.

The floor beneath my feet shook. *Breathe, Susan. Just breathe. Nobody died. Nobody was dead.*

He could have died, though. I remembered the screams, the bricks falling...

Just breathe.

My eyes still shut, I heard Cecil tap a hoof on the floor. "Don't worry, Violet. She's just having a moment."

I sensed movement; Donovan took a step back from me. "We need to do something about her."

Cress sounded dubious. "You want me to kill her? Now?"

"No, Cress," he sighed. "She needs to be taught. Eryk, did you find out if the múinteoir is still alive? His people are the only ones with the knowledge on how the Chosen works her magic. Apart from certain monsters, of course, and we do not want *them* teaching her."

"The múinteoir, Molinere, is not on the death roll. The stars will shut the portal by sundown, your Highness. So, if you wish me to go and look for him, we need to go now, otherwise we won't be able to go back to the Upper World without a new blood key."

He let out a grunt. "Both of you go now, and see if you can find him. Come back here before the portal closes."

Finally, I got my breathing under control and opened my eyes to find Donovan's face far too close. "Cress and I will come with you today. I will keep you safe."

It took me a long time to respond. "Fine."

CHAPTER
SEVEN

The offices of Budget Base Insurance were downtown, tucked away out of sight of the main streets and the swankier, more expensive suites, occupying three stories in a skyscraper, sandwiched between an old, crusty law firm, a co-op of financial planners, and a property management agency. I power-walked into the lobby—a stark, gleaming black marble tribute to the late eighties—and nodded to Bert and Luis on the desk as I strode towards the security gates. "Morning, gentlemen!"

"Heya, Susan. How are you doing on this fine day?" Luis was the only guard who ever replied to me; he was a cheerful, soft-spoken man, always happy to shoot the breeze whenever I came in. Bert, his giant craggy-faced security guard partner, was apparently from Yugoslavia, but you wouldn't know it, because he never said a word. In fact, I didn't think I'd ever seen him blink.

"I'm great, thanks, Luis. How's the baby?"

"*Mios Dio*, that girl, she's got some lungs on her!" Luis wiped his brow. "We be up all night, trying to get her to calm down." His eyes widened dramatically. "But she's loud. I'm thinking she got my mother-in-law's powers. That woman and her sisters are banshees. Always screamin' about somethin'."

I smiled back, trying to force my face to relax. My hallucinations all agreed to weave glamor spells around themselves so they could follow me into the office, unseen. I sold it to them as a security measure, but I was hoping it would be easier to ignore them if I couldn't see them.

While they were working on their spells, I showered in my new fantasy ensuite bathroom—under a sparkling waterfall in a fairytale cavern, with spongy moss-covered rocks beneath my feet—and went to my dressing room to change. Cecil picked out my outfit, obviously also a hallucination, since it appeared to be a brand-new Lierna Couture pencil skirt and matching double-breasted jacket.

Cress and Donovan spent a good amount of time creating green sparks and knitting them into a fabric-like sheet, then molding them into cloaks that they could drape around themselves. Now, they waited behind me, flanking me on either side. I couldn't see them, but I could feel them.

Especially Donovan. He was too close, both white-hot and freezing cold at the same time. He leaned down and murmured in my ear. "Who is this man, Chosen? And why does he lie? Humans cannot breed directly with banshees. That is unheard of."

For a second, I lingered by the security desk, smiling at Luis, my pulse beating fast. Do you see them, Luis? Did you hear him, just then? Donovan's voice had been loud enough for the sound to carry. Am I really crazy?

But Luis was still grinning, shaking his head. "I don't think I've had more than three hours sleep in the past week and a half, Sue. My daughter is a monster."

"Of course she is a monster," Donovan rumbled behind me. "She is a half breed banshee-human abomination."

I exhaled, and a little tension left my body. I really was nuts. "She's only a month old, Luis. She'll get used to this life and settle down. Make sure you let Gloria take her naps, okay?"

"Oh, yes ma'am, I will. I don't want to poke the beast."

"What manner of beast is she? If her mother is a banshee?"

Ignoring Donovan, I tapped my card on the reader and walked through the gate, quickly slipping into the bathroom to change my tennis shoes into what appeared to be a brand-new pair of black patent red-bottom kitten heels I'd found in my new closet. Luis didn't comment on anything weird, so hopefully I was actually wearing my normal business casual white-shirt-and-trouser combo, and not my flannel pajamas.

Before I left the bathroom, I checked myself in the full-length mirror. The pencil skirt was the perfect length to show off my legs without being too provocative; the black raw-silk fabric looked terribly luxurious and expensive, and my blood-red shirt was pressed to perfection. It didn't matter that I was the only person that could see it. I looked great, and I felt amazing.

Go with it, my father's voice echoed in my ear.

For the first time in two years, I sashayed out of the bathroom with a hint of my former confidence. The twin spots of icy-cold heat drifted behind me again, and together, we walked up to the elevator bank. I pressed a button.

The elevator dinged, and the doors opened.

"Wait," Donovan rumbled in my ear. "We must inspect the space for enemies."

I hesitated. It was still early. I was alone. "Be my guest."

I felt him move past me on one side. Cress, a less blisteringly hot spot, moved forward on the other side. "Your workspace is ludicrously small," she called out.

I pressed my lips together.

"I was under the impression that you were the leader of a team of workers. There is no 'team' in here for you to manage."

"Well, I always make a point to be the first to arrive," I said, trying not to laugh.

"Your underlings must be miniscule creatures." Cress's voice was filled with disgust. "There is no space for me to even swing my sword in here. Why do you not commandeer some of that cavernous space out front for you to conduct your business? Perhaps next to the banshee's husband? Or beside the troll?"

"This tiny cubicle is totally unsatisfactory." I heard a knock on the elevator wall; Donovan was tapping it, trying to see if he could magically widen it. "How could you work in such conditions? It is an insult, even to the likes of you—"

The doors began to slide close.

"Chosen!"

The doors snapped shut. I giggled like a schoolgirl, watching the buttons light up as the elevator ascended, first floor, second floor, third floor...

Silence. Blessed silence. My head was clear; there were no mythical creatures surrounding me. I took a deep breath, pushed the button again, got into a different elevator, and hit the button for the thirty-third floor. The lift didn't stop on any other floors; the building was probably still mostly deserted.

I always came to work early. It was a power move I'd learned in my broker days. If you came to work a little early, you got the jump on the day before anyone else had the chance to throw back their double-mocha Frappuccino and shamble inside the office. I didn't come too early, though. I was a workaholic, not a psychopath.

Well, I was also a psychopath, apparently. But this time, I hadn't hurt anyone.

Not yet, anyway.

The call center of Base Budget Insurance occupied a full level of the thirty-third floor of the building. Just above us, on the thirty-fourth floor, was the product team, compliance, accounts, and human resources, and above that, the executive offices and board room. The technical team, for some reason, were in the basement of the building, level minus zero-one—something to do with the servers needing to be close to the ground to stay cool. Occasionally, one of the pale, dead-eyed wraiths from the tech team would stumble out of an elevator on the thirty-third floor, float through the call center with dead, empty eyes, lurch over to whatever poor idiot had summoned them, and wordlessly switch their desktop off and back on again.

The lights of the call center automatically flicked on as I walked through, illuminating the whole floor and highlighting the soul-sucking worn gray carpet, the concrete-colored cubicle dividers, and the pee-yellow walls. Four small glass offices in each corner of the open-plan floor were the only redeeming feature of the place; three were department manager's offices, one, a large meeting room.

I had my eye on the one on the far side—the Client Experience and Support Senior Manager's office. That was the next rung on the corporate ladder, one step up from where I was as Client Experience and Support Team Leader. I'd get there if it killed me.

Only two years ago, I used to have a private office suite, with Judy, my scary-as-hell executive assistant, in a vestibule outside my door. Now, I coveted one of the tiny glass fishbowl offices in the corner of an open-plan office hell. How the mighty had fallen.

Swallowing my grief, I straightened my shoulders and marched over to my desk. The other team leaders had been confused when I pulled my designated double-wide cubicle away from the wall, removed the partitions, and put my seat on the other side, creating more of an open space—a desk in front of the window instead of a pokey box to hide in. But, thanks to a careful arrangement of my team in their cubicles into a square U shape in front of me, I cut the rest of the call center off and provided myself with a tiny bit of privacy. Unlike the other team leaders, I wanted to be seen, and I put myself in the perfect Feng Shui power position where nobody could approach me without running the gauntlet through my team's cubicles first. It was the little things that made all the difference.

I sat down, switched on my desktop, and logged in.

A billion new emails lay in bold font at the top of my inbox. I scanned them all quickly, deleted the pointless ones, filed the ones I didn't need to respond to, and started working my way through the endless drudgery of customer complaints, staff requests, petty squabbles over budget allocations, over-excited declarations from the social committee...

This meeting could have been an email. This email could have been a cage fight.

Slowly, some of my team began to drift in. Once called "call center operators," then "customer service officers," then, briefly, "client relationship development and liaison partners," the twelve Client Experience and Support Representatives in my team could be roughly divided into two distinct camps. Ironically enough, in my head, I'd always called them the sprites and the dragons.

The sprites were all young and flighty, full-time or part-time students trying to fit a paying job around college, where they studied art or design or some kind of sports-related science. This job was a means to an end; they didn't put much effort in. Bare minimum only.

The dragons were all older men and women—career call center workers, hoarding their knowledge of the outdated tech systems we used, grunting to each other moodily at their desks, and guarding their cartoon bobble-head figurines in their cubicles like piles of gold and silver.

The dragons always came in first, and none of them ever said good morning to me. I always made a special point to call out to them as they arrived and started to log in. All of them had been working at Base Budget Insurance much longer than me, and they always defaulted to their normal grumpy state first thing in the morning. It never took me long to reestablish dominance, though.

I waved and called out to the head dragon, Thomas, and asked him how his mother's colonoscopy went yesterday, then deliberately called Cherry over to ask her about her leave request, forcing her to leave her desk and come to my territory.

Office politics. I lived and breathed it. I used to play the most high-stakes version of it. Now, it was more like checkers instead of war games, but I had to take my kicks where I could get them.

Stacey, a kinesiology major at USF, was the first of the sprites to arrive, swinging her satchel off her shoulders and shaking out her honey-blonde braided hair. "Morning, Susan!"

I gave her a wave, deliberately not looking at Owen, another sprite, who walked very slowly in behind her. "Hi, Stacey. How was your spin class?"

She blew out a breath, and her bangs flew up. "So good. Juanita, the instructor, she *killed* me. I *literally* died. Rest in peace, me." She dropped into her chair with a huff. "Oh. Hi, Owen," she said, her tone deliberately casual.

Owen, a cute young white boy with a shaved head—a graphic design student—dropped into the seat in the cubicle opposite her. "Hi, Stacey," he said loudly. "How are you this morning?"

"I'm great! *So* great."

"Great." He beamed at her. "That's great."

I turned back to my computer, hiding my smile. Owen and Stacey had been sleeping together for the past five weeks. They thought nobody knew.

Contrary to popular belief, office romances weren't necessarily a terrible idea, especially for sprites, who weren't known for their company loyalty in the first place. But, the way I figured it, if you were banging your colleague, you were more likely to show up for work, and you'd be far more cheerful about being there in the first place.

I'd seen the spark of interest in Owen's eyes when Stacey moved onto my team, and I'd seen how she stared at him when he wasn't looking, so I shifted their cubicles together and shipped them harder than a delivery from Wish. We were now six weeks into their affair, and both of them had shown up every day, on time. And neither of them had called out since.

At nine on the dot I stood up, did a quick headcount, and saw that everyone on my team was logged in and taking calls.

Business as usual. Everything was normal and boring. Perfect.

Smiling, I sat back down and started working my way through more emails.

"You tricked us," Donovan's voice growled in my ear.

Goddammit. With enormous effort, I forced myself not to react.

"That box carried us away, up to the top of the tower, and deposited us in a den of vampires."

I frowned, and quickly put my headset on so I didn't look like I was talking to myself. "Vampires? What are you—" I remembered watching the floor numbers flash. The elevator had taken Donovan and Cress to the thirteenth floor. "Oh, no," I said, chuckling. "Not vampires. They're lawyers. Vladovich and Sangine are a law firm."

"Whatever you call them in this realm, it doesn't matter. You deliberately evaded us." Donovan's fury vibrated off him, cold and intense. It felt like there was a freezer with its door open behind me. "You do not understand the danger you are in, Chosen. You have no understanding of your powers; you have no knowledge of the creatures who hunt you." His voice lowered dangerously; despite the chill, I felt warmth spread in my belly. "Do *not* evade us again."

I took a deep breath and sighed it out. "Fine," I whispered. "Just... just stay back there, and try to be quiet." With enormous effort, I went back to my emails.

Suddenly, the room darkened. A sinister, slimy feeling crawled up my arms.

Oh, no. What fresh preternatural horror—

I saw him. Ah. Not a preternatural horror. Just a mundane one.

Richie Curran—tall and skinny and wrapped in a cheap shiny midnight-blue suit and a skinny black tie, with his long, greasy black hair pulled back into a low ponytail, and a supercilious smirk on his face—loped through the office.

I cringed, moving sideways a little, hoping my monitor would block me from his—

"Susan!"

Fuck.

"Susan *Moore*," he said, deliberately emphasizing my

last name. He sauntered past my team, coming to a stop right in front of my desk. Ignoring the chair, he leaned forward cozily, resting his hands on my desk. "How are you this morning, Susan *Moore?*"

I took the precious few seconds to finish the email I was drafting, glanced up, and raised a brow. "Why aren't you with your team, Richie?" I went back to my emails, clicking, filing, deleting, not bothering to look at him. "Don't you have any work to do?"

"Oh, I'm letting them fly solo for a few minutes. They'll have to get used to being without my support soon, of course," he said. "I thought I'd do a morning tour of the floor, seeing as I'll be department manager of the whole Client Experience and Support Contact Center by next week."

I huffed out a laugh. "There's a fine line between confidence and arrogance, you know, Richie. You seem to have stomped over both, dragging your knuckles, and landed straight on blistering entitlement." I glanced up, curling my lip—a perfect combination of vague disinterest and disgust. "You don't have the stats to back up your claims of being the best team leader in the office, and everyone knows it. Nobody mistakes confidence for competence anymore, so this swaggery schtick won't work."

That wasn't actually true. I knew better than anyone what it was like to be passed over for a promotion in favor of an incompetent, arrogant jerk in a suit whose only real talent was to steal your ideas and talk over you loudly. Unfortunately, sloppy bosses were still drawn to loud, brash confidence, favoring it over quiet competence.

The difference now was I'd gotten more skilled at manipulation. I found it easy to point out I was more qualified, more experienced, with a better track record at achieving results than any other candidate, and I was good at making light-hearted jokes at the end of the interview about how I hope they'd be able to defend their decision in court.

That was the trick. As soon as your boss realized a discrimination lawsuit lurked on the horizon, they looked at the facts, and realized quickly who the best person for the job actually was. And it was *never* their whisky-sodden loudmouth friend.

Richie's easy smile twitched for a second, but he glued it back on. "My team is thriving."

"You're never with them. You get Carol to do most of your admin work while you swan around having unnecessary 'meetings' with your friends."

"See? I'm a great mentor," he said, puffing out his chest. "Carol is working hard for the chance to get my job when I'm promoted."

I pursed my lips. "Except you told Daniel you would put in a good word for him." Poor Carol was going to get walked over by another loud, entitled man, even though she'd been effectively running Richie's team for the past six months.

"Ah, well." Richie grinned, unashamed. "A little competition is healthy. I build people up, Susan. I encourage them to reach for the stars."

I sighed. "I'll give you some advice, Richie. You seem quite focused on the wrong things." My voice dripped with disdain. "If you spent as much time actually supporting your team so they could do their jobs better, you would have *already* been offered the department manager promotion. Instead, you sleaze around the office talking to your creepy buddies all day. I've only been here six months and Yvette is considering me instead, because I've stabilized my team, reduced turnover to zero, improved our performance, and blown our KPIs out of the water. Do you know how I've done it?" I raised my eyebrows. "I'm at this desk every day, working hard to make sure I'm doing everything I can, so my team can do their jobs better. *That's* what a manager does. We work for our team, not the other way around."

Richie leaned back and laughed. "Nice speech. Did you learn that in the *mental institution?*"

I stiffened.

"With your fellow *lunatic murderer buddies?*" Richie gloated.

My mouth went dry. I could hear my heartbeat in my ears. Woosh, woosh, woosh. A wild heat built in my stomach, a rumbling volcano deep within me—

A heavy hand fell on my shoulder and squeezed gently. "Chosen."

Fucksticks, Richie wasn't wrong. I was nuts. The evidence for that was right behind me, hiding under a magic invisibility blanket.

Richie, sensing blood in the water, smiled widely. He bent back down to put his hands on my desk. His neck stretched towards me, snake-like and grotesque; I forced myself not to flinch away. He leaned in close, and inhaled through his nose deeply, like he was breathing me in. "Mmm." His eyes hooded. "Maybe I didn't make myself clear enough yesterday. Listen carefully, Susan Moore. You'll tell Yvette you're dropping out of the running for the promotion *today*," he said slowly. "Or I'll tell the whole office who you really are. I'll tell them where you have been for the past two years. I'll tell them what you did." His eyes glittered with malice. "Nobody will be able to look at you with any respect ever again. You'll always be the crazy old lady who tried to kill her husband."

CHAPTER
EIGHT

I watched Richie saunter away slowly, calling out greetings to my team in an overly casual way. My heart was beating too quickly. I couldn't slow it down.

Cress leaned in close. I could tell it was her; her energy was less terrifying than Donovan's. "I do not understand," she said, her voice a harsh whisper. "Are you not offended? He insulted your honor. Why did you not run him through with your blade?"

"I don't have a blade." The words came out in a mumble.

"I see. We will rectify that immediately. But... Chosen... You didn't even strike his face with your hand. Please do not tell me that you allow men to speak to you like that? To say such horrible things?"

"He's wrong." I swallowed. "I'm not a murderer." My lips felt numb. Damn it, I let him get to me. "I didn't kill anyone."

"That's even worse. Why not?" Cress hissed, outraged. "You should have. You should have taken that weasel man's life. You are lucky that Donovan has insisted that I obey your command to stay hidden, or I would have carved a cross into that man's face myself."

Her words gave me an unexpectedly warm feeling. My hallucinations were very supportive. "Thanks, Cress. That's really lovely of you."

Richie finally disappeared from my line of sight, heading around to the other side of the floor, probably to schmooze with one of the other Client Experience and Support Representative teams. There were five teams in total, but out of all the team leaders, only Richie and I were in the running to take Yvette's job as department manager when she left to join the executive team.

I took a deep breath and exhaled heavily. "Unfortunately, we can't kill Richie Curran, Cress."

"Nonsense. It would take me less than three seconds with a quick thrust to his carotid. If you wanted him to suffer first, I'd hit his kidneys. It would still be silent," she added. "Fast, and very painful, but silent. Death by kidney strike is so excruciating, he'd be in too much pain to even scream."

"Thanks for the offer, but no. Murder is illegal in this realm. Even attempted murder is frowned upon."

I knew that better than anyone.

"That is ridiculous," she snorted. "How do you resolve anything in this realm? How do you rid yourselves of your enemies?"

"I'll come up with something. He's given me until the end of the day to withdraw my application for the promotion." I chewed on my lip for a second. "Maybe I should go and throw myself on the mercy of the Human Resources ogres now. I won't get the promotion, but if I confess, at least I won't get fired. Maybe..." I added gloomily. Bart was right; I didn't exactly lie in my interview. I didn't have a criminal record. Not guilty by reason of insanity was still not guilty.

The back of my neck tingled. "You must not take any other quests today, Chosen," Donovan growled in my ear. "We do not need to see the ogres. I believe the ogre stone is still deep in the center of their realm, and it is very well guarded. No, we must leave soon to try to pursue the mermaid's siren stone. Make haste with your arrangements."

"Donovan," I groaned. "I can't leave work. I've got a team to manage. And just to clarify, the women in HR aren't *actual* ogres. They just act like ogres."

"Regardless. We must go soon." His voice lowered. "My brother's mind works in the same way as mine. If he cannot get to the scribe stone, he will be searching for a Mer to trick. He will need one to take him to their realm. We must beat him to it."

"Sorry to burst your bubble, but I don't know any mermaids, Donovan." My fingers tapped my keyboard listlessly, trying to concoct a reply to a customer complaint that was more diplomatic than *go fuck yourself*.

"Of course you do. You must know some mer. The mer infest the mortal realm like ants on a sugar lump," he said. "Their own realm is too small to hold them all, and their lust for praise and admiration consumes them. They cannot keep themselves away from humans."

"Well, I don't," I murmured, tapping out a reply to the complaint email. *I'm sorry my team's service did not reach your expectations today. We're always looking at ways to improve, and I would like to thank you for your valuable feedback. If you call to speak with any of my team again, you can rest assured we will not end the call before a resolution is reached. Even if you scream the most disgusting, vile abuse at my team like you did last time, please ask to be transferred to the manager, and I will be happy to call you a cunt and hang up on you myself.*

"I honestly can't think of any." I deleted the last line of my email, signed off, and moved to the next one. "I know for a fact that I haven't seen any half-fish people around lately."

He scoffed. "They have magic, Chosen. They wear charmed necklaces to change their tails into legs so they can walk among humans, and always return to their own home before night falls."

"Why before nightfall?"

"Their charms are solar-powered."

"Ah. Well, if they look like us, how would I know who is a mermaid?"

He let out an exasperated grunt. "Molinere should have taught you how to expand your vision so you can see the magic in front of you."

"Well, he didn't," I murmured, tapping out another gracious reply to a customer who was outraged that he couldn't get insurance coverage without actually paying for it. "Molinere got ratfaced drunk and disappeared with my dad."

Donovan moved closer. I couldn't help it; I shivered. "You will be able to sense them," he murmured. "You are the One of Every Blood; you have a trace of Mer heritage. You will know your own kin. Think well, Chosen." His lips were so close to my ear. Too close.

I slumped over my keyboard. Suddenly, I wondered why the hell I was answering my emails when I was probably going to get fired before the end of the day, anyway. The only thing in my future was me, hitting the streets, looking for a minimum wage job that wouldn't ask too many questions.

I might as well have some fun before I get fired. "Fine," I

sighed. "I'll think... er... *well*, as you so poetically put it." I reached for a marker and a scrap piece of paper and wrote *mermaid* on it. Underneath that, I wrote *only here during the daytime.*

"What else? You said they're vain, right?"

"Yes. Physical beauty is very important to them."

I wrote *vain* on the paper. "You said they love to be admired. Do you mean for their beauty, or something else? Am I looking for a model, or an actress, or—"

Cress snorted. "They sing, of course, Chosen. The Mer love to beguile with their voices."

A weird tingle raised the hair on the back of my neck—a strange sense of the familiar. I tapped the page and wrote down *singers*. "And they have to wear a necklace?"

"Yes. It will not be a small trinket. Transformation magic requires a large vessel, so the pendant will be quite conspicuous."

I scribbled *chunky statement jewelry* underneath *vain*, and pursed my lips. I could already think of the perfect person who matched this description.

It figured. "Of course." I should have already seen where this was going. "Hyacinth," I muttered. "That bitch is just about as insane as I am." She'd even referred to herself as a siren on stage a handful of times.

This was crazy.

Cress bristled. "A water flower?"

"Hyacinth is not a flower. She's my nemesis," I said.

There was a pause. "You will have to elaborate on that further, Chosen."

"As part of my treatment, I was encouraged to find a creative outlet to express myself, to try and channel the overwhelming..." I hesitated and sighed heavily. "You know what, I'm not going to go into it. To cut a long story short, I found that I enjoyed singing, especially to a little crowd. My therapist Bronwyn said that it was understandable—I always found it cathartic to bring my audience on an emotional journey through song."

"Obviously," Cress muttered. "You have mer blood."

"You crave to be understood," Donovan corrected her. "Go on, Chosen."

I shifted in my chair uncomfortably. It's not shameful to admit when you need help, I told myself firmly. "When I started here at Base Budget Insurance, I knew I needed an emotional outlet, just in case I got overwhelmed. I found a K-bar in a basement only a block away."

"K bar?"

"Karaoke bar," I explained. "It's like… a tavern. An alehouse, where you can drink, but you can also get up on stage and sing a song. There's usually a half-dozen or so people like me down there, acting out their rock-star fantasies. It's actually really sad," I said, a huff of laughter escaping me.

"Why is it sad?" Cress sounded confused. "I have accompanied many a lute player with a lusty tune in an alehouse. It is a wildly enjoyable way to release tension after battle."

I suppressed a smile. "That's a good point, Cress. Anyway, I started going there on my lunch breaks. Hyacinth is always there. I don't even think she has a job. She's a stuck-up bitch, she hogs the microphone, and she acts like she's the hottest thing to ever grace a stage. The others seem to like her more than I do."

"Well, if she is a mermaid, then she will not be employed," Donovan said. "And her magic will weave through her song, so she would appear to mortals as a beautiful creature. You would be immune to her siren magic, as you carry mer blood."

The musty-smelling drunks in Karaoke Cove *did* seem

entranced when she sang. And she didn't have a very good voice. I was no Mariah Carey, but I thought I had a better voice than she did, yet Hyacinth always got a higher score on the applause-o-meter than I did. Maybe she was a mermaid. It would explain a lot.

Reality smacked me in the back of the head. No. This was insane. I was delusional.

"We will go now," Donovan put his hand on my shoulder again, and all my resolve disappeared immediately. "We must find this Hyacinth."

What the hell. I might as well make time for my creative outlet. "Fine. I guess we're heading into the Karaoke Cove for my lunch break."

"Good. Make haste, woman. Gather your things."

CHAPTER
NINE

I took an abrupt left turn past Sammy's Sandwich Shop, skipped down a flight of stairs that smelled overwhelmingly like pee, pushed open the heavy metal door, and walked inside.

The door shut behind me firmly, cutting off the sounds of the city, I waited until my eyeballs adjusted to the sudden darkness, and listened to someone murdering a rendition of an eighties power ballad. It was Gary, by the sounds of it. He was always partial to hair bands.

The Karaoke Cove was the epitome of a dive bar—a seedy old basement with a handful of rickety tables and chairs in front of a tiny corner stage and stained, sticky carpet that might have been red once upon a time.

Cress huffed. "This place smells atrocious." She whipped off her cloak, popping into a full, blisteringly sexy vision beside me.

"What are you doing?"

"We only agreed to hide ourselves in your place of employment, Chosen. I'm not skulking under a glamor cloak in here."

"But—" I cut myself off abruptly. It wasn't like anyone

else could see them, anyway. Just then, I realized that I couldn't sense my other hallucination anymore. "Where the hell is Donovan?"

She sniffed. "He walked in ahead of you, of course. He is still upset with you for tricking him with the tiny moving office. He will be scouting this tavern for danger, to ensure you are safe."

Tension simmered in my stomach; I forced my hands to unclench. *Just pretend they're not here*, I told myself. *Because they're not. Get up on stage, sing a couple of songs, release some tension. Go back to work, finish your day...*

And pack up your desk because you're about to get fired, anyway.

I blew out a breath. "Fine. Before we go through to the bar, Cress, what is it you want me to do with Hyacinth? Should I just ask her for the stone?"

"Gods, Chosen, are you mad? A common mermaid will not have the spark stone. The sea witch guards the siren stone. She would never let it out of her sight."

"So..." I raised my eyebrows. "You want me to ask Hyacinth to go and get the sea witch and come here?"

Cress reared back, horrified. "What is *wrong* with you? Of course not! Why would you think it would be a good idea to invite the dark malevolent power of Jengrakenzlore into the human realm? Are you *mad?*"

"Yes, apparently I am." I held up a finger and gave her a stern look. "If you have feedback for me, Cress, please make sure it is constructive. You need to remember I don't have a clue about any of this, so you need to be clear with your instructions."

She stared at me sullenly. "Find this Hyacinth. You will need to either strike a bargain with her or trick her into taking us to a Mer portal. Once we are in their realm, we will need her to guide us to the lair of the great sea witch. She guards their spark stone."

"Okay." Easy-peasy, lemon-delusions. "Do I want to know what I'll have to do once we get to the sea witch's lair?"

"No. I do not wish to scare you."

I grimaced. "Fine. Let's go." I swished the curtain back and strode into the little basement bar.

I was right. Gary, a fifty-something actuary from Wisconsin, was standing onstage with one foot up on the speaker, head thrown back, tunelessly screeching about how much he missed the rains down in Africa.

My eyes adjusted to the red lights slowly. Apart from Banoy, the bartender, the place was practically deserted, but that was normal for lunchtime on a Thursday.

Banoy waved at me from behind the bar as I walked in, giving me a big smile. "Hello, Susan!"

"Hey, Banoy. Have you had a chance to get up there today?"

"No." He shook his head sadly and slid a diet soda onto the bar for me. "We're too busy today, Susan. Maybe tomorrow."

Banoy wasn't allowed to get up on stage when there were people in the bar to hear him; it upset the singing enthusiasts too much. Not many people realized that karaoke was like a national sport in the Philippines, and nobody liked getting their delusions of grandeur crushed by a skinny old Filipino man who could murder any rendition of any nineties power ballad you could think of.

I'd heard him once; Banoy sang like an angel. His voice literally brought me to tears.

I wandered inside, weaving through the empty tables and chairs which were placed too-close together. Cress drifted away from me, melting into the darkness around the corner from the bar.

A prickle shot down my shoulder blades. There was Donovan, leaning up against the velvet curtains in the back corner in almost total darkness. His deep emerald eyes flashed in the gloom, focused, poised, in full stalking-predator mode.

My stomach flipped when I caught sight of him; both him and Cress had changed into their battle leathers. The hard, tight midnight-black suit wrapped around his powerful legs perfectly, and the sculpted armor over his tunic highlighted every hard muscle, every taut and poised line in his body. Michelangelo would weep at the sight of such perfection—such powerful proportions, such a perfect balance of predatory beauty, feral grace, and supreme power.

Nobody seemed to notice him. Then again, there was barely anyone in here, only a couple of people slouched at the tables right in front of the stage. I recognized both of them—Timothy, a retired alcoholic with a penchant for very long blues songs, and Jackie, a stocky bus driving lesbian who enjoyed belting R&B classics. Jackie must have had a route to run later since she was still in her uniform; a very tailored and sharply pressed beige ensemble that gave off Gestapo vibes.

Aha! There she was. Hyacinth stood to the right of the stage, quivering with expectation and fingering her own bejeweled microphone she'd bought from home. Now that I looked at her, it was no wonder my broken brain had decided she was a mermaid. Hyacinth was probably my age —mid forties, or so, with a thick head of long, wavy dark-honey colored hair. She was curvy and always dressed to show it off, favoring fifties-style pin-up fashion. Today she wore a low-cut blue and white polka-dot dress, showing off her ample boobs, a waist-cinching, thick white patent belt, and a tight knee-length skirt that hugged her thighs.

My eyes focused on her huge necklace; chunky orange beads with a large resin starfish hung between her boobs. She always wore statement jewelry. Mindful that I only had one hour for lunch and I should wrap this up quickly, I marched over to her. "Hey, Hyacinth!"

She glared at me. "You're not cutting in today, Susan. I'm next. Banoy has already programmed my song."

I held up my hands in surrender. "I'm not going to cut in, Hyacinth. I would never dream of it. Besides." I smiled. As soon as she called me a psycho, my delusions would be satisfied, and I could leave and go back to work. "You've got an adoring crowd to seduce with your siren song. You can't let your fans down."

"Ah ha." Her eyes narrowed further; I could almost feel her picking me apart. "You've finally decided to put your cards on the table and challenge me, haven't you? Took you long enough."

A trickle of unease ran through me. Working to keep my face relaxed, I made my mouth move. "Whatever do you mean?"

She snorted. "Oh, Susan. Do you think I'm stupid? I can tell you right now, you'll never beat me. My voice is pure magic. You might have a little talent, but you have maybe one-hundredth of my power, you know?"

The trickle of unease turned into a river of foreboding. "I don't actually know, Hyacinth. But that's quite mean."

"Cut the crap." She tossed back her hair. "I am a siren. My song seduces all who hear it. I don't know who you are, but you're a weak-as-piss version of me." She squared her shoulders, thrust out her chest, and got right in my face. "You'll never be *me*, Susan, as much as you might want to be."

Oh, right. Hyacinth was as nuts as I was. This wasn't new information.

It was time to go all-in. What did Cress say? Make a deal? Trick her?

"Well then, bitch," I murmured, smiling sweetly. "If you think you're so amazing, let's make a deal."

Her overplucked eyebrow rose. "I don't need to make deals with you."

"Oh, you're scared, are you? Scared of a little competition when it comes to singing?"

She snorted. "I'm not scared. I'll destroy you."

I needed to taunt her a little more. "You *think* you will." My lip curled in a smirk. "I've been holding back."

Her jaw ticked. "You have not."

"I have."

She studied me carefully for a second. "It won't make a difference. You don't have the power I have."

"Well," I sighed. "I guess you'll never know."

We glared at each other for a whole moment. I waited patiently. Finally, she cracked. "What's the deal?"

Here's where I found out how crazy she actually was. "Duet," I snarled, holding her gaze. "The Boy Is Mine. I'll do Brandy, you do Monica. If you win, I promise to never come into this bar ever again. But if I win..."

I took a breath, composing myself. You never got used to people's scorn when they realized how insane you actually were.

I swallowed. "If I win, you take me and my friends through a portal to the mermaid realm."

There was a long, long moment of silence, while Hyacinth and I stared at each other. I cringed a little bit. God, this was embarrassing.

Finally, her cherry-colored lip curled. "I wondered what those sexy Fae bastards in the corner were up to. You're doing this for them, aren't you? They want you to get them into my home realm, don't they?"

I relaxed slightly. Hyacinth was playing along. "Maybe."

She looked away, suddenly uncertain. "The portals to the mer realm are supposed to stay secret. Security reasons, y'know?"

"Oh, yes, I know," I nodded, as if I understood. A bubble of slightly hysterical laughter escaped my lips.

Luckily, Hyacinth was still thinking. She chewed on her lip for a while. "It's not like you're actually going to beat me, anyway..."

"I might. You never know."

Her eyes flashed. "I do."

"You've got nothing to be afraid of, then."

Her jaw hardened. "Fine. You've got a deal. Whoever is first to get to Superstar level on the Applause-o-meter wins."

I grinned, and held out my hand, and shook hers firmly. "Deal." I turned and walked towards the bar. "Banoy? Change of plans. Queue up number four-oh-nine-five and reset the Applause-o-meter to two-player mode.

"Yasss, girl!" Banoy did a little shimmy of delight and tapped on the monitor behind the bar. "It's battle time!"

Gary's song had finally come to an end. I climbed on stage, gave him a pat on his very sweaty back, and plucked the microphone out of his hands.

Hyacinth, thrusting out her chest, joined me on the stage, stomped to the center of the tiny space, and jabbed me in the ribs with an elbow at the same time. "Move over, bitch," she hissed.

I grimaced and conceded a couple of inches, my stomach sinking. I should have thought this through more thoroughly. I knew I was a better singer than Hyacinth, but she always seemed to get the highest scores on the Applause-o-meter. Damn mermaid magic.

Doubt nudged me. Maybe I wasn't as good as I thought I was.

If I lost, I wouldn't be able to come back again. I'd lose my creative outlet, my way to blow off steam. I needed this seedy underground dive bar. It was my dirty secret. Nobody I knew would ever come in here. And there was nothing else like this in a twenty-block radius.

Damn it. Well, it was too late now. I was going to do this like I did everything. Once-hundred-percent effort, play to win.

The song started; both of us began to sing the intro. Breathy voices, soft vibrato. Hyacinth swayed next to me, batting her eyelashes at Timothy and Jackie, our only audience.

Hyacinth sang the first line; I took the second, then, it was her turn again. She rolled her hips seductively as she sang. Timothy winked at her and let out a hoot.

The needle on her side of the Applause-o-meter crept up.

I sang again, putting a little more emotion into my performance. Jackie hollered appreciatively, but it wasn't enough to move my needle past Hyacinth's. She butted me aside with her hips and sang again; both Jackie and Timothy hooted. Her needle moved up again.

An idea hit me. Whoever got to Superstar first won. That meant whoever got the audience to make the most noise while they were singing would win our bet.

All I had to do was get Timothy and Jackie to scream.

Hyacinth, doing a little shimmy, turned around so her back was to the audience, and she could sing seductively over her shoulder. It was a sex-kitten maneuver I'd seen her pull many times, something that usually elicited lots of appreciative catcalls and loud hoots. She wanted to wrap this up quickly. Giving a sexy pout, she lifted her bedazzled microphone to her lips and opened her mouth.

I did a spin around her and punched her in the stomach.

Hyacinth gasped, winded, and mouthed like a goldfish, suddenly unable to sing her verse.

I walked to the front of the stage, belting my verse out. And since I had no self-respect left, anyway, I ripped open my blouse, displaying my lacy black bra, and shimmied my boobs vigorously right at the edge of the stage.

Timothy and Jackie both leapt to their feet and screamed in tandem. "Yesssss! Oh my *goddddd*! Wooo *hooooo!*"

The needle on my side jumped straight to Superstar.

I turned to Hyacinth. Her face had turned red. "Game over, fishgirl." I dropped the microphone.

CHAPTER TEN

"You *bitch*," Hyacinth gasped, one hand on her chest, as we both climbed off the stage. "You cheated!"

"Maybe I did," I grinned at her, walking to the back corner of the bar, trying to salvage the buttons on my blouse. One had popped off completely, leaving me with quite a plunging neckline, but it was nothing indecent. As long as I didn't make any sudden moves, I'd be okay. "But if I cheated, then you did, too. We were both using more than our voices. You were using your siren magic to win. I just used my boobs."

"You punched me in the gut!"

"You elbowed me in the ribs when you went on stage. I was just getting my payback."

She huffed, her face turning even redder. "The deal is null and void, then."

"The deal stands." Donovan loomed out of the dark like a specter. "She beat you fair and square, siren."

Hyacinth hissed at him, baring her teeth. They were suddenly very white, triangular shaped, and very very sharp.

Uh oh. There goes the last fragment of my sanity.

Just go with it, my dad's voice whispered in my head.

Cress stepped in front of me. "She beat you fair and square, mer-bitch. You have to show us to the portal."

Hyacinth pouted. "Why do you want to go to my realm anyway?" she rubbed her stomach sulkily. "What are you doing here? Have you gotten sick of bullying the creatures in the Upper World already? You high fae are all the same; you think you should be running everything."

Donovan grew very still. "I would caution you to hold your tongue, sea hag. If you want to keep it," he added quietly.

Hyacinth bristled, but she didn't respond.

"Come on, Hyacinth." I said. "We had a deal."

She glared at me for a few more moments. "Fine," she finally huffed out. "I'll show you the portal." She stomped across the floor, heading towards the tiny corridor at the back of the bar, walked in, and kicked open the door to the ladies. "If either of you tell anyone about this, I'll—"

"You won't do anything," Cress said. "You're too embarrassed about losing your bet."

Hyacinth scowled and kicked open a cubicle door. "At least tell me what you're going to do in my realm. I won't put my people in danger."

Cress and Donovan stared at her stonily. In the long silence that followed, I checked my watch. Damn it, my lunch break was almost up already. I had to wrap up this little breakdown in a few minutes and get back to the office.

"We need to see the sea witch," I piped up.

There was a long pause. All three of them stared at me.

Hyacinth's mouth dropped open. "You... you need to see the sea witch?"

Donovan let out a groan.

"Apparently, yes."

Hyacinth's eyes lit up, and her cherry-colored lips

curved up in a big smile. "Oh. Oh, okay. That's fine, then. If you want to pop into the portal and go and visit the sea witch, you're more than welcome."

I frowned. "Something tells me that I suddenly don't want to go and see the sea witch."

"No, you don't," Hyacinth said, her tone gloating.

"And why is that?"

"She's going to eat you."

"Oh." I hesitated a moment, then shrugged. "I can't imagine being eaten by an imaginary sea witch would be too painful. Let's just get on with it, shall we?"

Hyacinth pouted again, obviously not getting the required terrified response. After a minute, she brightened. "If you must go, I'll take you right to her lair myself."

Donovan moved close to me, looming over my shoulder. "Cress and I have a plan to infiltrate her domain, Chosen. We were going to break in, steal the stone, and have you close it."

My irritation spiked. "I don't know *how* to close stones." I shook my head, frustrated. "You know, if this was a real-life team project, you would be a terrible team coordinator, Donovan."

Cress bristled, one hand on the sheath of her dagger. "The prince commands an army of fifty thousand fae warriors," she snapped. "His leadership is exemplary. How dare you—"

"When you want people to work together as a team, you have to provide communication and training. In this case, both have been non-existent," I told her, meeting her furious stare calmly. "We both know you're not going to stab me, Cress, so maybe take a couple of deep breaths instead, okay?"

Actually, that was a good idea. I took one of my own, hoping everyone would just disappear. When they didn't,

I glared at them. "Look, I don't mean to be rude, but I have to wrap up this little episode quickly and get back to work. Can we just flop around here in the ladies' room and pretend to be swimming, and then I'll fight an imaginary sea witch with my magical powers and get back to work?"

Hyacinth peered at me, tilting her head. "You are quite mad. Did you know that?"

"Yes." I nodded. "Come on, let's get this over with. Where's the portal?"

"Here." She pointed at the toilet bowl.

I frowned. "Not a chance in hell."

"You wanted it, girlfriend, so you got it. It's the only portal in a fifty-mile radius. Why do you think I spend so much time in the Karaoke Cove?" She pointed. "If you want to go to the mer realm, you need to dive into the bowl."

This was getting ridiculous. "How about you go first?"

She chuckled. "You want these two sexy brutes to come with you don't you? Well, you have mer blood so you can pass through the portal, but they'll have to hold on to one of us to go through." She pointed at Cress, who was still glaring at me. "I'll tell you what, I'll take Lara Croft here first, and you follow with her big scary boyfriend."

"Ugh. Fine."

She reached out and grabbed Cress by the shoulder. "Let's go."

Suddenly, Hyacinth jumped high into the air, leaping towards the toilet bowl, and hit the starfish pendant around her neck at the same time. A pulse of energy punched me, surging through every atom in my body.

I gasped. Before I could believe what I was seeing, there was a flash, and an enormous red glittering tail splashed down into the bowl instead of legs. The bowl expanded with split-second timing; the water sparkled a fiery blue, swallowing Hyacinth, who pulled Cress down head-first with her.

They both disappeared.

I gaped down into the bowl.

Donovan nudged me gently. "We must follow quickly, Chosen, or we may lose them in the currents."

"Oh.... kay." My body wasn't obeying me, though. I couldn't move.

"Come." Very gently, he reached out and took my chin, turning my head so I was facing him. "Don't be afraid. I will protect you." He slipped his hand into mine, his firm, strong fingers holding me with a sure grip, and jostled me into position in front of the bowl. "Jump."

"Jump?"

"Jump."

I closed my eyes and jumped.

CHAPTER
ELEVEN

Water swallowed me completely, and the shock of cold jolted my senses. I waved my arms around wildly, Donovan tugged one hand, squeezing my fingers.

"Open your eyes." His voice sounded muffled. Oh, shit, we were underwater, deep underwater; I couldn't feel anything below me. I opened my eyes, bracing myself for the sting of salt and frantically looked up.

Blue. Just endless blue. I couldn't see the surface.

Panic gripped me, and Donovan tugged me back down to face him. Something was covering his face; a bubble of air was suspended over his mouth and nose.

"Just breathe," he ordered.

I shook my head frantically. Where the hell was *my* portable oxygen bubble? My chest was getting tight.

I started kicking. I had to find the surface, or I was going to drown any second. But... Where was the surface?

Donovan let out a growl, let go of my hand, and clamped both of his hands over my face, pulling me down to face him directly. To my surprise, I realized I could see as clearly as if I was wearing goggles; my vision wasn't reduced by the water surrounding me. I could see every detail of his shockingly handsome face, the rigid lines of his hard jaw, his sculpted cheekbones, his furious, blazing green eyes.

"Breathe," he ordered, shaking me gently. "You have mer blood. Reach into yourself, find your magic, and let yourself breathe."

I shook my head again, too scared to waste any of the oxygen in my lungs to reply. *I can't*, I mouthed. *I'll drown.*

My head started to spin. Oh, God, my chest was too tight. I kicked out, trying to break free, but Donovan held me in an iron grip. He wouldn't let me go.

"Breathe," he growled, clamping his hands tighter on my face. "Now."

Panic overwhelmed me. I had to get away. I had to find the surface, now. Without thinking about what I was doing, I sank down a little, reached out, grabbed Donovan by the hips, and kneed him in the groin as hard as I could.

"Oof." Shock blazed over his hard expression, and he let me go. I took the opportunity to kick out, trying to head to the surface. I had no idea where it was, though. There was only endless blue as far as my eyes could see.

A hand caught my foot; I squeaked. It dragged me back down, pulling me through the water almost effortlessly. Donovan turned me to face him again, his expression furious.

"Are you completely incompetent?" he shouted through his air bubble. "You think that *I'm* a terrible leader? I'm communicating to you, but you have no idea how to follow instructions!" He shook me again. "Breathe, you incompetent, foolish woman!"

What did he just call me?

A fire lit up my belly, going from a tiny spark to an inferno in just a millisecond. It felt like I was no longer a woman—I was a volcano, and I was about to erupt. It was too late, too late to stop the explosion, I couldn't take deep, slow breaths and calm down, there was no time to repeat mantras or call Bronwyn or take one of my pills...

My whole body pulsed; an electric current burst through me, sending a shock of intense, blistering outrage through me. I poked Donovan in his ridiculously hard chest. "Listen here, you arrogant bastard," I snapped back. "You don't throw someone into a project without preparing them properly first. You have given me zero instructions."

"I have told you exactly what you must do, and you are fighting me." His eyes narrowed, burning into mine with a blazing intensity. "You know what you are? You are difficult to work with."

I gasped; he'd hit me right where it hurt. As far as I was concerned, that was the worst insult he could have come up with. "Donovan, I am *not* difficult to work with. I am a professional. You have *literally* thrown me into the deep end. How am I supposed to—"

One corner of his lip twitched just a fraction. A smug light sparked in his eyes.

"Oh."

I could breathe. Huh.

Donovan didn't smile, but a definite lightness lifted the hard lines in his face. Bastard.

Carefully, mindful of my delicate mental state, I reached out with my faculties to try and make sense of what I was feeling. It didn't exactly feel like breathing. Water wasn't rushing into my lungs, and they weren't expanding or deflating, either. Instead, I felt a kind of... flow, a very gentle drift, and a light, pleasant tingle behind my ears.

Hesitantly, I reached out and stroked the tingly spot, and felt three ridges back there, as if the curve of my ear had been duplicated a few more times.

I looked at Donovan. "Have I got gills?"

"Yes."

"Huh. Well, they definitely weren't there before."

"You finally accessed your power, Chosen. You are the One of Every Blood. You can move within all the realms effortlessly, so your magic will provide you with exactly what you need to adapt."

"Took you long enough," a voice below me snorted. "I thought you were going to thrash around like a puffed-up pufferfish all day."

I spun around in the endless blue, awkwardly trying to get into the right position. Hyacinth and Cress floated below us. Cress's face was also covered by a bubble of oxygen, but I could see her clearly, scowling.

For a second, I gaped at Hyacinth's tail. It really was absolutely stunning, long and powerful, with shimmering reddish-orange scales morphing into an enviable flat stomach. Her breasts were only barely covered by her floating golden hair. She saw me looking and waved her tail smugly. "Bet you wish you had one of these, don't you? You might have mer blood, but you'll never be like me."

I sighed. "Let's just get this over with, shall we? Where is the sea witch's lair?"

Hyacinth smirked. "This way. Follow me." With a flick of her tail, she darted off, heading straight down, disappearing into the endless blue almost instantly.

"Hyacinth," I called, using my "stop fucking around" voice. "If you want to escort us, you will need to make allowances for our pace."

There was no response.

I sighed. "You don't want to get in trouble for showing us the portal, do you?"

She darted back, her tail flicking powerfully behind her

to propel her quickly through the water. "Ugh. Fine. Come on."

Awkwardly, I spun my body so I faced downwards and kicked. Cress floated just in front of me, slicing through the water with more grace than I could summon. But then again, she was wearing her skin-tight battle leathers, which made her sleek like a seal, while I was still wearing my shirt and pencil skirt, which I'd hiked up around my thighs so I could kick my legs more freely.

I could feel Donovan behind me. Covering my six, I suppose he would say. He'd be getting an eyeful of my panties right now.

"This sucks," Hyacinth moaned, barely moving her tail to propel herself downward. "How the hell can you possibly live like this? If I had to swim this slowly all the time, I think I'd die of boredom. I'd die of hunger, definitely. There's no way you could catch anything going this slowly. I'd have to go vegan and eat seaweed for the rest of my days. Bleeack." She faked a gag.

"Be kind, please, Hyacinth," I reprimanded her gently. "We are doing our best."

"I can feel the barnacles growing on me," she moaned, scrubbing her shoulders with her hands. "I'm going to have to get someone to scrape them off."

Shapes came into focus in front of me. I tuned out Hyacinth's moaning as the seafloor came into view, first, a field of bright-green seaweed swaying gently in the tide, then, a rocky reef rose up. It was a glorious underwater garden, bright with all colors and shapes and sizes of coral—vivid pink rosettes rising up from rock, claws of bright-orange, long spikes of purple, big, bulbous round green protrusions, and a giant yellow thing that looked like a brain. Little fish zipped in front of us, hiding in the pudgy tentacles of fat anemones that lay between the coral. A black-and-white striped angelfish, bristling with spikes, nudged into the reef, flat-shaped silver fish sparkled as they dashed left and right, and a giant grouper drifted by, mouthing stupidly, as if outraged at our mere presence.

My eyes boggled. It was an enchanting sight.

"Come on, slowpoke," Hyacinth called. A smug smile pulled at her lips. "The sea witch's lair is this way."

She led us down further, where the seafloor dipped down between two reefs. The coral grew less bright, the colors more muted. The light dimmed, as we went down and down along the bare sandy seafloor. Soon, I realized we were being funneled into the bottom of a deep trench, the top seemed to get further and further away, and the light was rapidly disappearing.

A feeling of danger pricked my senses. I glanced behind me and caught Donovan's eye. "Are you sure this is a good idea?"

"No," he answered, his tone grim. "But we must get to the siren stone before my brother. Its power would be terrible in his hands. Be brave, Chosen. Cress and I will fight if we have to."

A spiky figure loomed up ahead. As we got closer, I realized it was a skeleton of something huge—a whale, probably, bones picked completely clean.

"Well, this is not ominous at all, is it? It's like something out of my nightmares." I gazed around at the oddly prickly-looking walls of the trench, realizing that they were littered with smaller bones, too.

"Not far to go now, not far at all!" Hyacinth flicked her tail, propelling herself forward through the cracked bones of the giant whale, spinning elegantly around the ribs until she was on the other side. I swam through the enormous dead creature tentatively, using the rough bones to propel myself forward. This giant skeleton felt like a warning. Danger. Keep out. Enter and die.

Hyacinth floated on the other side, waiting for us. She pressed her finger to her lips, indicating quiet, and waited for us to swim closer.

My senses screamed at me. Quickly, I looked around, checking out all angles. To the left and right, the walls of the trench stretched upwards as far as I could see. Behind us, the whale skeleton seemed to block our exit.

Up ahead, the trench narrowed to almost a point, ending in another weed-covered rock wall. I narrowed my eyes, peering through the gloom, and saw an enormous round shape etched into the wall. It looked a little like scales.

No, not scales. They were shells arranged in a large rosette pattern in the wall, bone-white and shining with an odd, preternatural pearl-like luster. It should have looked pretty, but it didn't. It looked terrifying, like a door made of shining human teeth.

Hyacinth waited until we were next to her and pointed. "There you go." Her voice was a hushed whisper.

"That's the sea witch's lair?"

"Yep."

I frowned. "So... it's a cave?"

She beamed. "That's right."

"No other doors? No emergency exit out the back? No side windows to let in a little sunshine?"

Hyacinth shook her head. "Uh uh."

Cress and Donovan began muttering to each other behind me, while I studied the creepy door. Whatever their plan had been, it didn't involve a frontal assault.

"Hey." Hyacinth suddenly spun around to face us and spread her hands expansively. "Do you guys want to play a game?"

I caught the wicked spark in her eyes and held up my finger in a warning. "Hyacinth—"

"Let's play..." Her coral-pink lips split into a huge smile. "Ding dong ditch!" She flicked her powerful tail and darted away from us, heading straight for the door, then smacked it with both fists, causing it to clatter loudly like a snake's rattle. Without hesitating, she turned around and sped past us at a lightning pace, cackling in glee and spinning effortlessly through the bones of the whale, and disappeared into the distance.

A sickening pulse thudded through the water around us, and my heart sank. The door cracked, then swung open, smacking against the rock wall with a terrifyingly loud clang.

Before I could move, before I could even breathe, enormous silver-blue tentacles erupted from the hole, slithering like snakes, peeling up the sides of the trench. I froze.

A woman's voice—deep, thrumming with an alien power—echoed out from the darkness within the cave as the tentacles kept coming and coming, long and thick and absolutely horrifying. "Who dares disturb me?"

Donovan was suddenly in front of me, a shining dagger in each fist. A tentacle shot towards him, lightning fast, and wrapped around his arms, squeezing them to his sides.

The voice cackled. "Got you!"

He swore, threw his head back and shouted a word in a foreign tongue; a flash of green light sparked in the water. The tentacles unraveled and slithered away.

"Ouch! What the—ooh, you just wait until I get there, you little bastard." The voice echoed, getting louder. Those enormous tentacles snaked closer again. Donovan, now with his hands free, swiped at them with his daggers, and they flinched back. "You want to use magic on me?" The sea witch's voice rose through several octaves. "On *me?*"

A tentacle reared back and shot forward, wrapping around Cress's leg and tugging at her. Another circled her arm, holding it tight. Quickly, she whispered a spell under her breath and slipped out of the creature's grip like she was boneless. Still, the silvery-white tentacles kept coming, getting thicker and thicker.

Donovan whipped around, facing the door and brandishing his daggers. He roared a challenge. "Come, monster! Face me!"

Cress dropped down and planted her feet on the sea floor in front of me, one leg stretched out, in a classic predator crouch.

"Oh, don't worry, I'm coming, you little shit," the sea witch spat out from the depths of the cave. "Just you wait." The enormous tentacles kept spilling out of the hole. "Just wait." There was a pause. "I really should get this entrance widened one day."

"Come, sea hag!" Donovan roared again. "I will have your head!"

This was stupid. I heaved a sigh. "Stop."

"What?" The sea witch's voice echoed out from deep within the cave.

"Not you," I called out. "I'm talking to my companions."

Donovan turned his head and glared at me furiously. Cress didn't move. Her huge eyes were fixed on the open doorway, watching the enormous monster's tentacles spill out and unfurl like intestines falling out of a stomach wound.

"Just... just stop," I told Donovan. I kicked my feet, swimming past him. "You're being terribly rude."

His emerald eyes flashed with fury. "It's the sea witch," he hissed. "She is a vicious monster."

"Donovan!" I spun around in the water to face him.

"That's also very rude. You don't know her personally, do you?"

"She's a predator, Chosen! Of course I know all about her. The legend of the evil sea witch of the mer has reached every single corner of our Upper World."

I pursed my lips. "I'll take that as a no. You *don't* know her personally."

"Everyone knows of her! Her dark magic powers are—"

"Ah." I nodded smugly. "Now I get it. That's what all this is about, isn't it? This is what this little episode is all about. I've never really let myself be comfortable being a powerful woman, have I?"

"Chosen..." Donovan shook his head, exasperated. "What are you talking about? She's literally a monster, and she will kill us and eat us."

"No, Donovan," I said patiently. "She's a woman with power, and you're going to insult her and bring her down and call her a witch and a monster. Well, I've got news for you, buddy." I wagged my finger at him. "You can't silence us anymore. Gone are the days where you can take an intelligent, powerful woman and burn her at the stake. Powerful women are *not* evil. We are not monsters."

Cress twitched. "Donovan..."

His eyes flicked behind me and widened.

Now that I realized what this delusion was about, I was determined to not to be distracted. "Focus, please," I said. "We're having this little talk now, Donovan. A woman with power isn't a witch. She's not a hag, and she's definitely not a monster," I added, swishing my hands so I could turn around to see what he was staring at. "A powerful woman can still be soft; she can still be gentle. We can command respect. We don't have to be unyielding or hard, or masculine-presenting to get ahead. For too long, the patriarchy—"

The words died in my throat.

There, outside the sinister shining shell door, the silver-blue tentacles stretched out in all directions, thick and dexterous as boa constrictors. Right in the middle was the most terrifying-looking woman I'd ever seen in my life.

Huge, at least four times my size, and humanoid apart from her terrifying tentacles that branched out from her thick waist. She had a human-looking face, except for her mouth—too wide, stretching out from one ear to another. The huge maw dropped open in a big wide O, displaying a full circle of razor-sharp triangular teeth. Her enormous round eyes were coal-black, with no trace of whites on either side of her iris. Long, tangled stringy-green hair drifted around her head. To complete the picture, two huge bare breasts floated out from her chest, waving gently from side to side in the drift of the tide. Her skin shined silver-blue, with an odd preternatural luminescence that raised goosebumps all over my skin.

I swallowed roughly.

The sea witch closed her mouth, blinked, then opened it again. "Go on," she finally said. "What were you saying about the patriarchy?"

I chewed on my lip for a second. This is me, facing my demons. "Uh, where was I? Oh right." I took a deep breath and felt my gills tickle. *Just go with it, Susan.* "For too long, the patriarchy has been demonizing strong women, trying to bring them down, because they fear our power. We are not evil just because we are smart and strong and brave."

The terrifying woman nodded slowly. "You're right," she mumbled. "I'm not evil. I'm just powerful."

I nodded stiffly. "Exactly. You are a beautiful, magical creature."

Her enormous mouth split open again in a horrifying grin. "You think I'm beautiful?"

I swallowed again. "Beauty is subjective, of course. But that's beside the point. Even if you weren't beautiful, that doesn't mean you are evil."

"That's right. Well, maybe I can occasionally be a little evil. When there's a ship to sink, or a bratty mermaid kid to curse to an endless, agonizing existence as a screaming sea-wraith," she added, hitching her bony shoulders in a shrug. "But I can be soft. I can be gentle."

"You can," I told her. "You can be anything you want. You are a strong, powerful, beautiful woman, and it's unfair to demonize you."

She nodded to herself thoughtfully for a moment. "I crochet," she said, raising her thin eyebrows. "Did you know? No, no one knows that. I make handbags out of kelp and decorate them with shells. They're so pretty." She pouted. "But no one ever says, *oh, look, there's that talented, wonderful sea witch who makes those pretty kelp handbags*, do they? They just swim away screaming, *oh shit, it's the sea witch! Run away, she's going to eat us!*"

"I can commiserate," I told her, trying not to look at her enormous tits as they bobbed along sideways in the current, then back again. "When people fear your power, they can be awfully mean, can't they?"

Her chin wobbled. "Yes. And the other merpeople can be so mean to me."

I kicked my feet, moving closer to her. Face your demon...

A hand grabbed my leg and yanked me back. "You are insane. She's literally going to eat us," he growled. "Get behind me, woman."

I sighed heavily. "Look, Donovan, if she eats us, I dare say we deserve it. We've gone about this the wrong way. We should have knocked on her door and politely asked her to talk to us."

"Oh. I still would have eaten you," she called out from behind me.

"But instead," I barreled on, ignoring her. "We rattled the door to her sanctuary and attacked her when she tried to come out. That's not a polite way to introduce yourself, is it?"

"Yes," the sea witch called. "It was *very* rude."

I paddled with my arms, facing her again. "Please accept my apologies... uh, I'm sorry, I didn't catch your name."

Her lip wobbled again. "Nobody has asked me my name in centuries. Everyone just calls me the sea witch."

"Well... what's your name?"

"It's Jengrakenzlore."

"Nice to meet you, uh, Jen. I'm Susan Moore." I held out my hand.

She looked at it and licked her lips. Her sharp teeth flashed.

I snatched it back.

"Sorry," she said cheerfully. "Force of habit."

"Listen, Jen." I sidled a little closer. "I was wondering if you could help us with something. I've heard that you guard your realm's spark stone."

Her eyes suddenly narrowed. "What's it to you?"

"Well, first of all, it shows you how much the other merpeople respect your power. If you're the strongest, most magically capable creature in this whole world, and they've given you the stone to guard, it means that they value you enormously."

She puffed out her chest. "You're not wrong there, love. Well," she wobbled her head from side to side. "*Technically*, they didn't give it to me. I took it, and nobody could stop me. I've been using it as a centerpiece on my dining room table for the last few hundred years."

"But you obviously know how important it is, so you guard it with your life."

She shrugged. "Not with my life. Just with my teeth. And to be fair, I don't really have to try too hard to secure it."

I edged closer. "I'm sorry to have to tell you this, but the spark stone is in danger right now."

"How?"

"There's a—" Hmm. I probably shouldn't mention that the thief was Donovan's brother. "There's a fae man running around the Middle World who intends to steal it and devour it."

"Really?"

"Yes."

"Hang on. This rings a bell." The sea witch pouted her thin beaky lips and tapped a black-clawed finger against them. "Honestly, it's hard to keep track of all the prophecies that soothsayers and oracles spout, but I've heard this one a few times. Hmm." She peered at me. "I suppose he is trying to absorb its power?"

"Yes. Exactly."

"Right." She huffed out a long breath of bubbles, a long sigh. "This *has* been foretold. The great Devourer, coming to destroy the magic of all the worlds." She looked at me, frowning. "You're the Chosen, I suppose. The One of Every Blood."

"Apparently, I am. I'm supposed to close the stones."

Her eyes roamed around my body for a second, her thin eyebrow raised. "You're not what I expected. I thought the Chosen would be some hot chick in black leather. Like her." She jabbed a thumb at Cress, still in her Black Widow pose —tense, taunt, and ready to fight.

"I'm sure Cress would make an excellent Chosen One."

"No, she wouldn't." The sea witch sniffed. "I would have eaten her and spat out her bones. And there's barely any flesh on her, anyway, so it would have been *deeply* unsatisfying."

"Well, I guess it's lucky you've got me," I said, smiling at her warmly, trying to maintain eye contact while her boobs drifted all the way to the right, then back again. "I don't think I'd be much help in a fight, but in conflict situations I believe in diplomacy, first and foremost. Jen, we are both smart women. I know we can reach a mutually beneficial outcome with a little discussion. But in the interests of full disclosure, you should know that if I close the stone, your people will cease to evolve."

She wrinkled her nose. "We're already damned perfect. I can't see how we can get any better."

"Fair enough," I said. "So, that's the only downside to cooperating with us today, Jen."

The sea witch tapped her chin again, thinking for a moment. "I can't just give you the spark stone, you know. I've been looking forward to fighting someone over it for centuries."

"The Devourer will still come for it," I reassured her. "From what I understand, he is obsessed with power, and he'll try to eat all the spark stones. We'll keep this between us, and hopefully he'll still come to fight you."

She nodded with relish. "Good."

"And I don't need to take it away from you. I just need to close it, so he can't absorb the magic if he does try and eat it. Is that right, Donovan?" When he didn't answer, I glanced back at him.

Oh, God, he was doing the same thing as Cress—he was frozen, eyes blazing, daggers bared, every line in his body tensed and ready to attack.

I turned back to the sea witch. "So, how about it, Jen? Let me close the spark stone, and you can just relax, kick back, and wait for the Devourer to show up, and you'll get a good fight out of it. You won't be risking anything, because if he does by some miracle manage to eat your spark stone, it will be closed, and you won't lose your magic."

She furrowed her brow, scowling deeply. "That's actually a good point. I can't imagine not having my magic. An eternity of not being able to curse bratty merkids will get boring quickly. Hmmm." I waited patiently for a whole minute. "Okay, fine," she said. "Wait here."

She swiveled around and shot back into the hole, her tentacles trailing behind her. "I'd invite you inside," her voice echoed out from the darkness of her cave. "But the kitchen is a bit of a mess. I was making lunch when you banged on my door." A low moan drifted out of the hole. "Quiet, you," she admonished. "Give me five minutes, I'll be right back."

I glanced back at Donovan and gave him a reassuring smile, but he was still tense, his eyes glued to the hole.

The tentacles erupted again, spilling out the doorway and fanning around the rocky seawall. Good grief, she really was a terrifying nightmare. If this was real, I'd be absolutely pooping my pants. "Sorry it took so long," she puffed, finally emerging. "I had it glued to my dining room table. I learned the hard way that when I let my dinner wander around the cave, they can't help themselves and keep picking it up. Sticky fingered little bastards." She whipped her hand out from behind her back. "Ta dah!"

I gasped.

"Pretty, isn't it?"

My eyes bulged. "It's glorious!" The mer spark stone was the size of a cantaloupe, perfectly round, with a hundred natural facets that caught the dim light in the trench, setting it to a heavenly, otherworldly glow—a shimmering deep aqua color, sparkling with silver flecks.

"Go ahead," she said, holding it out. "Close it."

"Er..."

She sniggered. "You don't know how, do you?"

"Not exactly, no." I cast another glance back at Donovan, but he and Cress were still in attack-mode, eyes darting left and right, waiting to make a move. "I must admit I'm new to all this, Jen. Could you give me some pointers?"

She sighed dramatically. "Fine. All you have to do is draw your power up within yourself and focus it on what you want. In this case, you want to ask the atoms of the stone to move, to condense, if you will, so that they harden on the surface, creating an impenetrable shell. That way, the stone will still vibrate on the inside, but the shell will stop the magic from emanating out of it."

"That sounds simple enough," I said, nodding. "So... er... how do I draw up my power?"

She stared at me. "You've got to be fucking kidding me."

I sighed. "Please be kind, Jen. It's been a long day, and like I said, I'm new at all this."

"Kindness is not in my wheelhouse, sweetheart," she said.

"Then we're both trying something new today, aren't we? Please," I begged. "Give me some pointers."

She huffed out another exasperated sigh. "Well, what does it feel like in your body just before you work your magic?"

"I... uh... I don't think I've ever worked any magic."

She snorted. "Of course you have. You are the Chosen. You can manipulate matter. You can't contain that kind of raw power, girlfriend. If you don't focus on it, it can erupt out of you whenever you're scared or angry. You could quite literally tear down mountains."

"I'm quite good at regulating my emotions," I told her. But a tingle ran down my spine as the memory hit me. The heat within me, it was overwhelming, I couldn't contain it, and it erupted out of my belly, pouring through my limbs and electrifying every part of me. Walls shaking, plaster cracking. Bricks falling inwards, hitting the bed, bouncing on the mattress. Screams.

Loud screams. I'll never forget the screams.

The sea witch snapped her fingers. "You managed to grow your gills. How did you feel just before that happened?"

With effort, I forced myself to focus. I remembered. Donovan was calling me incompetent. The heat in my belly overwhelmed me. I opened my mouth to shout at him, and I realized I could breathe. "The heat," I whispered. "Of course. My hot flashes. The menopause." I shook my head, finally understanding. "I'm subconsciously trying to reframe my early menopause symptoms into something not bad." I chuckled softly. "This all makes sense now."

"Whatever, weirdo. Listen, can we hurry this up? My lunch is probably trying to escape." She held out the glittering stone.

"Right." I took the enormous crystal in both hands and jolted with shock as it tingled on my skin. "It feels… alive."

"It is alive, stupid," she snorted. "It contains the magic of the merpeople. It literally *is* life. Come on. Get on with it." She nudged me gently once. Wait, no, that was her boob, drifting in the current, bumping into me. "Focus. Draw on your power."

I nodded and stared down into the brilliant sparkling aqua depths of the siren stone. Now that I was holding it, I felt... different. The tingling sensation almost pulled at me, tugging on the heat in the core of my belly, like its power recognized me and wanted to reconnect. It felt like a best friend, soulmate, a kindred spirit, like, like...

Sadness suddenly overwhelmed me; a cry of anguish escaped my lips before I could stop it. The stone felt like my old dog, Rusty, happily trotting to meet me when I came home, licking my bare leg, doing a little happy dance with his front paws.

God, I missed him. Rusty was my best friend, a little white yorkie who never left my side. Vincent had given him to me for my thirty-fifth birthday. When I was arrested, I begged my lawyer to take care of Rusty. When I saw her again a month later, she told me Vincent was looking after him.

She lied. Probably deliberately. Vincent informed my lawyer that Rusty ran away almost immediately, probably trying to find me. She didn't tell me until I was let out of the hospital.

I rang every single rescue in the city. Finally, a very sympathetic vet nurse told me that Rusty had been brought in, but he'd been put to sleep well over a year ago.

The heartbreak nearly killed me. I didn't think I'd ever recover.

But I did. I recovered. Because I *always* did. I was a lot of things, but at my core, I was a survivor. And I would survive this.

Carefully, I let the emotions swirl through me, my love for Rusty tempering the pain of loss. Instead of violently erupting, the heat blossomed slowly, and the tingles spread, growing in intensity.

A vibration—that was it. The stone was vibrating, and I was matching its resonance. This is how I could speak to it.

"Good," the sea witch said. "Now ask it to close. Tell it to protect itself."

I imagined myself stroking Rusty, telling him to be brave, to prepare himself for loss, to harden himself, to protect himself. *I don't want anyone to hurt you*, I told the stone. *Close yourself. Hide away.*

The stone tingled underneath my fingertips sharply; a buzz shot right through my whole body, strangely warming the lump in my throat. Then, it relaxed, and I felt it obey me.

Good grief, I could definitely feel it; I could sense the stone rearranging itself, the vibrations moving inward as the magic retreated to the core of the stone beneath its new hard shell. The brilliant, transparent sparkling aqua stone became opaque, then solid, but it remained as beautiful and shining as ever. Finally, the vibrations under my fingertips dulled, then retreated completely.

It felt like it was asleep. It was done. The stone was closed. I turned to Donovan, and grinned. "I did it!"

He didn't relax, his eyes never straying from the sea witch, floating next to me.

"Good job," the sea witch nodded, plucking it out of my hands. "Did it gift you any magic?"

I cocked my head. "Er... no?"

"Well, then." Her lips curved up in a grin. "Now that the stone is closed and safe from the Devourer, I suppose you can stay for lunch, too."

Donovan let out a low growl.

"Jen." I shook my head in disappointment. "Let's not resort to stereotypes—"

She lunged at me, teeth bared, tentacles spread out, boobs disappearing into her armpits as she surged through the water to grab me.

Panicking, the heat in my belly erupted out of me. **"Stop."**

The witch froze, mid-lunge, mouth wide open, fingers curved into claws. Frantically, I kicked away from her, but a wave of exhaustion hobbled me. "Donovan!"

He grabbed my hand and pulled me beside him. "Go!" We swam as fast as we could, up the grisly bone-covered narrow walls of the trench, pure adrenaline pushing through my overwhelming fatigue to drive me forward.

I looked up; a sliver of pure blue lay above us like the hint of sky—the open ocean. I kicked desperately. I felt as weak as a kitten. Donovan pulled me upwards, powerful legs propelling him.

A hideous screech echoed up behind us. "Get back here, you raggedy bitch!"

"Faster!" Cress shouted behind us, pushing me. "She's following!"

The terrifying clatter of bones on rock sounded like it was coming from all around us; I glanced down and watched the sea witch as she squeezed her enormous body up through the trench, knocking old bones loose, her silver-blue tentacles stretching towards us, reaching closer and closer.

"I'm going to filet you alive and make shish kabobs out of your ass!" she screamed. "How *dare* you use my own powers on me? That friggin' *hurt!*"

Donovan tugged me hard, pulling me up. "Take her," he ordered Cress. She grabbed my hand and kicked away. He whirled around, tugged a metal object out of his leather pants, put it to his lips, whispered, and tossed it down into the trench just as one giant tentacle shot out, coming straight towards him—

The metal thing flashed bright green and exploded.

The sea witch screamed.

"Go!" Donovan roared over the rumble of rockfall around us; the trench was collapsing. I kicked harder than I'd ever kicked before as the walls on either side of us gave way, tumbling inwards, sucking us down. Oh good grief, this was hard. I was too tired; we were going to be buried under a million tons of rock under the sea...

We popped out into the clear, brilliant blue open ocean, leaving the muffled curses of the sea witch behind us.

CHAPTER

TWELVE

My feet squelched, making fart noises in my fancy shoes as I power-walked back to the office. There was nothing I could do about it, though. I'd wrung out my skirt and jacket as best as I could. The fabric of my shirt still clung to me.

"Chosen," Donovan murmured from beside me. "You do not have to go back to your place of employment."

I swallowed roughly, a sickening fear churning in my gut. "Yes, I do, Donovan. You don't understand. I'm so late. I'm *so* late." My hands shook. I was going to get fired. "Please... just let me be."

"As you wish." He drifted back behind me.

God, I was tired, bone tired, exhausted, and absolutely sick to my stomach. Only five minutes ago, I popped back to reality in the bathroom at the Karaoke Cove, panting in fear and absolutely soaked from head to toe.

My phone was dead. And I had no idea how long I'd been out for.

The whole thing had obviously been the wildest hallucination—the worst one I'd ever had. But this part—the aftermath—was like a nightmare, one of those recurring dreams where you're late for something important, a flight, or an important client meeting, but your phone isn't working, the calls won't connect, you can't find the right contact in your contact list to ask for help...

I raced down the block, arms pumping, heading for my office, and saw the digital clock outside the bank flash the time in big red numbers. Five-oh-nine.

Oh, no. No no no.

I'd been gone for almost five hours. I disappeared at lunchtime and hadn't gone back. The workday was already over.

I was going to get fired.

No job, no money. No money, no apartment. No apartment, I was homeless, living on the streets, trying to survive in shelters...

No. I had to get back to the office and put things right. Everyone else would have gone home, but Yvette would still be there. She was putting in extra hours to smooth the transfer from her Department Manager role to Executive. I had to find her, I had to explain—

What? What the hell was I going to tell her? That I'd lost my mind in the ladies at a scummy basement karaoke bar, blacked out, and splashed around on the wet floor like a dying fish for five hours?

I had to try. I had to try *something*. Panting, I rushed into the lobby of the building, dodging the last of the office workers pouring out of the elevators, skidding on the smooth black marble floor. I slapped my security pass on the reader, waving at Luis as he called out to me from the desk. "Susan! Hey, Susan, Wait! You have to sign—"

"Sorry, Luis, I have to run!" I bolted for the elevators, hit the button for my floor, and tapped my foot impatiently as we rose upwards.

Emptiness surrounded me. Even Donovan and Cress

had abandoned me. I couldn't feel them next to me. I was alone.

The doors dinged and slid open. The floor was in almost complete darkness—there, Yvette's light was still on in the corner fishbowl office, right on the other side of the floor. I could see her sharp salt-and-pepper bob bent over her laptop.

I hurried over, dread sinking into the pit of my stomach. How was I going to explain myself?

A tall, black-suited figure stepped out of the meeting room on my left suddenly, blocking my path, looming over me. "Well, well, well."

I stopped. My breath left my lungs in a defeated sigh. "Richie."

He chuckled. "You took a *very* long lunch, Susan Moore," he gloated. "Spectacular timing, don't you think?"

I clenched my jaw. "Richie—"

"Your prolonged absence was noted, you know." He smirked and put his hand on the wall, leaning against it casually, still blocking my path. "Yvette's been trying to get hold of you all afternoon. She's pissed that you aren't answering your phone. She even did a couple of loops of the office, looking for you." He laughed again, shaking his head. "To think I went to all that trouble digging up dirt on you, and you've gone and sabotaged yourself, anyway. I shouldn't have bothered. Of course an unstable old cow like you wouldn't be able to hold down a job for very long." He let out a bark of laughter. "To think I once considered you a threat to my career."

My ears began to ring. Panic was starting to overwhelm me. *Breathe, Susan. Breathe. Don't let your anger explode...*

"In any case, I'm still going to let her know everything about you. Just in case she feels sorry for you and decides to keep you around after this little disappearing act this afternoon. She needs to know what you're capable of. You're a liability, Susan."

My chest felt so tight; suddenly, I couldn't breathe. "Don't do this," I whispered, panting softly.

"It's already done, sweetheart," Richie replied, eyes glinting. "I'm on my way to talk to Yvette now."

"Don't..."

"You know, you should have played nice months ago," he said, wagging his finger. "This is what you get when you go up against the big guns, baby."

This wasn't happening. This couldn't be happening.

Richie put his finger on his lip, pretending to think. "I'll tell you what. I'm a nice guy. I can cut you a deal. How about you do what I asked you to do on the day you started here, and I *might* think about keeping your little secret for you." He waved a hand towards the little meeting room. "In here. Nobody else has to know."

My mouth dropped open; words refused to come out. "You— You—What?"

"You heard me." Richie's almost-black eyes roamed around my body lazily, lingering on my shirt, still clinging wetly to my skin. "Yvette might not fire you if I keep my mouth shut. And... If you keep playing nice, I'll be a good boss to you when I've got her job." He let out a soft chuckle. "Maybe."

My pulse roared in my ears. Outside, a crack of thunder boomed. The thin carpet beneath my feet trembled slightly. Was that me?

"Come on, Susan. Don't waste my time. I know you're out of options, so you might as well give it up already." He grinned widely. "Once you get over your pride, you'll find it easy to get down on your knees for me."

Breathe, Susan. Just breathe.

"Let's get—" Richie glanced behind me, his eyes suddenly wide. "Hey. Who are you?"

A huge, dark figure stormed past me, brushing my shoulder. A low furious tone rumbled through the corridor like thunder.

"How *dare* you speak to her like that." Donovan reached out and grabbed Richie by the throat with one huge hand.

Richie let out a strangled yelp. Donovan's hand squeezed harder, and he shoved Richie backwards into the meeting room behind him.

Flailing wildly, Richie lost his balance, stumbling on his feet, but Donovan held him upright by the throat as if he weighed nothing. He threw Richie back against the meeting room wall, still holding him in the air, letting his cheap, shiny shoes dangle helplessly six inches above the ugly carpet.

"How *dare* you." Donovan's voice was filled with such fury, it shocked me out of my stupor.

"Donovan! Stop!" I raced into the meeting room, swinging the door shut behind me.

He didn't stop. He held Richie up in the air by his throat, his dark emerald eyes almost burning into him. "You are a worthless snake," he growled. "A revolting waste of matter. You do not deserve to even speak a word in her presence, slime."

Richie's face rapidly changed from white to purple. His weedy arms flailed around uselessly, smacking at Donovan's bare muscular forearms. Good grief, the power in those arms, the insane strength...

Richie might as well be trying to fight a statue made of stone. Donovan's grip didn't even falter. Richie spluttered, a dribble of spit escaping his lips and dribbling down his chin.

Donovan was choking him to death. He didn't look like he was going to stop. I licked my lips. "Donovan!"

My imaginary fae prince leaned closer, staring at Richie's trembling face. "Listen to me carefully, scum. From this day forth, you will never look directly at the woman you call Susan Moore. You will not make eye contact. You will never seek to sully her name by even uttering it with your diseased tongue." He bit the words out with effort. "Do you hear me, you worthless sewer rat?"

Richie's eyes bulged. He choked out a gurgle.

"Please let him go," I whispered. My whole body felt numb. Was this real? Because if *this* was real...

Donovan's fingers twitched and relaxed just a fraction. Color surged back into Richie's cheeks as he choked for air.

Slowly, Donovan turned to face me. The fury in his eyes had died down, just a fraction, but it still simmered just beneath the surface. "I will not kill him, Chosen. Not today, anyway."

Richie let out a moan of terror. I caught an unpleasant whiff of what smelled like the subway after dark, and I realized that he'd peed his pants.

Donovan frowned, looking at the dark stain spreading on Richie's crotch. "Allow me a moment to speak with this disgusting wretch in private, Chosen," he said quietly. "Cress is waiting for you in your employer's office now. Go and join her."

My whole world was collapsing around me. No... my whole world was exploding.

"Please," Donovan added, his voice dropping a whole octave lower, vibrating through me, shaking me to the core. "Go."

I mouthed like a goldfish, nodded, then walked stiffly out of the room, then carefully shut the door behind me.

What the fuck? What the actual *fuck?*

Numb, almost robot-like, I walked down the corridor and around the corner, heading towards the light in Yvette's office. She was there, at her desk, brow furrowed, nodding seriously at a large police officer sitting in the chair in front of her.

Without thinking, I walked straight in.

"Susan! Oh, thank goodness, Susan!" Yvette leapt to her feet and rushed around her desk towards me, her sharp silver bob swinging with her swift, bird-like movements. Yvette was ten years older than me, thin, wiry, and very quick-witted. "I've been so worried." She stopped just in front of me, her dark brows pinched together in concern. "When you didn't come back from lunch, I knew something terrible had happened." She tilted her head. "Are you okay?"

I opened my mouth. "I— I—"

"It's okay," she said, taking my hand gently. "You must be very rattled. The officer here filled me in on what happened."

I glanced at the police officer and blinked. My vision had gone funny. He was a little blurry. And... glowing. A green glow, like an aura, blazed around his body.

"Okay," I managed.

"You're an extraordinarily brave woman, Susan," Yvette went on, her voice soft. "I don't know what I'd do if I walked into an active hostage situation. The police officer said you distracted the villain, saved the jewels, pulled the fire alarm, and got everyone out safely."

She was waiting for a response.

"Uh. Yes, that's right," I said.

"You're so brave. Oh, and my dear," she sighed. "You're still soaking wet!"

This *was* real. This was all real. I had to say something.

Say something, Susan! I licked my lips. "I'm sorry, Yvette. My... uh... my phone. It died. I couldn't call you."

She reached out and squeezed my hand. "Of course it did. The officer said that the sprinkler system flooded everything."

The officer stood up. I glanced at him again, but the strange green blaze hurt my eyes. "She was very brave, but quite foolish," the officer barked. "She insisted on coming back to work as soon as we could clear the scene."

Yvette glanced at the officer sharply. "Susan is not foolish, officer; she is merely dedicated to her work." She turned back to me and smiled. "It's an admirable trait. I would have come back to work, too."

"Indeed," the officer rasped. The green glow shifted, and I caught a glimpse of Cress's slim form in the middle of a rounder cop's body. "If only she could devote her time to a more worthy cause."

My boss glared at the officer again. "Susan is to be commended for her bravery, and for her commitment in coming back to work."

The officer eyeballed Yvette, his face a stony mask. "If you say so."

Yvette turned back to me. "My dear, I'm just glad you're okay. Go home, rest up." She tilted her head. "Will you need a few days off work?"

I swallowed and gathered myself up. This *was* real. "Oh... no, Yvette. Thank you so much." I managed a smile. "I'll be back in the morning, bright and early. I promise."

"Good." She smiled. "Go home and rest."

"I shall escort you," the officer said, stomping to my side.

"Thank you." I turned and walked out of the office.

CHAPTER
THIRTEEN

"Cress?"

She stalked beside me down the corridor, her lithe, sexy catwalk gait completely at odds with the rotund cop she appeared to be. "Yes, Chosen?"

Up ahead, at the far end of the floor, I watched as Donovan walked slowly out of the meeting room. He turned and saw us coming. The tension on his face eased. He leaned up against the wall and waited.

"I think I'm about to have a proper breakdown."

"Another one?"

My lips twitched. "Don't be a bitch." I walked a little slower. "I'm being serious."

She let out a long sigh. "What is it this time?"

"I didn't think any of this was real," I whispered.

She frowned. "I don't understand."

I held my breath as we approached Donovan, waiting for us in the corridor beside the meeting room. As we passed the open door, I glanced inside. Richie was there, huddled in the corner. Moaning softly, rocking, hugging himself, eyes squeezed shut, tears pouring down his cheeks.

He looked real. He sounded real.

Donovan waited until we drew near, then stepped aside, moving to his usual position, just behind me, with Cress just in front. We walked into the elevator bank. Woodenly, I hit the down button. All the elevators were stuck upstairs.

Cress pushed the button again. And again. "What were you saying, Chosen?"

I hesitated for a brief moment. "All this time, I assumed you guys were hallucinations."

"Really?" Cress looked amused. "Why on earth would you think that?"

"Well, for starters, because magic is not real."

"Of course it is," she replied. "Look at me. This is a simple glamor charm, and it fooled your employer." She hit the button again. "I must admit I was a little shocked at how well that worked. In this realm, anyone can put on a uniform and sling a couple of firearms on their hips, and the rest of your people roll over and show their bellies like scared dogs."

"You don't even need a uniform," Donovan rumbled softly, still on guard, eyes flicking left and right, checking the exits.

"*You* don't need a uniform," I said, turning to face him. "What did you do to Richie?"

"Nothing. I merely continued to emphasize my displeasure that he would dare to speak to you in such a manner. Or at all." Donovan turned away from me and muttered something else under his breath.

"Sorry? What was that? I didn't catch what you said."

He turned back. "I said I may have also broken several of his fingers during the conversation."

I pinched my eyes shut and counted backwards from ten. When I opened my eyes again, Donovan was still there in front of me, massive shoulders tensed, guarding all the exits.

Cress was still pushing the elevator down button. "That doesn't make it come any faster, you know," I said, my voice faint.

"No?" She swiveled to face me, outraged. "That's absurd. Why not? How else will it know that someone requires its services urgently?"

"It doesn't work that way. It's, uh, technology. It doesn't work the same way as..." I hesitated and swallowed. "Magic."

Damn, I really was going to entertain this. "If this is all real, why isn't magic out in the open in this realm? Why don't humans know about it?"

"Witches do. Sorcerers, oracles... They are a breed apart, but still mostly human."

"Yeah, but... what about everyone else? How come nobody else knows about magic? And why don't witches flaunt their powers?"

"They keep their magic secret for the good of the whole Middle World. To protect the other realms within it from humans."

I didn't understand. "But... but humans don't have any power."

"They don't have *magic*. But they have weapons, and too many bodies to act as shields." She wrinkled her nose. "Humans breed like rodents."

My head was spinning. "So magic is a secret to protect the other realms? That doesn't make sense, Cress. If humans can't do magic, what's the point of keeping it a secret?"

She let out a delicate snort. "Please, Chosen. I've read your history books. I know what humans are like. The other realms within the Middle World are not only rich in magic, but they're also rich in natural resources." Her lips thinned. "You give a human a whiff of oil on an anthill, and they're going to invade, kill the creatures inside it, colonize it, then rewrite the history books to show that they've always been there." She pressed the elevator button a few more times. "The centaur realm in particular has endless plains with rare minerals buried just under the surface. And it's an easy realm to get to from here. If any of your governments ever got wind of it, within two new moons, it would be nothing more than a giant quarry, and centaurs would be nothing more than mythical creatures."

I opened my mouth and closed it again. "I suppose that's fair enough."

Donovan turned his head to meet my eye. "You really thought you had gone insane?"

"Not gone. I *am* insane." My chin quivered; I willed it to stop. "I have a whole list of medical diagnoses. I've hallucinated things before. I've become paranoid and violent, and I assumed this was more of the same. But you just made my worst enemy piss his pants, and Cress just used magic to impersonate a cop so my boss wouldn't fire me."

She shrugged elegantly. "You seemed very insistent on maintaining your employment. It was the least I could do, considering everything you achieved today."

I looked at my soggy shoes. It was too hard to imagine that the trip to the mermaid realm and the battle with the sea witch had been real. "I don't know what to think now. Oh, God." I clapped my hand over my eyes. "If it is real, that means I actually flashed my boobs on stage at the Karaoke Cove."

Donovan stared at me. "This whole time... everything you've done so far. You thought you were hallucinating?"

I nodded.

He gave one sharp nod. "Now I understand. Your

bravery in confronting the sea witch was incomprehensible to me."

"Not brave," I muttered. "Just nuts."

"But it worked," he said quietly, almost in an undertone. "You skillfully negotiated with a monster, and it worked."

I took a deep, calming breath. It didn't help. How was I going to know for sure? How would I really, truly know that this was real?

The elevator dinged, and the door slid open.

Bart stood there. He spotted me, and his huge teddy bear body sagged with relief. "There you are, Susan! I heard you went AWOL at lunchtime. I was worried about you! I had to borrow Luis's lanyard to get up here—"

Donovan moved closer beside me, emerald eyes flashing.

Bart saw him and gasped, clutching his chest as if he was about to have a heart attack.

There was a long, long moment of silence.

Donovan nodded. "Shifter."

Bart dropped into a swooping bow, going down on one knee. "Your Highness."

CHAPTER
FOURTEEN

Bart sat on an armchair by the enormous window in my new drawing room, holding a cocktail glass and wearing an expression of unbearable smugness. He looked like Winnie-the-Pooh had just won the lottery. "For the record," he said. "Can I just emphasize the fact that I had no idea you were the One of Every Blood?"

It was hard to hear him properly under all the layers of pink tulle that Cecil was trying to force over my head. "So you said. A million times."

"To me, you were just Susan, my lovely, but completely batshit crazy ex-convict friend."

I spat out a mouthful of tulle. "Again. Thanks, Bart. And again, technically I am not a convict."

"We are in your debt." Donovan's intense, deep voice echoed from where he stood by the window, surveilling the cityscape outside.

Eryk and Nate were out there somewhere. While I'd been arguing with a bitchy mermaid, choking on seawater, and cozily negotiating with a terrifying, woman-eating sea monster, they'd been scouting the city for traces of Connor the Devourer.

They'd found a handful of portals to the other realms in the Middle World, and apparently found evidence of Connor's servants—creatures they referred to as banwyns—around Professor Owen's manor house, which was apparently a terrible thing, worthy of several minutes of incomprehensible discussion in very serious voices. When we got back to my apartment, Eryk and Nate took Cress with them to show her what they'd found, while Cecil shoved a cocktail in my hand and started shoehorning me into evening gowns.

Donovan chose to stay with me. He would be accompanying me to Professor Owen's manor tonight. He was already dressed for dinner. Cecil, the bitchy miniature-pony duocorn, was apparently an in-house stylist as well as my interior designer. He'd produced a perfectly tailored suit—midnight-blue pants and a sharp jacket with a crisp white shirt, no tie, and two buttons at Donovan's neck undone to reveal a hint of his collarbones and creamy tan skin.

Donovan in his battle leathers was like an erotic fantasy come to life. Donovan in a suit was just...

It was too much. I could barely even look at him. The suit was tailored to perfection—hugging his broad chest, defining his muscular shoulders, giving only subtle hints of his huge biceps, showing off his flat stomach, and skimming his long, strong legs perfectly. His long black hair was pulled up in a topknot, highlighting his perfect high cheekbones and chiseled jaw.

It wasn't just the clothes, or his body, or his brutally handsome face. The power he exuded was almost overwhelming. It was just too obvious he wasn't human—he moved like an apex predator, like a warrior prince. When I caught a glimpse of him from the corner of my eye, I had to remind myself to breathe.

At least I wasn't as bad as Bart. He was acting like a

blushing schoolgirl in Donovan's presence. "It was nothing, Your Highness," he said demurely.

"It was everything, Bart," I said. "I'll never be able to repay you."

Donovan turned away from the window to face him. "You protected the Chosen, gave her sanctuary and a means of employment when no other person would help her, without realizing her true nature or her destiny. Such a noble deed will not go unnoticed when this tale is written into history, Shifter."

Bart let out a high-pitched giggle. "Thank you, Your Highness. Susan has always been a great source of comfort to me. I was just happy to help my friend in her time of need."

"Your family will hear of it, and your entire ancestral line will be honored by your deeds."

Through the tulle, I watched Bart snigger into his martini glass. "Ooh, I can't wait. They're going to *hate* this," he whispered gleefully.

"So, what's the deal there, Bart?' I asked him. "You and your family are shifters from the shapeshifter realm, is that right? I mean, of *course* you are, because why *wouldn't* my closest friend in the world secretly be a supernatural creature?" I added, a little testily.

"Well, to be honest, it's not hard to keep secret. I haven't shifted in years. Gone native," Bart explained. "And, to be fair, Susan," he said, a smirk pulling at his lips, "*everyone* knows I'm a bear."

"I thought that was a gay stereotype!"

"It is. In my case, it just also happens to be literal."

I huffed out an exasperated breath. "And I thought you were from Washington DC?"

"Our realm is called The Woods," he explained, while Cecil tussled with the layers of tulle, trying to find my head somewhere amongst the explosion of pink fabric. "Most of us are expats, though; almost all shifters live in the mortal world. We've evolved alongside normal humans, but our people took care to keep our realm as close to nature as possible. The human realm is our home. The Woods is more like a cabin we all go to when we need to get back to the wild. Some shifters live there full time." He frowned. "They're a bit crazy."

Cecil yanked me sideways, and I wobbled on my knees. The bare floorboards were a bitch to kneel on. "Can I get a carpet or a rug or something, here, Violet?"

My house rumbled in a noise that I'd started to think of as acquiesce, and fuzzy beige wool pushed out of the vintage oak floorboards, sprouting like a thick carpet of tiny mushrooms. My knees sank into the soft fabric gratefully.

"Thanks," I whispered.

"That's nice," Bart said approvingly. "Scandinavian alpaca wool blend. I saw that at Evonne's Atelier a few months ago, and it cost her a fortune. You really got the hang of this quickly, Sue."

I swatted the fabric out of my face. "I think it's because it's absolutely ridiculous, Bart. I still haven't decided if my sanity has completely deserted me or not. For all I know, I'm back in the padded room at Serenity Ward, talking to the walls."

Donovan gave a low, rumbling grunt, deep within his chest. "Chosen. You are being asinine. You were never insane in the first place."

I froze. No, that couldn't be right. If I was never crazy in the first place, that meant all the hallucinations I had before were real. And if they were real...

A hoof stomped on the sole of my foot. "Ouch! Cecil!"

"Calm down, Chosen," he said snippily, clomping around me and yanking the dress over my head. "We have to do this as quickly as possible. I have twelve other gowns for you to try on, and we still have to do hair and makeup." With one last tug, he pulled the pink jeweled bodice down, throwing his beautiful white mane back, and ran his eyes over me.

"Can I get off the floor now?"

"No," he snorted, curling his lip. "You look stupid. We will have to try another one." He clapped his hooves together. "Come on. Arms up."

A low chime rang through the air, and I flinched. "What was that?"

"It's your doorbell," Cecil muttered, trying to lift the tulle skirt. "Someone's trying to buzz you."

I frowned, wriggling out of Cecil's oddly dexterous hooves. "I've got a visitor?"

"So it seems."

I scrambled to my feet, looking around my enormous drawing room—an almost-replica of the morning room at the Palace of Versailles. The intercom phone by the door wasn't there anymore. Neither, in fact, was the door. From the hallway outside, it looked like a normal-sized beige door with a standard silver handle. However from this side —the inside—my little apartment door was a huge cream oak double-door with gilt carvings all around it. "How do I check who it is?"

Cecil let out a huff. "I'm not putting that horrible plastic device back on the wall."

I groaned. "Cecil. Please."

"No. It's an eyesore. An abomination!"

"How am I supposed to know who's at my door, then?"

He sniffed. "They should have made a prior appointment with you, like a civilized person. Then you'd know exactly who it was."

"Violet." I hiked up the enormous skirt and started

shuffling towards my front door. "Please put the intercom back where I can see it."

My house obeyed me immediately, and my gray intercom phone popped out of the wall by the door. Cecil was right; it was as attractive as a giant zit on a model's cheek.

"We don't have time for this, Chosen," Cecil said bitchily. "You've got twelve other gowns to try on. Ignore it."

"I can't." I reached out and picked up the phone. "Yes?"

The phone line crackled. A young woman's voice rang through like a bell; a soft, lilting Irish accent. "Hello, Susan."

I frowned, recognizing the voice instantly. "Seraphina?"

"Yes. I need to speak to you."

My heart started pounding. What the hell was she doing here? I licked my lips and hit the buzzer. "Come on up." I waited until I heard the downstairs door click, then I hung up the phone and exhaled heavily.

"Who is it?" Bart asked.

It took me a moment. "It's Seraphina."

Bart gasped softly. "No."

Donovan tensed, then marched towards the door, pulling two daggers out of thin air with a menacing zing. "Get behind me, Chosen. I will deal with her."

I almost laughed. "You can't stab her, Donovan."

"You *should* stab her," Bart muttered under his breath.

Donovan marched towards the door, brandishing his daggers, planting himself in front of me. "Who is this Seraphina? An assassin? A sorceress?"

"No," I sighed. "She's my husband's fiancé."

"Your husband?" Donovan glanced back at me, his face thunderous.

"Ex-husband." My stomach churned. My bowels felt

watery, like I desperately needed to poop all of a sudden. My old reality kept colliding with my new reality, and it was throwing me off. Just as I got used to one version of myself, I got flipped back to the old version.

"Tell her to fuck off." Cecil lit a cigarette, took a puff, then blew it out slowly, eyes narrowed against the smoke. "We've got work to do."

"Cecil," I hissed. "You can't smoke in here."

"Of course I can. I'm doing it right now. See?" He inhaled again and blew out another plume of smoke.

"This is a non-smoking building. The super will—" I huffed out a breath. "You know what, I can't deal with this right now," I muttered, trying to walk through a sea of tulle, backing away from my gorgeous door. "Donovan, step back. It's fine. Seraphina is twenty-four and only one-hundred pounds soaking wet."

"She could still be dangerous, Chosen."

"She's not." As soon as the words were out of my mouth, I wasn't so sure. I glanced at Bart. "Is she?"

"Seraphina is completely human, as far as I know," he confirmed. "The jury is out on whether she's dangerous or not," he added under his breath.

That was a can of worms I wasn't ready to address yet. I straightened my shoulders. "Violet, can you please reconstruct my tiny apartment? Just around the door, please."

Walls slid into place in front of us, rising up effortlessly from the floor. A low ceiling sprouted from the walls, capping off the tiny, boxy apartment. I watched it in wonder, horrified by how tiny my old apartment had actually been, especially in context of the huge vaulted-ceiling drawing room with the glorious, domed stained-glass skylight above my head. My old apartment really was the size of a shoebox. It only cut off one corner of the room we were standing in right now.

There was a sharp knock from within the box. Seraphina was at my front door.

"Thanks," I said to my House. "Can you please give me a way to get inside?"

A door grew in front of me from a tiny speck, popping up like a pimple.

I turned and narrowed my eyes. "Please stay quiet," I ordered the others. I bundled up the layers of tulle in my hands, opened the door, and marched inside.

The door shut gently behind me, and I stared at my old apartment. A feeling of intense vertigo overwhelmed me so violently, I stumbled. The apartment was back to exactly what it looked like before—one tiny room, the kitchenette to the side, the slightly ajar sliding door leading to the tiny bathroom. My bed was folded up, the curtain drawn. My soft, cushy green-velvet armchair was waiting for me by the window.

I shook myself. If it wasn't for the bedazzled bodice and layers of tulle around me, it would be easy for me to think that the last twenty-four hours of my life were a crazy dream.

Knock, knock.

I walked forward and opened the door.

Seraphina stood in the hallway. She was alone. My heart cracked a little. I'd been hoping...

She smiled softly. "Hello, Susan."

Seraphina always reminded me of a beautiful deer, tall and willowy, reed-thin, with delicate features, long silky strawberry blonde hair, a pointed chin, huge vivid-blue eyes and a smattering of freckles on her button nose. I had a deep appreciation for beauty, and I'd always loved looking at Seraphina. She was stunning—a softly-spoken, fragile, delicate flower.

My eyes traveled downwards and noted the gentle curve of a bump on her belly.

My throat went dry. "*Erachhh.*"

Seraphina blinked. A tiny crease appeared in the smooth skin of her brow as she frowned. "Are you okay, Susan?"

I swallowed the enormous lump in my throat. "I'm, um, I'm fine."

"Can I come in?"

"Of course." I had to back up all the way to the far wall to let her in. The skirt of my gown was ridiculous.

"I see you're playing dress-ups." Her voice, as usual, was so quiet, I had to strain to hear her. "That's nice. Good for you." There was no hint of maliciousness in her gentle smile, no trace of bitchiness in her soft tone.

"Uh. Yes." *Come on, Susan. You're a strong, smart, capable woman.* "I'm just trying on a few things."

Seraphina drifted effortlessly over to the window and glanced out. "I love your apartment. It's so... uh... cozy." Her huge, innocent eyes blinked around at the tiny box surrounding her.

"Thanks," I managed.

"You've made very efficient use of the space." She paused again by the window and leaned against the counter, posing like a model, so effortlessly elegant. Her belly jutted out a little further. "I love how you've decorated it."

My hands were beginning to shake. "Is there something I can help you with, Seraphina?"

She blushed and looked down demurely. For the first time—for the very first time—I wondered if it was all an act. Who can blush on command, though?

"This is so embarrassing," she whispered. "I'm sorry to

barge in on you like this, Susan. But your alimony check didn't arrive."

I opened my mouth. Nothing came out.

I closed it and tried again. "Oh."

I'd sent it, just the same as I'd done every month. It wasn't due until tomorrow. I always posted it a couple of days early, so Vincent always got it a couple of days early. It wasn't even late yet, but they'd both taken it as a sign that something was terribly wrong with me.

"Please don't worry yourself," Seraphina said hastily, holding up her hands. "Vincent doesn't mind. He was just..." She blinked, tilting her head, watching me carefully with concern in her eyes. "He doesn't need it, of course, so it doesn't matter. We don't mind."

I swallowed again. This damn lump in my throat was going to choke me. "Of course."

A strange noise floated through the walls. It sounded like a horse's huff.

In fact, it sounded like a horse huffing out the word *whore*.

I barely noticed. Seraphina was right; Vincent didn't need my money now. Now that we were divorced, his parents had written him back into their will. They were the ones who'd given him the money to rebuild and restore my house. The alimony was court-ordered, though. I still had to pay him most of my salary.

"We thought it might have something to do with the building deed transfer," Seraphina went on. "Our lawyer called and told us about your purchase this morning. He was really angry, he thought..." She trailed off again, and her eyes widened. She'd obviously noticed the look of confusion on my face.

We stared at each other in silence for a second. "What, Seraphina? What building deed transfer?"

Seraphina hesitated, then her tense expression relaxed a little. "Don't worry about it, Susan. I'm sure it was some kind of mistake. Maybe someone put the wrong name down. Your, uh, your surname is common, so it was probably a different Susan Moore, and our lawyer got angry over nothing." She smiled. "We know you're not the type of person that would hide assets. I'll tell him to back down."

My stomach churned again.

"It's just..." Oh, she wasn't done. "When the alimony check didn't show up yesterday, Vincent got worried about you." Her eyes were suddenly shining with unshed tears. "We were both worried, so I thought I better come and check on you. Last we heard, you had this great little apartment, and a good job, and you were doing really well."

I clenched my fists to stop them shaking. "I am."

Seraphina nodded slowly. "So, everything is okay at your new job? You're... uh... you're holding it together okay?" She watched me carefully, looking at me in the same way the doctors watched me, analyzing every little twitch and quirk in my expression.

"I'm fine." I had to bite the words out from between clenched teeth.

"Good," she said finally. "I'm glad you're getting better, Susan. I hope we can go back to being friends one day."

The fire in my belly sparked. I clamped down. *No. Not now. Not here. I am in control. My emotions do not control me.*

Seraphina had never been my friend. She was only ever an employee—one of Vincent's interns, an art student, just one member of a gorgeous group of young, dazzlingly brilliant up-and-coming artists who supported Vincent. In truth, Seraphina wasn't even much of an artist; she was just a beautiful, delicate ornament that hung around at parties and gallery openings and exhibitions.

I'd been a mother hen to all of Vincent's interns. They

were all poor students, so I always made sure they helped themselves to food from my refrigerator. I bought them booze and condoms and cigarettes, because if I was going to be a mom, I was going to be the cool mom. I even introduced Seraphina to the immigration lawyer who helped her get her green card. I paid for it, too.

She gave me a gentle smile. "Don't worry about the alimony for now. Just mail the check when you have a moment free."

"Okay."

"Oh, and... Susan?" Seraphina shifted on her feet uncomfortably.

"Yes?"

She pointed to a little bronze sculpture of a ballerina on my bedside table. "I don't want to be rude. I really don't. But Vincent did get that Marlanique in the settlement."

I felt like I'd been punched in the stomach. Vincent got *everything* in the settlement. My house, all our belongings, our entire collection of art...

"We were wondering where it went," Seraphina went on in her beautiful, lyrical accent. "We were worried it had been stolen."

The Marlanique was my favorite piece. And it *had* been stolen. I'd stolen it when the police escort took me through my house to get my clothes. My whole house had been filled with carefully curated, beautiful things, and that little sculpture was the only thing I had left.

A vision bloomed in my head; me picking up the bronze and smashing it into Seraphina's face.

She had to leave now, before I hurt her. "Take it," I bit out, my voice ice-cold.

She flinched, like a beautiful doe in a meadow startled by a loud noise, enormous eyes staring at me, horrified. She made me feel like a monster. "Susan... I *am* sorry. You know that Vincent and I didn't want you to be hurt. We only want you to get better."

I plucked the statue off the table and held it out in front of her. "Take it, and leave."

She stumbled back as if I'd slapped her. Tentatively, her hands shaking, she reached out and took the Marlanique in her thin, tiny hands. "Susan, please. Don't be like this. I'm sorry for how things turned out, I really am. I know it all started when you went through menopause, and you couldn't give him a baby, but you have to understand—"

Heat flooded me. The voice that came out of my mouth wasn't human. "**Get out of my house. Now**."

Seraphina jolted. Her eyes flew wide in an expression I'd never seen on her face before—true, horrified shock. Moving strangely, her natural grace gone, she shifted bolt upright, swiveled left, swung her arms, and marched out of the apartment like a robot.

The door slammed behind her.

"That's right!" Cecil's voice called out, muffled behind the wall. "Fuck off and don't come back, you slimy little paddy bitch!"

CHAPTER
FIFTEEN

My tiny apartment walls melted away immediately, leaving me back in my luxurious drawing room, face to face with Donovan. Or face-to-chest anyway. The man was so tall.

After the horror of sharing a tiny space with Seraphina and the memories of the darkest time in my life, the sight of Donovan was such a relief, like a cloud of cool mist on a blistering hot day. I had to fight the urge to sink to my knees.

He was real. Magic was real, my sentient House was real, my bitchy miniature duocorn personal stylist was real.

But if everything that was happening to me *now* was real, then that meant—

Donovan stared at me, those blazing dark-emerald eyes boring into me, like I was a puzzle that he couldn't quite figure out. "So, it *did* happen."

"What happened?"

"The siren stone gifted you some of its magic. It emanated right before you closed it."

I frowned. The sea witch had asked me if it had, too,

and at the time, I'd said no. I didn't feel any different. "No, I don't think so."

"It did. You sank magic into your voice and used it to command, just like a siren. When you faced the sea witch, you ordered her to stop, and she froze."

He was right. I hadn't spent much time thinking about it, because I assumed it wasn't real to start with.

"And just now, you ordered that... that... *girl*—" He sank so much derision into his tone, I almost melted with gratitude. "You told her to get out, and she left."

"Oh. Oh, no. I think she realized I was about to punch her."

"Nope," Cecil snorted. He clomped over and shoved a fresh passionfruit margarita into my hand. "You did siren magic. I heard it loud and clear. That was what Connor was after, you know. That's why he's trying to devour all the stones." He chuckled. "You're getting the power he wants, and you don't even have to eat them. The stone gifted you the magic of the merpeople."

I stared up at the fae prince. "That's why your brother wanted the stones? So, he'd have the power to order people around?"

Donovan's eyes iced over. "Yes." I waited for him to say more, but he turned away, and took up his spot by the window, glaring out at the city. The tension returned to his shoulders.

Bart saluted me with his cocktail glass. "It's your power now, Sue, honey."

Absently, I rubbed my throat. "Huh." My voice had sounded different when I told Seraphina to get out. And she *had* left very abruptly. It wasn't like her at all. Seraphina usually drifted around gracefully, floating like a delicate soap bubble. She didn't march jerkily like a robot. "But... mermaids lure people in. They don't push them away."

"They only lure people in when they want to eat them," Bart explained. "They can also make nosy researchers go away by commanding them to scram. If you draw some magic up and express it from your throat chakra, you can probably do the same thing."

I took a breath and blew it out. "I'm not sure I'm comfortable with that kind of power."

Bart chuckled. "You command people every day. You're a manager, Susan."

"I don't *command*. I gently request that my team do their jobs. And if they don't, I gently manipulate them until they do." I furrowed my brow, rubbing my throat again. "This feels... too much. I would never want to take away someone's free will."

"Get used to it," Cecil said cheerfully, throwing back the rest of his martini. "You've got it now, and you can't give it back." He pointed with a hoof. "Now, honey, get out of that dress. You've got twelve, maybe thirteen more to try on before we do hair and makeup."

I groaned. "No more dresses." Stirred up by my exasperation and confusion, the hot feeling in my belly flared again.

"It's a black-tie dinner." Cecil struck a pose, still standing upright, one hoof on his hip. "We have to get this right, Chosen. This is your rebranding. Your coming out party. You have to strike exactly the right note. You—"

I drew up a little heat from the depths of my belly and sank some power into my voice. "**Go get the red one.**"

Cecil jolted. He tossed his empty glass behind him, fell to all fours, and pranced stiffly like a dressage pony, clip-clopping straight out of the drawing room, his tail flicking behind him.

Bart chuckled, shaking his head. "You are a fast learner, Sue."

I still felt unsettled and edgy, so I paced back and forth a few times, my enormous tulle skirt rustling in the silence of the drawing room, breathing in and out, trying to rid myself of all the excess energy swirling in the pit of my stomach. The feeling of imminent catastrophe was hard to shake, but it was dissipating slowly. I knew how close I'd come to losing control in front of my husband's new fiancé. I could have killed her.

"Are you sure Seraphina is a human?" I asked the room in general. "She's the only person who's been able to really get under my skin like that." I shook myself, bristling, and tried to brush off the lingering sadness and despair that clung to me.

Ugh. Grief. That was the one emotion that was so hard to shake. I'd lost the love of my life, but he was still alive. Maybe I'd never be able to shake it. "I'm a good judge of character," I went on. "And Seraphina always seemed so genuine. She comes off as the sweetest, most innocent young girl." I shook my head. "But..."

"Considering her current circumstances," Bart replied. "I know exactly what you mean. She's human, though. I've never sensed a trace of magic around her."

I chewed on my lip for a second, thinking. Cecil trotted back into the room, holding a scarlet dress in his teeth. "Seraphina's such a delicate creature," I said, almost to myself. "And she's so scared of me, Old Crazy Susan. But she came here, to my apartment, alone, to ask me where Vincent's alimony check was. That's not something you would do if you were scared of your partner's ex." Suddenly, I remembered something. "Did you hear her saying something about a building deed?"

"We heard everything," Bart replied.

I rubbed my lip where I'd bit it too hard. "I wondered

what that was about. She said her lawyer thought I was hiding assets."

Cecil spat the red dress out on an ottoman next to me. "Their lawyer probably got his hands on the purchase notification." He scowled deeply, moved back up onto two legs, tossed back his hair and lit another cigarette. "I wonder how that happened?"

I was too confused to complain about the smoke. "What purchase notification?"

Cecil stared at me like I was an idiot. In the background, by the window, I noticed Donovan's shoulders had tensed even further. "The building purchase notification," Cecil replied slowly.

I sighed. "Can you elaborate on that a little more, please, Cecil?"

"Lord have mercy." Cecil echoed my sigh even more dramatically and tossed his bangs out of his eyes. "I can't graft the bones of a Domicile onto a piece of land you don't own, Chosen. You didn't own that tiny box you called your apartment."

"Oh. So... you bought my apartment?"

He curled his lip. "Ew. Gross. No."

"Oh."

"The magic of the Domicile has to be grounded to work properly, and it must be secured to the master of the House for it to grow."

I frowned. "I'm confused."

"The mistress of Violet House must own the ground she sits upon. When his Highness installed me here, we found out you were"—he shuddered dramatically—"*renting*. So, we quickly purchased the building."

My mouth dropped open. "You... You what?"

"We purchased the building. And transferred it into

your name. So, I could graft the bones of Violet House to your living space properly."

I mouthed stupidly for a minute. "How? How the hell did you buy the whole building?"

Cecil threw his hooves up. "Don't look at me. His Highness ordered the purchase."

From his spot by the window, Donovan threw me a quick glance over his shoulder. "I did what needed to be done, Chosen."

"How?"

His massive shoulders hitched in a shrug. "We have human agents in this realm who look after these things."

I gaped at him. "You... you can't just buy an entire apartment *building*. This is San Francisco!"

"He's the prince. Of course he can." Cecil gave a supercilious snort. "It's not even difficult. The royal family's agents here hold several billion dollars in cash ready to make these kinds of purchases as needed. I doubt that the Queen's treasurer even noticed the withdrawal from the mortal accounts."

"But... but you transferred it into my name? You can't do that. Donovan. It's... it's insane."

"Technically, you bought it from me for one of your mortal dollars." He turned slightly, barely meeting my eye. "So, you owe me a dollar."

"You can't do that." I shook my head slowly, unable to comprehend it. "It's too much. It's too much. Donovan... you can't give me a whole *building*."

Cecil snorted. "If you're worried about that leggy redhead bitch and her lawyer trying to take it from you, don't worry. The Prince and Princess's human lawyers will eat her for breakfast."

"I'm not worried about that." I wasn't. The terms of our

settlement were very clear. Alimony would be half of my salary until Vincent remarried, and anything I purchased with my own money after our divorce was mine.

And all the beautiful things I owned before our divorce belonged to him, including my dream home, my heritage-listed dream home up in Pacific Heights.

It would be rude to say it out loud, but I'd trade the whole building to get my old life back. Instead, I faced Donovan. "This building would have to be worth hundreds of millions of dollars. It's beyond generous."

"I didn't give it to you. You bought it from me. And it is nothing." He turned back to the window again.

Cecil bristled. "It's not the building you should be thanking him for."

"Cecil." Donovan's tone held a warning.

The duocorn shut his mouth, picked up the red dress, and tossed it at me. "Put it on," he said, a touch hastily. "I'll get my makeup kit." He shimmied back out again.

"Donovan..." My own voice held a warning. "What else should I be thanking you for?"

"Nothing."

Bart chuckled into his cocktail glass. "The *building* is nothing."

"Is it Violet House? Is that the thing you would consider generous? Is that the thing I should be thanking you for?"

"You need not thank me for anything. Consider it payment for services rendered." A strange expression drifted over his face. "You have already done more to stop my brother from growing more powerful than any of my company has done in the last half century or more."

I shook my head, confused. "Half-century? Connor has been at it for *fifty years?* I thought you were the older brother? You don't look a second older than thirty-two." I paused and held up a finger. "Actually, let's circle back to that. I noticed you didn't answer my first question."

Donovan let out a gruff noise. "Violet House was a mere fragment of bone when she was grafted into the foundations of this building. Domiciles like Violet are fairly common in my realm," he explained. "They are like... like pets, I suppose, but you don't know what kind of Domicile you're going to get until the bones are grafted in place and watered with magic." His eyes drifted around the luxurious drawing room. "As luck would have it, she has turned out to be possibly the most magnificent Domicile I have seen, but she was not valuable when I had Cecil install her here."

"So what is the—"

"Me," Cecil said, clomping back in, wheeling a huge suitcase behind him. "It's me. I'm the generous gift."

Donovan growled. "Cecil."

He bowed. "I'm sorry, Your Highness. She's going to find out eventually. We might as well get this over with."

I stared at him. "You?"

"Of course, me." He struck a pose. "I'm what we call a *foilynre ey bateromont*. Loosely translated, it means 'spoils of war.'"

"You're a spoil of war?"

"That's right. My herd was foolish and stubborn enough to go to war with the Kingdom of the Crystal Gardens many years ago. We lost, and as part of the ceasefire negotiations, my family had to offer up a sacrifice to enter into the Royal Family's service."

I gasped softly. "They gave you up? As a sacrifice?"

"I volunteered, actually," he said, a little snippily. "Back then, I would have done anything to get away from that herd of stuck-up arrogant assholes. I'm a bit of a black sheep, if I'm being honest, Chosen. An outsider. A lone wolf."

"You are? Is it... is it because you're short?"

He gasped. "No, you bitch. It's because I have two horns. The rest of my herd are standard unicorns. I'm too extra for the rest of those losers."

Behind him, Donovan shook his head. *Because he's short*, he mouthed.

"And because I have two horns, I'm blessed with extra magical abilities," Cecil went on, oblivious. "I've always had an affinity for working with Domiciles, so I would credit most of Violet House's magnificence to my presence."

Donovan shook his head again.

"But most of my talent is in ambience. I can make anything beautiful. Including you." He pointed a hoof at me. "Please, put that dress on now, Chosen. We're running out of time."

Dutifully, I unzipped the red dress and stepped into it. I hadn't felt embarrassed about standing around in my underwear, firstly because Cecil had already supplied me with the most exquisite lacy black shapewear, which covered all the bits that needed to be covered, pushed my breasts up and out proudly, sucked in my tummy, and slimmed my hips. I'd lost most of my pride when I was incarcerated, and when you spent twenty-three months of your life in either orange jumpsuits or hospital-issued pajamas, you tended to want to show off when you could.

The shapewear was amazing. I hadn't looked this good in years.

"Unfortunately for me, my raison d'etre doesn't quite vibe with the rest of my herd," Cecil went on, adjusting the red dress as it fell around me. "Making things beautiful is an act of service to society at large, and unicorns don't do service. They are proud and haughty creatures. None of them liked me changing the wallpaper in their stables.

They get really snippy when you put foil highlights in their manes while they're sleeping."

"Ungrateful fools," I said, carefully draping the gown's straps over my shoulders.

"Yes! Exactly! *Thank* you, Chosen." Cecil huffed out a sigh. "I have a talent that cannot be held in. I must work my magic, or I will explode."

"That's why you volunteered as a spoil of war?"

"Yes. I figured that at the very least, I'd be doing what I loved—making things beautiful. Of course, if I had known that the Queen would mothball me for years, I might have just put up with living with my herd. I realized quite quickly she was hoarding me with the intention of gifting me to someone worthy of me. I have his Highness to thank for liberating me and bonding me to you."

I frowned. "We're bonded?"

"Of course!"

"How so?"

"Well, it's like a marriage..."

"It's not like a marriage," Donovan rumbled from the corner. "It's a magical contract. He is *foilynre ey bateromont*. Cecil has been gifted to you from the Royal Family. He belongs to you now. He's your servant, and you're his mistress."

Cecil gasped, offended, but he closed his mouth, and didn't say anything else.

I didn't want his feelings to be hurt, so I patted his mane gently, only for him to whip around and bite at me with his horsey teeth.

Ooh, he was pissed. I didn't really blame him for snapping. "So, er, *you're* the very valuable thing I should be thankful for, Cecil."

He eyed me suspiciously. "I am."

"Far more valuable than a multi-million-dollar building. More valuable than a magical sentient house."

"Yes."

"You're highly prized. Coveted. And powerful, just like a genie."

He looked a little mollified. "I suppose I am. In fact, when combined with the strong magic of a Domicile like Violet House, I am very much like a genie." He wrinkled his nose. "Except I am infinitely better looking."

"I bet the Queen is going to be mad when she finds out you're gone." I was just trying to make him feel better, but for my sake, I hoped the answer was no.

"Oh, she's going to be furious!"

Damn.

"I am one of her most precious things, a *foilynre ey bateromont,* and a duocorn, too. I could have been a present for a foreign tyrant that she wanted to appease, or a very expensive gift of appreciation for a powerful ally, or a dowry for one of the future princes or princesses. Instead, the Heir had me stolen from the treasury and bonded to..." He waved his hoof dismissively. "*You.*"

I glanced over at Donovan. He was still looking out the window. He didn't turn.

There was a long moment of silence. "Am I in danger?"

All three of them answered simultaneously. "Yes."

"The Queen is the least of your worries, Chosen," Cecil said, fussily smoothing down the dress and fixing the straps to fall over my shoulders. "She cannot do anything now that Prince Donovan has gifted me to you."

I spoke to Donovan's back. Too late, I realized he wasn't being rude; he'd turned away while I was undressing. "What will she do to you?"

He let out a rough breath. "Nothing. My mother and

father have instructed me to do whatever I have to get Connor to stop what he's doing and come home."

Something about his tone gave me pause. There was an edge of hurt in his words. "Just the four of you?"

"It did not have to be me personally, but I felt it was my duty." He didn't turn, but after a second, he nodded. "Discretion is necessary."

I understood. Donovan's spoiled brat brother was on a power trip, and Donovan had been sent to quietly reel him in. Despite the fact that Connor's actions could destroy countless realms, hobble multiple different species of magical creature, and turn him into an overpowered tyrant who could destroy the very fabric of all the Worlds, his parents—who sounded like elitist assholes themselves—wanted Donovan to take care of it quietly.

Bart threw the last of his martini back and got up out of the armchair reluctantly. "As much as I want to hang around and see the results of your makeover, Susan, I have to go. Mikhael wants to go to the ballet tonight."

"Thanks for coming over, Bart," I said warmly. I had no idea who Mikhael was. Bart had an endless parade of beautiful young men and women he went out with on weeknights when he wasn't babysitting me. "And thanks for... you know." I waved my hand in the air. "Everything."

He kissed me on both cheeks. "I have to be nice to you now, you're my landlord." He chuckled.

A blush warmed my cheeks. "Well. Guess who is going to be living rent-free from now on?"

Bart patted my shoulder. "I wasn't paying rent anyway," he said smugly. "It's not my lease. Gavin and Montero have a contract in Barcelona for the year, I'm just housesitting for them." He smiled at me fondly. "I'm so glad. You deserve it all, Susan." He turned and bowed to

Donovan. "Your Highness." He moved back upright, suddenly uneasy. "I know I don't have to—"

"She will be safe, Shifter," Donovan said, his voice cold. He didn't turn. The Prince was back to brooding-mode. "I will see to it."

"Er. Good," Bart said. "Have a great night." He looked around the massive room. "How do I get out of here again? Is it through those white and gilt carved doors or the marble archway over there beside the Ming vase filled with the blush peonies?"

"Come," Donovan said. "I will guide you back to your apartment." They walked out; Bart, lumbering like a big teddy bear, and the Prince, just as tall, but moving like a warrior, like a tiger stalking through the jungle, with a barely contained tension simmering inside of him. I understood why he left. He needed to move.

Cecil finished fussing with my draped straps, jumped on top of the ottoman and ran a critical eye over me. "I think that's perfect. I was right all along—the red one was the best."

I knew it the second I'd seen it; that's why I told him to get it. He had been planning on making me try on a dozen other dresses. I decided to let that one go. "Oh, it is."

"I just need to do your hair and makeup."

I groaned. Getting dolled up was fun, but I always resented the time it took. Full glam makeup took hours. Life was too short to sit with my eyes half-shut so my mascara wouldn't smudge before it dried. And the fun of getting glammed up sort of dwindled as you got older—cakey makeup sank into little wrinkles, making them seem even deeper, and lipstick feathered out from lips that were just a little less plump than they'd been ten years ago. "Just a little, please, Cecil."

He whipped open the case behind him—trays and tray

of pallets, with every shade of lipstick and eyeshadow and blush you could think of in shimmers, mattes, sparkles, and nudes. Creams and powders and liquids in perfectly clean little bottles. A hundred soft brushes of every size and shape. The sixteen-year-old girl within me let out a squeal of glee.

"Stay still," he ordered, brandishing two brushes stuck between each hoof. "Actually. You better close your eyes for this. You're new to this, and I don't want you freaking out."

I lowered my lids dutifully. A blast of air hit my face, a flurry of movement whirling in front of me.

"Done!" Cecil declared.

I opened one eye. "What?"

"I'm finished."

"Finished what? Finished applying my left eyeliner?"

"No, you silly cow," he said, holding out a beautiful antique silver hand mirror.

I took it. "Are you allowed to call me a silly cow?"

"I can call you whatever I like. My sentence is in service, not in politeness. Now, gaze in wonder at the fruits of my labor."

I looked. "Holy shit," I whispered. In less than three seconds, Cecil had managed to apply the most exquisite natural-looking makeup. Smooth tan skin, slightly rosy cheeks, a hint of shimmer on my cheekbones. My lips were blood-red, perfectly moisturized and lined so they looked as full as they had twenty years ago. My eyelids were shadowed with dark gold, making my blue-green iris glow in an almost preternatural way. A thin, expertly applied simple black liner with a tiny wing gave my eyes a sultry look. My lashes were full and lush and one-hundred percent real. There was nothing fake, nothing contoured, nothing outrageously sculpted. Just skillfully chosen and applied colors to enhance my features perfectly.

I'd never looked better. "Wow."

"The canvas is a little dated, but still good for painting on." Cecil sighed dramatically. "It isn't my best work, but it will do."

"I'd love to see your best— Wait." Something weird caught my eye. "What... What the hell is this?"

"What is what?" Cecil said, his tone innocent. He reached out with both hooves to take the mirror out of my hands.

I yanked it back. "Cecil."

We tussled over the mirror for a minute. "Give that here, you uppity bitch."

"No! Did you dye my hair, Cecil?"

"No." He pouted.

"You did!"

"It's not dyeing. It's called *coloring*," he said patronizingly. "And it's just a few foils," he sniffed. "Calm down."

"I will not calm down!" I'd never colored my hair before. I wasn't necessarily against the idea; I'd always liked my natural color well enough. But Vincent had loved it—a deep and lush dark chocolate with vivid plum shades in the sunshine. Vincent begged me not to change it, and since I liked it, I never did. And when I started to find a few gray hairs sprinkled through my part line, I put a lot of emotional effort into being okay with it.

Vincent had loved my hair. He would spend Sunday mornings winding his fingers through it, stroking me like a cat. Grief stabbed me in the heart all over again.

I was too far gone to try and "process" this grief, so I squashed it down for once instead. This wasn't Cecil's fault. I was still pissed, though.

"How the hell did you dye my hair?" I glanced at my reflection in the mirror again.

Not only was my deep chocolate hair now artfully and

subtly streaked with caramel and cream highlights, camouflaging my gray hair completely, he'd somehow arranged it into perfect waves draped over one shoulder, with a deep side-part over my left eye.

"I put in a couple of highlights while you were freaking out about your brand-new siren powers." He yanked the antique hand mirror out of my hand and tossed it carelessly behind him. The ottoman slid sideways by itself and caught it with a bounce.

"How did I not notice you putting *foil* in my *hair?*"

"I don't know. Maybe you're just not very observant." Cecil heaved another dramatic sigh. "You might as well get a proper look at yourself now that you're all finished. Violet, can we get a full-length mirror over here?"

A gap appeared between the floorboards, and a gold-framed mirror slid out, propping itself up in front of me. I stared.

The red dress had caught my eye from the start—pure silk, the color of freshly spilled blood, with a long skirt that hugged my thighs to the knee and blossomed out like a tulip, giving me a sexy silhouette. The dress had a deep split to mid-thigh for ease of walking, and was cinched in at the waist, rising up into a structured corset top that shaped my breasts perfectly. Gathered and draped straps hung off my shoulder, making the sexy gown seem a touch more regal— the kind of thing a former princess might wear to a diplomatic function the week after her divorce. Considering this was the first event I'd been invited to since I'd been released from the hospital, it was stupidly appropriate. I was no longer the poor man's Jessica Rabbit. I looked like Crown Princess Jessica Rabbit, Duchess of Sultryland.

The door opened, and Cress stalked in, her expression thunderous. Eryk and Nate stomped in behind her. They saw me and paused, eyes flaring wide for a brief moment.

The boys both bowed their heads deeply. Cress lifted her chin, studying me carefully. "Well. If I had known that Cecil could perform miracles, I would have stolen him for myself decades ago."

Cecil sashayed back to the wet bar and picked up the cocktail shaker, muttering under his breath. I caught a handful of words, mostly swear words.

I laughed. "Do you think I look pretty, Cress?" There was nothing more satisfying than having a lovely young person tell you that you looked nice. Normally, young adults enjoyed nothing more than telling you that you look old, dried up, and crusty.

"You look stunning." She stared at me. A strange heat bloomed in her eyes, and suddenly, I felt a little awkward.

"Thanks."

The heat disappeared, and she arched an eyebrow. "But where will you put your weapons?"

"Umm." I patted my beautiful gown. "I don't know. Nowhere? I'm not really a weapons kind of girl, Cress."

"You must." She marched over, pulling an assortment of blades and daggers out of various sheaths in her skin-tight leather vest and pants.

"Leave her alone, Cress," Cecil poured a measure of tequila into the shaker and tossed in a shovel of ice.

"No," she said stubbornly. "It is my duty. I am *isanayrin ayawa*; I must make sure she is armed."

"Mistress of the blade," Nate supplied helpfully.

"The company weapons expert," Eryk added.

"Right." I nodded thoughtfully, as Cress knelt before me. I hadn't had a chance to figure out the dynamics of their company yet; they obviously had established roles and specialties. Donovan, the prince, was obviously in charge, and Cress, his scary warrior princess girlfriend was the second, with Eryk, the fire

165

elemental and Nate, the battle mage, deferring to both of them.

It didn't surprise me in the slightest that Cress was the weapons expert. I let out a little shriek as she knelt before me abruptly and slid her hands up my thigh, caressing my skin gently. "What are you—"

"You will have to wear a sheath," she muttered, lifting the hem of my gown and getting right in between my legs. I felt a slap of leather. A cold tingle of a buckle brushed my skin as she fastened something onto me. "There. You will have room for at least four blades on that sheath. You will have to carry your throwing knives in your purse."

There was a crash, as Cecil slammed the shaker down on the bar. He spat out the words between clenched teeth. "She's *not* putting throwing knives in her Joy Linman crystal-embellished clutch!"

The door slammed. "Cress." Donovan's voice was as cold as the grave. "She has no need for weapons. She will be with me." His tone dropped even further. "Step back. Now."

Ooh. Donovan didn't like Cress touching other people, including women. That was interesting. No wonder he took her everywhere. Someone clearly had trust issues.

She stood up and turned to faced him. "There is banwyn excrement all over this city, Donovan," she said, her voice just as icy. "Connor is here with at least a hundred of his vicious lower-realm minions. She will need to be armed with at least a crystal blade to repel them, since she is not in control of her own magic."

He let out a low noise—a gruff grunt of exasperation. "Fine. One blade. Tourmaline." He checked his watch. "And hurry. We must go now; it is almost time. I am concerned that the scribe stone may be stolen when Ahdeannowyn opens up his Domicile to his guests."

"The professor's place isn't a magic manor, Donovan. It's just a regular house."

Cress curled her lip. "It is a Domicile." She plucked out a small black dagger from a hidden spot at her ribs, flipped it, and handed it to me. I took it.

"Thanks." It felt cold in my hands. "Can you fill me in on what the hell a banwyn is, so I know what to stab?"

"A demon-like creature from a realm in the Lower World," she explained. "They are lower-vibrational, vicious beasts who feed on fear and desperation and thrive in chaos. Connor consumed their spark stone many years ago and imbibed their power. The banwyn now follow him as he offers them a chance to feast in other realms. Like this one," she added darkly.

"What's their power?"

"They can sense when someone is weakened, panicked, and easily overwhelmed."

"That doesn't seem like much of a magical power. You'd just look for the person with a sweaty brow, a fidget spinner and anti-anxiety medication in their handbag."

"It is subtle but useful magic. A malevolent person would use it to their advantage to find people who are easy to manipulate, something that Connor already excelled at. The banwyn need the power to select their victims. They are small creatures, not physically powerful by themselves, so they need to choose their meals wisely. They swarm their victims, biting them with small, sharp teeth. They do not imbibe blood nor flesh, however. They feed on their victim's fear and panic, and if the attack is prolonged, the victim will go insane."

I made a face. "Yeesh. So, what do these little demons look like?"

"They look like human children."

I looked at her. "What?"

"They would appear to your eye as normal human children," Cress said patiently. "From between four to seven mortal years old."

"Are you kidding me? They look like kids?"

"They have very sharp teeth," Eryk added helpfully. "They bite. And they swarm. They run in a weird way, like they're not sure what to do with their arms."

"You're literally just describing human children, Eryk."

Nate raised his hand. "Their iris will flash ultraviolet when you shine a light in their eyes."

I huffed out a breath. "Now we're getting somewhere. Thank you, Nate. And I was starting to worry."

Cress looked confused. "Why would you worry?"

"I don't want to go around stabbing little kids by accident, Cress."

She frowned. "Why not? You cannot do too much damage with the tourmaline blade, Chosen. It is better to stab a few human children by accident than get overwhelmed by banwyn." She whipped another small, shining black blade out of nowhere and handed it to me. "Put that between your breasts, just in case."

I opened my mouth and closed it again. "Okay."

"We must go," Donovan said gruffly, looking at his watch again. "Come."

Over at the bar, Cecil poured himself another cocktail. "Doesn't the Chosen look lovely, your Highness?" There was a bitchy note in his tone.

Donovan raised his head and met my eye. Apart from a few quick glances, it was the first time this evening he'd properly looked at me. I caught a hot spark deep in the depths of his gaze, then, his expression hardened.

No, not just hardened. His face iced over. He looked like a man who was staring at something he *hated*.

He hated me. I was messing up his company's mission,

and he hated it. He was forced to deal with a dried-up old bag of a woman with no knowledge, no experience, no skills, and no idea what the hell she was doing.

I couldn't blame him. I was doing a fantastic version of failing up—somehow managing to secure spark stones against his brother without any understanding of *anything*.

A long moment passed.

"Her appearance is satisfactory," he muttered. "Let's go."

CHAPTER
SIXTEEN

My skin broke into goosebumps as soon as I walked out of my building thanks to the icy wind chill coming off the water. Autumn had settled on the city—the days were still sunny, but the nights had turned cold.

Cress, Nate, and Eryk melted into the darkness immediately—apparently, they were going to be shadowing us, watching for signs of Connor and his creepy banwyn army in case they decided to ambush us en route.

"Where is your carriage?" Donovan asked.

"I don't have a carriage."

"Your mount, then. Where is your stable?"

"No mounts either," I said, thumbing my phone. "And sorry, we're all out of stables." I had just enough money left on my credit card to grab an Uber, but it was going to have to be the cheapest ride. Idly, I wondered if Professor Owen would give me some leftovers to take to work for lunch tomorrow.

"Susan!" Audrina, my lovely teenage songbird neighbor, loped towards me from across the street, long limbs swinging awkwardly. Those long arms were handy when they were wrapped around her guitar, but she still hadn't figured out how to walk with them without looking like a neanderthal dragging her knuckles behind her. She stopped a few feet away, eyes round with wonder. "Wow. You look... wow!"

I smiled. "Thanks, Audrina."

Her eyes swung towards Donovan and widened further. "*Wow.*"

"Yes. Audrina, this is my friend Donovan. Donovan, this is my neighbor, Audrina."

Audrina seemed to have lost the power of speech. She just stood and stared at Donovan. I could hardly blame her; the man looked like he'd just stepped off a catwalk.

His eyes flashed. "This is the one you called the Chosen. The one you sent us to—"

I shushed him. "Uh, yes. This is the lovely Audrina, the songbird of Nob Hill." I frowned. "Okay, don't put that on an album cover, it sounds weird."

Just then, I noticed she had her guitar slung on her back, and two large duffel bags over each shoulder. I frowned. "Where are you going?"

She still stared at Donovan.

I clapped my hands, and she flinched. "Audrina, where are you going?"

Her eyes filled with tears. "Mom took the boys for ice cream in the park today. They saw me singing."

Oh, no.

"I didn't spot them until it was too late. I was in the middle of a song, and I had my eyes closed. Something cold smacked me in the face, and when I opened them, I saw my brothers laughing like hyenas. One of them tossed his ice cream at me. They thought it was the funniest thing they'd ever seen, but Mom went ballistic." The tears spilled down her cheeks. "She dragged me home. I'm grounded. Forever, apparently. Mom said she'd never been more humiliated in her life. Apparently, me busking is the most embarrassing thing to ever happen to her."

"You're running away, aren't you?"

She nodded.

"Audrina," I sighed. "You can't run away. Anything might seem better than living with those bullies, but you have to be practical. You'll get eaten alive on the streets."

"I can't go back there." She let out a sob. "I can't, Susan. Everyone thinks I've got such a privileged life. Yeah, we're so rich, Mom and Dad were famous, but it's *hell*. My brothers think that bullying me is a sport. They actually compete to see who can be the first to make me cry every day. Mom tells me to suck it up, and I just have to get thicker skin, and nobody can make me feel anything I don't want to feel. But I can't. It hurts so much." Audrina's face turned blotchy as tears poured down her cheeks. "I can't take it anymore. I even told my mom I was thinking of ending it all. And she... she..."

Nausea lurched up in my gut. I knew what Audrina was going to say. Her mother was fucking awful. Jessica was the kind of person that saw everything in her life as an object to be used. She used her talented and handsome sons as trophies, and she used her husband for his money and status. But to her, Audrina was worthless.

"Mom's eyes lit up when I said that," Audrina whispered, her voice hitching. "She was actually excited about the idea of me committing suicide. She'd get everything she wanted. I'd be gone, I wouldn't be around to embarrass her anymore, and she'd get more attention and lots of sympathy. I could see the thoughts ticking in her brain."

I sighed sadly. Audrina wasn't being dramatic. Jessica

was probably already planning the name of the mental health charity she would set up once her daughter was gone.

"Chosen..." Donovan was suddenly standing too close. My thoughts scattered.

Oh, yeah. We were already late. "Please, Donovan. Just wait a moment. I can't leave her out here like this."

He let out a soft grunt, then turned, and whistled a low note.

Suddenly, Nate was standing next to us. Audrina froze, mid-sob. Donovan spoke to him. "Take this young woman upstairs to Violet House. The *guest* quarters," he said pointedly. "Keep Cecil away from her, but inform him that she will need..." He frowned. "All the things that young mortal women need to keep her occupied."

Audrina's eyes widened again. "You'll let me stay with you?"

"Of course," I said. "Just until we can figure out a plan. You need to let your family know you're safe, though. But don't tell them you're staying with me," I added hastily. The last thing I needed was to get arrested for kidnapping.

She nodded frantically. "I will. I'll do anything, Susan. Oh, thank you!" She threw herself forward, but instead of hugging me, she veered away at the last second and wrapped her arms around Donovan's waist and squeezed him around the middle, pushing her face into his hard stomach. He froze. She rubbed her cheek against him like a cat, desperate for affection.

I held back a laugh; Donovan looked almost alarmed. After a moment, he patted her on top of her head once, then again. "There, there."

Gently, Nate untangled her and led her away. Just in time, too. My phone buzzed in my hand. Our ride was here. "Let's go," I said to Donovan. I walked up to the red hatchback that had just pulled up, swinging my hips and relishing how the silk brushed over my skin as I walked.

Somehow, Donovan got there before me. He opened the back door, looked inside, then hesitated. "This is not your carriage."

"Yes, it is," I said brightly, shuffling past him. I stuck my head inside. "Hello, Amir," I said to the driver.

The driver turned and gave me a huge smile. He had a thick pelt of black hair and the most impressive black handlebar mustache I'd ever seen in my life. "You are Miss Susan? Yes?"

"Yes, I am! How are you this evening?"

"Good, good. Haight-Ashbury, yes?"

"Yes." I shuffled in next to the two other passengers—two teenage boys, both wearing thick glasses and shirts with anime characters on them, both clutching comic tote bags to their chests. "Hello," I said, smiling.

Both of them blinked at me and held their tote bags tighter. Neither responded. "Donovan, you'll have to get in the front."

He didn't move. I glanced up and saw him clench his jaw. "Chosen. This is *not* acceptable."

"This is our ride to the Professor's house, Donovan. Get in."

"You have small flightcraft in this realm. You have long vehicles with partition screens and small bars installed in them, I have seen pictures. Why are we sharing this small carriage with commoners?" He glared into the back of the car. The two teens cringed into their seats.

Amir hit a button on his phone. "Wait time fee, Miss Susan. Sorry, sorry."

"That's fine, Amir," I said, letting out a sigh. The wait time fee would chew up the last of the money in my account. I turned back to Donovan. "I *am* a commoner," I said, a little sharply. "This is perfectly decent transportation, Donovan, and it's all I can afford right now."

He frowned. "You cannot afford a carriage of your own?"

"No."

He glanced at Amir. "Are you an honorable man?"

"Yes, yes," Amir said, smiling so wide I thought his face might break in two. "Five-star rating. Three months driving in this country, my home, United States. You check."

"Then the Chosen will sit in front." Donovan's tone indicated there would be no arguing. He stepped back.

"Fine." I shuffled back out of my seat, while he held the front passenger door open. I settled into my seat. Donovan leaned in one more time and glared at Amir.

"If you touch her, I will disembowel you with a fork and use your entrails to string you from that bridge."

"Donovan!"

Amir giggled. "No problem, no problem, my friend. No need to disembowel today. I do best service. Five stars! We go now, yes?"

"Yes, please," I said faintly, as Donovan got in. I didn't want to look, but I heard a whimper of fear from the two young men in the back seat, and I couldn't help but turn my head. Donovan, huge, long-legged, wildly intimidating, sprawled out behind me, the picture of terrifying grace and menacing power. He took up most of the space in the back seat. The boys looked as scared as if they were sharing a backseat with a hungry panther. Both of them were sandwiched up against the other window, staring at Donovan like he was a god.

Amir pulled out onto Pine Street, heading towards Haight-Ashbury, and we weaved through the nighttime city traffic in silence for a few minutes. Mostly silence, anyway. I could hear one of the boys in the back breathing heavily through his mouth. Panting, almost. "We must get you your own carriage," Donovan said gruffly. "This is unacceptable."

"Five stars!" Amir's mustache quivered in outrage. "I have five stars. You will not take my stars away from me."

"It's okay, Amir. We'll give you five stars."

His mustache pouted. "I am good service."

"You're doing great. Thank you."

"Good." He flung his hand towards the dashboard, gesturing. "You want music?"

"Oh." The tension caused by the near silence in the car was so thick I could cut it with a knife. And it would be nice not having to hear the two boys in the back whimpering and panting in fear. "Yes, please. Music would be lovely."

"Pop? Country? You like rap?"

"Whatever you like, thanks, Amir."

Amir hit the console. A heavy trap beat boomed through the car, soon accompanied by a woman's voice rapping the most sexually explicit lyrics I'd ever heard in my life. A different woman joined in with even more X-rated chorus. Amir happily nodded along to the beat. I had to press my lips together to stop laughing.

While the woman sang and rapped about how much she liked having her butthole licked, I risked a peek in my vanity mirror. Donovan was no longer brooding like a thundercloud. His head was slightly cocked, his brow furrowed, as he listened carefully to the music. "Is this... these... these female bards. They are popular in your realm?"

"Oh, yes, my man, yes," Amir said. "Very popular. Top ten in charts, always."

Donovan listened for a little while longer. "Your friend. The songbird. Does she perform ballads like this one?"

I lurched upright. "No!" Oops, that sounded very judgmental. "I mean, no, she doesn't. This music is lovely, but

Audrina sings folk songs and plays her guitar. Less of a heavy beat," I explained. "More ballad-like."

"Hmm." Donovan met my eye in the vanity mirror. "You are kind to offer her sanctuary."

"I'm hardly going to leave her out on the streets. She'd be trafficked in a heartbeat. The poor girl doesn't even have a phone. Her father is never home, and her mother is a tyrant."

"Tyrants do not give up their prisoners easily," he said quietly. "If this mother finds out the songbird has escaped and is seeking sanctuary with you, she will strike out at you."

"I know," I sighed. "I will have to manage her in the same way I manage everyone else."

He looked almost interested. "You will do battle?"

"In a way. Management is all about helping people get onto the best path for everyone. And the best thing for Audrina is to get her away from that family, and the best thing for her mother is to let her go so she's not constantly confronted with her disappointment every day."

I exhaled wearily. I was a big believer in redemption, but practical enough to know that sometimes, you just had to throw the whole person in the trash. "As you said, tyrants don't give up their prisoners easily, and since Audrina is underage, Jessica won't let her leave home." I looked out the window, thinking. "Audrina's mother cares about one thing and one thing only; her image. She's cold and heartless, so there's no point appealing to her sympathy. No." I sighed. "I'm going to have to threaten to ruin her reputation."

"How will you do that?"

"She prides herself on being seen as a good mom. Mom of boys," I clarified. "She's based her whole personality on it. I just have to publicly threaten that image. I'm thinking we'll film a few clips of Audrina talking about how hellish her life is and how horrible her mother is, interspersed with some videos of her singing, just to gain additional interest. Then, we'll send them to Jessica and threaten to release them on social media—and tag her, of course, so her humiliation is as public as possible. Then, we just have to offer Jessica some options, so she feels like she's in control of the outcome. I bet she'll let Audrina either stay with me, or she'll enroll her in a boarding school somewhere far away, until she's ready to go to college."

Donovan nodded slowly. "And if it does not work, we can kill this Jessica tyrant," he said softly. "We will 'tag' her publicly."

"Um..." I'd been wondering how much of what I was saying he would understand. "Let's call that plan B."

Donovan furrowed his brow, listening to the explicit lyrics of the song again. "It is interesting. The women in the front box of your carriage sing songs like the warrior goddesses of fae lore. Do you have the same warrior goddesses in this realm? They sing of the same things. Is this a hymn to the old gods?"

"Uh. No? How are they... uh... similar?"

"They sing of destroying men's bodies, gripping them, and forcing them to beg for mercy. Wrestling pythons. Devouring predatory cats all night long. And... eating equine beasts like baked goods?"

"No, no, my friend," Amir chipped in. "Eating *ass* like a *cupcake*."

My cheeks burst into flame. "Oh, look," I said brightly. "We're here!" Amir turned onto a dark street lined with huge cypresses. It felt like we'd turned into another dimension. One second, we were on a city street; the next, we were driving down a dark road lined on both sides with mansions and stunning gardens. "Professor Owen's manor house is just there."

The wrought-iron gates were wide open. A strange blue glow lit the space between them. "That's weird," I said, narrowing my eyes. "I didn't know he had laser security."

Donovan grunted. The two boys sandwiched up against the window next to him flinched. "It is a ward, Chosen."

"Huh."

Amir pointed. "I drive in, yes? He has circular driveway?"

"Yes please, Amir."

"No." Donovan said firmly. "The ward may not allow you to enter. You will find your flesh pushed through the metal of this carriage like raw beef in a sausage press. Even these younglings will not survive the passing."

The teens squeaked.

"Just stop here, thanks, Amir," I said.

He pulled up to the curb. Before I could open the door, Donovan was there, holding it open for me.

"Have good fun, my friends!" Amir called out. He roared off, trap beat still booming.

I turned to face Professor Owen's manor house. Just beyond the glowing blue gates, I could see lights on and hear a faint tinkling of laughter.

I gulped. "Donovan?"

"Yes, Chosen?" He stood beside me.

"Never mind." I couldn't tell him how scared I was. Once upon a time, I'd been at dinner parties like this every weeknight. Vincent and I were invited to everything, and I blazed confidently through every gallery opening, every first night performance, every jubilee and centenary ball.

Now, I was an outcast. Persona non grata. A poor, pathetic, sad old lady—the crazy ex-wife who had lost everything. I was someone to be pitied, someone to be avoided in case the humiliation and shame were catching.

I was still me. The confident, happy Susan was still inside me somewhere. She'd just been beaten, bloody and raw, until she was almost dead. I just had to find her again.

Donovan moved closer and took my arm. "Come, Chosen. I am with you."

CHAPTER
SEVENTEEN

Professor Owen's maid, Gladioli, stood on the steps outside the manor house, silhouetted by the light of the open door behind her. "Hello, Mrs. Susan!" She waved happily as Donovan, and I walked up the long driveway.

"Hi, Gladioli!" I waved back, then did a double take. It sounded like Gladioli. She was wearing her usual uniform —pressed black knee-length skirt, crisp white shirt, black tie, sensible shoes— but she looked... different. She was a foot shorter than I remembered, and her skin was creased with a billion more wrinkles than usual. Her nose and chin were so long, they almost met in the middle of her face.

Her gray hair was green. My footsteps faltered.

Donovan felt me hesitate and squeezed my hand gently. "She is a brownie."

I spoke out of the corner of my mouth as we walked towards her. "How the hell did I not notice that before?"

"You did," he murmured back. "Your eyes saw her. Your mind may have refused to comprehend what you were seeing."

The brownie waved me forward excitedly, and I got over her odd appearance quickly. I kissed her on both cheeks. "It's good to see you, Glad."

"I was worried you would never come back, Mrs. Susan," she said happily. "I missed you. None of the Professor's guests ever offered to help with the washing up before. You were the first."

"And, if I recall correctly, you threatened to stab me in the chest with a dessert spoon and carve out my heart if I so much as picked up one plate," I said fondly.

"Of course I did. It was a terrible insult to me." She grinned back. "I would have done it, too." Her eyes drifted upwards, taking in Donovan's blisteringly handsome presence. Her lip curled in disgust. "I see you have mated again. Ugh. He is infinitely more disgusting than your last one."

I blinked. "Ah..."

"Well met, Brownie," Donovan rumbled. "I swear on my life, I have not laid eyes on an uglier creature than the one who stands before me right now."

"Donovan!" I gasped.

Gladioli's sneer disappeared, and she grinned, preening like a little girl with a pretty dress. "You are welcome here, sir." She bowed. "Please, go on in. The Professor is receiving his guests in the antechamber."

We walked inside. "What was that about?"

"Brownie diplomacy," Donovan murmured softly as we walked down a massive, red-paneled hallway lined with portraits of stuffy people peering down their noses at us. "Their beauty standards are the opposite to ours."

"So... you just told her that she is the prettiest creature you've ever seen?"

"Essentially, yes." A hint of a smile lifted the hard line of his lips. "And she thinks I am more handsome than your husband."

"Ex-husband," I corrected. And he was. By miles. Donovan was the most beautiful and terrifying man I'd ever seen in my life. Not that it mattered. He wasn't my date; we were here on a mission. My stomach churned again. "Speaking of ex-husbands, there might be a few people—"

"Susan!"

I looked. Professor Owen waved at me from an alcove up ahead, just before the closed doors of what I remembered was the formal dining room.

I smiled. Dean Owen looked like a living definition of a "wacky professor." Small and slight, bordering on skinny, dark-skinned, with scruffy white hair and a long white beard that brushed his chest, the professor wore a purple velvet three-piece suit, the waistcoat embroidered with what looked like tiny, stylized vaginas. A massive rottweiler sat at his feet, panting. A little puddle of drool lay underneath Bonbon's mouth.

The professor waved us forward. The massive hallway seemed almost a whole football field long. The manor house was obviously a Domicile. How had I not noticed it before?

Just before we reached him, his eyes swiveled towards Donovan, and they widened in shock. His mouth moved, and he muttered under his breath. I caught the words as they echoed towards us.

"Holy slimy pixieballs, it's the prince himself!"

As we approached, the professor stepped forward, clasped his hands behind his back formally, and bowed deeply from the waist, almost doubling over. "Prince of the Westerlands and all of the Southern plains," he boomed in a loud voice. "Conqueror of the Twelve Isles, Heir to the throne of the Crystal Castle. Your Highness, you are most welcome in my Domicile."

The enormous Rottweiler at his feet gave a rumble.

"Don't worry about Bonbon," the Professor added. "She's already given you the green light. You are who you say you are."

I bent down and gave her a scratch behind the ears. "Hello, Bonbon. It's good to see you again."

The enormous dog writhed under my touch.

Donovan stopped a few feet away and glowered. I glanced up at him, confused by his sudden hostility. "You're fooling no one, Ahdeannowyn," he said, his voice low and cold. "You are Elonn fae, the keepers of knowledge. You see how the chess pieces move before the game has even begun. You are not surprised to see me."

"Oh, I am." The professor kept his head sandwiched between his legs, still bowed. "Of course, the probabilities were there, but they were not in favor of you coming here yourself." He chuckled sheepishly. "You are High Fae, but even more than that, you are Heir to the whole Kingdom. None of us had our money on the fact that you would embark on this mission to stop the Devourer yourself."

Donovan let out an exasperated noise. "Does the entire Upper World think so little of us?"

Professor Owen hesitated. "Your brother is the Devourer, Your Majesty. We know what you are capable of."

My eyes swung between them, fascinated, and a little horrified. Maybe Donovan knew more about tyrants than he was letting on.

"I have responsibilities," Donovan said, his tone ice-cold. "You understand responsibilities, Ahdeannowyn. You are the guardian of your realm's spark stone. You knew it was in danger, so you brought it here, to the Middle World. You came here specifically to entice the One of Every Blood so she would close it for you."

"Of course I did. I would do anything to protect the

magic of the Scribes, even if it meant taking our stone out of the Upper World."

"You knew who she was," Donovan's voice grew impossibly colder. "You knew that Susan Moore was the Chosen One. You knew that she was unaware of... *everything*," he growled. "You could have helped her." Suddenly, the darkness in his eyes lifted, and he seemed a little uncomfortable. "You may rise."

Slowly, Professor Owen rose until he was standing. He placed his hands up, palms out, as if trying to placate a thunderstorm. "Before you rip my head off, Your Highness, please remember your own words. We value knowledge above all else. The Chosen remained unaware of her nature until now. So until now, she was quite effectively hidden from those who might have harmed her."

Donovan hesitated for just a second. "She has suffered."

"Diamonds are formed under pressure."

Donovan glared at him for a minute, then, finally, he turned to me. "Chosen. Will you leave us to speak in private for a moment?"

"No," I said immediately. "Oh, God, no. I don't want you to fight."

Professor Owen chuckled. "It wouldn't be much of a fight. That man could kill me with his pinky. In his sleep."

Bonbon let out a whine.

Donovan bent his head, staring directly into the hellhound's eyes. "I will not physically harm your master or you. You have my word."

"Okay," I said tentatively. "I'll leave you to it. I'll, uh, just go in, shall I?" Suddenly, my nervousness overwhelmed me, and it had nothing to do with Donovan or Professor Owen.

The professor opened the door behind him and bowed

deeply again. Soft music, cackles of laughter, and enthusiastic conversation drifted towards me.

I am a strong, confident woman. I am in control.

I took a deep breath, lifted my chin, and walked into the dining room. All the conversation stopped immediately. If this was a movie, I'd hear a record scratch.

"What the hell are you doing here?"

CHAPTER
EIGHTEEN

A dozen faces stared at me, expressions ranging from astonished to totally horrified.

I picked out the ones I recognized. Admiral Riley and his wife, Galena. The bone-thin blonde Saxby sisters, twins, Christina and Celina—distant relations to the Rockefellers and local socialites who had gotten too old for the party scene. The sleazy trust-fund baby Montgomery Walker, with what I assumed was his fifth wife, a very young woman called Ming. They all stared at me.

"Watch out, everyone." A bitchy voice broke the silence. "We've got a convict on the loose in here."

I sighed. "Hello, Juliette."

She smirked, clearly enjoying herself. Tall, athletic, with long brunette hair she always scraped back so tight in a ponytail to enhance her latest facelift, Juliette was an ex-tennis pro who had married the owner of a local broadcasting network here in San Francisco. In truth, she'd been a mediocre tennis player in her twenties and barely scraped into just a handful of Grand Slams, but if there was a tournament for social climbing, she'd win every single one. Now, with an army of reporters, a whole

TV station at her disposal and her husband's money greasing every wheel, Juliette was far too influential to snub at any party. I'd barely tolerated her before, but I did it for Vincent. Juliette's husband owned a lot of his paintings.

I glanced around, looking for her usual partner in crime, her best friend who accompanied her to all these functions. There he was, talking to an older woman who looked familiar, sprawled over by the wet bar—Dan Raine, the handsome meteorologist who worked for Juliette's husband, reading the weather reports on the evening news. Dan was generically handsome, orange-tanned, his artificially colored dark-brown hair sprayed with so much hairspray it looked like a helmet.

Dan had always hated Vincent with a passion. He was jealous of everything about him—Vincent's effortless charisma, his sexy-white-bad-boy good looks, and his phenomenal talent as an artist. Where everything about Dan Raine was fake—his real name was actually Wesley Arbuckle—Dan despised my husband for his unique, strong personality and almost cult-leader-like magnetism.

Juliette hated me because she was a salty bitch. Years ago, she approached me and Vincent, swinging her hips and licking her lips, and proposed a threesome. Both Vincent and I had made the mistake of laughing in her face. Ever since then, she'd been gunning for me, but I'd barely paid her any attention. I didn't need anyone to like me. I had Vincent, so I had everything.

It made her hate me even more.

Squaring her shoulders, she leaned over to the older, white-haired woman, dripping in diamonds next to her, and stage-whispered so everyone could hear her. "That's the woman who went insane, destroyed Bayview Cottage, and tried to kill her husband."

The woman's mouth dropped open. "*That's* the woman who destroyed Bayview?"

I sighed. Now I recognized the older woman they were talking to. It was Delia Bromley, the grand doyenne of San Francisco architecture. She'd visited my house several times to tour it for a book she was writing. I'd served her tea and let her take photos of all my things.

"She also smashed the Andresano's Modigliani. That was a priceless painting, and it was supposed to be Vincent's inheritance," Juliette went on, her tone scandalized. "She destroyed so many precious things and tried to kill her poor husband."

Delia bristled. "Why is she here? She should be in prison."

"Oh, she was in prison. She went to trial. Not guilty by reason of insanity. She just got out of an insane asylum."

I'd had enough. "I got out almost a year ago, Juliette," I said in a bored tone. "Probably only two facelifts ago, in your time."

Her mouth twisted.

Dan Raine approached me slowly, arms outstretched, faux concern all over his faux-tanned face. "How are you feeling, Susan?" He spoke loudly, like I was deaf. "Are you feeling calm?"

"I'm fine. Thanks, Dan." I smiled, even though the fury was starting to burn in my belly.

His voice grew louder. "And the menopause? Are your hormones stable? Have you taken your meds today?"

Fuck him. "No, actually, I haven't. In fact, since I got out of hospital, I decided to rawdog my menopause. Ride the wave, you know?" My smile grew wider. "Who knows what might happen tonight?"

Delia bristled. "I barely noticed it when I went through the Change. Barely even a hot flash. Women these days are soft, always want to be medicated up to the hilt. I never even lost my temper, not once."

A vicious glint appeared in Juliette's eye. She bent down and stage-whispered again, so the whole room would hear. "Oh, but it was *far* worse for poor Susan. See, Susan and Vincent had been trying for a baby for the longest time, but she couldn't get pregnant." She caught my eye and smiled like a snake. "Then, when she started to go through early menopause, the disappointment and sadness at being barren and childless forever drove her insane, and she—"

Bang.

Everyone flinched and turned to see a huge crack in the bay window behind Juliette.

Her eyes widened. "What the..."

Just then, Gladioli appeared out of nowhere and rang a little bell. "Honored guests, please take your places."

Slowly, everyone turned away from the window and walked towards the long dining room table. Conversation started again, and the guests teased each other over the seating arrangement and oohed and aahed over the beautiful violet and blood-red rose centerpieces. They found their seats, making jokes about how well the soft golden light of the candles in the antique candelabra disguised their wrinkles.

I couldn't move. My fists were clenched hard to keep them from shaking. All the pain, the panic, the despair of the past two years, all the rage that had festered inside me boiled like lava, and I felt like I was about to explode if I couldn't suppress it now. I closed my eyes and dipped my head, praying that nobody noticed. They'd call the cops. They'd call an ambulance. I'd never get out of the hospital again. *Breathe, Susan. Just breathe.*

I couldn't breathe. The floorboards began to tremble.

The door opened and conversation cut off abruptly. Someone gasped.

"We have a new honored guest this evening!" Professor Owen's voice echoed around the room, breaking the silence. "May I introduce a very old—er—friend. I hope," he added under his breath. "Please welcome His Highness, Prince Donovan y Tyrnn!"

One of the Saxby sisters, her mouth wide open, walked into the other one on the way to their seats. They both wobbled on their six-inch heels, clutching each other to keep from falling.

"Holy shit," Juliette whispered, her eyes bulging out of her head, looking like a strangled Pekingese. "Holy *shit*."

"Oh." Delia clutched the pearls around her neck. "Oh, my."

Donovan stood in the doorway, huge, brooding, his dark emerald eyes flashing. His beauty felt like a punch to the gut.

Dan Raine let out a squeak. "A prince?"

"Italian nobility," Professor Owen said hastily. "They're a democratic republic now, but they still have a royal family. They like to keep, er, a low profile. Because of all their money, y'know?"

Everyone froze and watched as Donovan sauntered into the room. His movements were languid and graceful, almost careless, yet vibrating with that intense, menacing power simmering just underneath the surface of his skin. The guests watched him, open-mouthed, looking as shocked as if the Morningstar himself had fallen to earth and stalked in to join us for dinner. Juliette tried to get to her feet to intercept him as he walked in, but he ignored her.

He ignored everyone, in fact. He walked straight up to me.

"Chosen." His tone held a warning.

My knees shook. I couldn't breathe.

Donovan reached out towards me and took my hand. Gently, he unfurled my clenched fist and deliberately wound his fingers in between mine, holding my sweaty palm against his own.

Those blazing dark eyes bored into mine, his gaze intense, overwhelming, but they also held a command that I couldn't ignore. *Hide your power, Chosen.*

Oh, good God, his hand. The touch of his skin, right now, in this moment... I'd never felt anything like it in my whole life, and I never will again. The power in his palm was so heady I almost blacked out. His fingers in between mine, thick, strong—they were gravity, holding me in place. They were torrential rain, dousing the wildfire that threatened to overwhelm me. He was ice; I was fire, and he was holding me together so I wouldn't explode.

I held his gaze, took a breath, and exhaled it slowly. The burning heat inside me dissipated.

The tension in his jaw eased. "Susan," he murmured. "*Mi amore*. I am sorry to keep you waiting. My business with Ahdeannoywn is concluded. You have my full attention."

I needed it. The fire inside me roared as he beat it back. I stared into his eyes and breathed in and out slowly.

Low mutters echoed through the room. "He's with *her?*"

"Like, her date? Did Susan bring an actual prince as her date?"

"The professor said that he's a friend, so he must be a real, actual prince. Look here, the internet says there's a whole Italian royal family, but I can't find any recent pictures. They must just keep a low profile, like Dean said."

"No way. No *way*. She must have bribed him. He might be one of those poor nobles who sell interviews to prop up their huge estates. I mean, I know better than anyone how expensive it is to maintain all my properties."

"She's broke, Juliette. Vincent got everything in the divorce. She doesn't have any money to pay him with."

The voice turned vicious. "Why the fuck is he here with her, then? She's a crazy dried-up old cow."

"Well... You have to admit, she looks incredible for a dried-up old cow, Jules. She never looked that good when she was with Vincent, and they were always the most beautiful couple at any party."

"Shut the fuck up, Saxby."

The other Saxby sister's high-pitched voice floated over. "They... they look like they like each other. He's staring at her pretty intensely. I mean, I'm sure they can both hear us, but they're ignoring us, and they're still staring at each other like they want to—"

"Susan? Your Highness?" Professor Owen's chirpy voice cut through the whispers. "You two lovebirds are over here."

Donovan raised his eyebrows—a silent question. I nodded. I was okay. He squeezed my hand, pulling me forward. "Come, *amore*. I am famished."

We walked towards the table. My heart sank a little when I realized the professor had put me right in the middle of the table, with Donovan opposite me. It felt like there was a whole ocean between us. "You're next to me, Your Highness," Juliette smoldered, patting the seat next to him.

Ignoring her again, Donovan held my hand firmly, leading me to my place at the table. He pulled out my seat for me. My heart thumping, I lowered myself stiffly into it, carefully arranging the red silk dress around my thighs. Donovan didn't push me in. Instead, he lifted the chair in his hands as if I weighed nothing, stepped forward, and placed the chair under the table.

Down the table, one of the Saxby sisters let out a little moan. The other one elbowed her in the boob, and she yelped. Donovan sauntered around the table to his own seat, all eyes on him, sat down, and leaned back, a vision of power and grace. He didn't look at Juliette or at Delia on his other side.

I swallowed, trying to remember my manners. To my left sat Ming, the young fifth wife of Montgomery Walker, eyes downcast, staring demurely at her empty plate. Thankfully, he was on the other side of her, away from me. Unluckily for me, Dan Raine was on my other side.

"I must admit, you're looking good, Sue," Dan said cozily, eyeing me like a piece of meat. "I expected you'd be a mess. You know, after everything that happened. Jail, the mental hospital, all that stuff."

I smiled tightly. "Thank you, Dan."

"Seraphina tells me you've got a new job, and you're doing much better now."

At the mention of Seraphina, my stomach churned again. "Hmm," I said, noncommittally.

Juliette grinned. "Seraphina is looking lovely," she said, her voice deceptively light. "I saw her just the other day, buying a stupidly expensive handbag in Jasper's." She plucked at Donovan's dinner jacket lightly; I wanted to rip her arm off. "Have you met Seraphina, Your Highness? Vincent Andresano's fiancé? His family is Italian, you must know them."

"I do not know them." Donovan didn't even look at her. "But I have seen her in passing," he replied. "She is a skinny redhead girl." There was so much derision in his tone, he might as well have said, *she's a disgusting bald troll.*

Juliette barreled on. "Seraphina was always a beautiful

girl, but now that she's pregnant..." She trailed off and sighed dramatically. "She's just stunning."

My smile disappeared. Why the hell was I playing this game? Why the hell had I *ever* played this game? Juliette was a monstrous bitch; just being in her vicinity was painful. Maybe I'd only ever played it before because I always won without even trying.

She took my expression as a win, a triumphant glint appearing in her beady brown eyes. "I was the same when I was pregnant with my boys. Clear skin, flushed cheeks, thick, luscious hair. There's something about pregnancy that really makes women glow, isn't there? Oh!" Juliette gave a fake gasp and clutched her chest. "I'm sorry, Susan. I forgot. You wouldn't know."

It would have hurt more, except Donovan's long legs had sandwiched mine under the table. He held me in place, like I was a sapling tree that had to be propped up in a storm so it wouldn't fall over. I could barely see Juliette anymore. My eyes had glazed over.

"And you never will," Juliette added, her tone icy.

"Hmm."

"Because you're too old to get pregnant now." Her barbs weren't hurting, and she was pissed.

Donovan leaned forward and picked up my wine glass, refilled it, and placed it in front of me. "One more glass, *mi amore*." He caught my eye, and held it, his gaze hot. "I do not want your senses dulled this evening."

The Saxby sisters both moaned in tandem. Juliette clamped her mouth shut, her cheeks reddening.

Holy hell, I loved this man. I couldn't help it—I giggled like a schoolgirl. "Okay."

Gladioli dished out the starter—a roasted fennel, burrata and prosciutto bruschetta.

"Thanks, Glad," I said as she placed the plate in front of

me. Everyone else icily ignored her, not even looking at their plates. I put the whole thing in my mouth and chewed. God, it was delicious—the prosciutto crispy and perfectly salty, the burrata creamy and smooth, the fennel lightly tingly on my tongue. "Mmm. Stunning, thanks Glad. You're a wizard."

Donovan scowled. "A wizard? This food is spelled?"

I kicked him under the table and mouthed, *not an actual wizard.*

"Are we eating carbs again?" One of the Saxbys blinked across the table at me, owl-like. One hand drifted tentatively towards her plate.

"No," Juliette snapped.

The Saxby pulled her hand back as if Juliette slapped her. Nobody else twitched.

Donovan picked up his bruschetta, put the whole thing in his mouth, and chewed once, then again with relish. He swallowed, then his eyes drifted down to Juliette's plate. He stared at her bruschetta longingly, then back up at me, a silent question in his expression.

I shook my head slightly. No, Donovan. You can't steal Juliette's bruschetta.

Delia turned her whole body towards him, her diamonds glittering in the candlelight, and started quizzing him on Italian architecture. Donovan answered in disinterested monosyllables and stole her bruschetta while she was monologuing about the Colosseum.

He kept looking back at me. Every time he did, I felt the blood rush to my cheeks. *No, Susan. He's taken. Cress would tear out your lungs with her bare hands and play them like bagpipes. And even if he wasn't already taken, he's so far out of your league it's not even funny. He is major league. You could barely qualify for little league.*

Dan Raine leaned towards me and put his arm around

the back of my chair, oozing cozy confidence. "How much did he cost you, Sue?" he murmured in my ear, and I stiffened at his closeness. "Inquiring minds want to know."

"Inquiring minds can fuck off, Dan," I said tightly, not looking at him.

He leaned closer. His breath tickled my ear. "Come on, now, Sue. He's not here with you, and we all know it. You're broke, so you must have rented that dress and got some kid to do your makeup. But how much did that prince cost you?"

"You." Donovan's low, cold voice cut through the conversation like a hot knife through butter. "Weather boy."

Dan tried not to flinch but failed badly.

"You are too close to the Chosen. Move away."

Dan froze. I could almost feel his ignorant bravado doing battle with the sudden heavy atmosphere of danger that had seeped through the room. The table fell silent.

"Now," Donovan growled.

Dan went pale underneath his orange fake tan. He took his arm off the back of my chair, leaning away, and plastered a shit-eating grin on his face. "I meant no offense," he said, holding up his hands. "Me and Susan are old friends, Your Highness." He was trying to act casual, but his voice shook. "I guess in the States, we're a little more casual with our friendships."

Donovan glared at him for a few more seconds, then, maintaining eye contact, he scooped up Juliette's bruschetta. "And in my country, I would slit a man's throat if he dared put his lips so close to the Chosen."

There was a long, uncomfortable silence.

"I love how you pronounce her name," one of the Saxbys tittered, trying to break the tension. "Susan. Chosen. Hee hee. Foreign languages are so crazy."

"No slitting throats at the table, please, Your Highness," Professor Owen called down the table.

"I make no promises." Donovan coldly ate Juliette's bruschetta.

Dan shifted his chair a foot away from me, now practically sitting in one of the Saxby twins' laps.

With effort, I turned to the silent Ming next to me, staring down at her untouched plate. "I hear congratulations are in order," I said warmly, forcing a smile. Gladioli moved in on my left, whipped Ming's bruschetta plate away, put it in front of Donovan, then placed a perfect square of her wagyu and roast cherry tomato lasagna in front of her. The poor girl stared at it, not moving. She looked miserable.

"Oh. Yes," she answered me in a tiny voice. "Thank you. I am well, and the baby is healthy."

"Baby?"

Montgomery's horsey face leaned over on her other side. "Ming just had our first," he declared. "Finally, I have an heir."

"I thought you already had kids, Monty," Juliette said. She shot me a nasty grin. "Some of us are lucky to be prolific life-bringers like that."

"I've only got girls so far, Jules," he replied, no hint of embarrassment in his voice. "This is my first boy," he said proudly. He leaned over and squeezed Ming's thigh so hard she flinched. "I'm so happy."

"Of course you are. Because girls are worthless, right?" I said, holding eye contact with Montgomery. "I'm sure your daughters *love* hearing that."

He shrugged. "I don't see them often, if I'm being honest, Sue. They stay with their moms most of the time."

"Oh. So, you're a deadbeat dad," I said sadly. "I understand."

He blustered for a second. "I pay them good money—"

"Oh, so you only support them *financially?* You're not actually there for them, though, right? You don't support them emotionally, or mentally, or physically, or spiritually, or socially, or in any other way that matters?"

"I pay them *a lot*," he hissed. "That's all that matters."

"Put some extra aside for therapy, Monty. They're going to need it." I turned to Ming. "Congratulations," I said to her. "How old is your baby?"

"A week," she whispered.

My mouth dropped open. "A week? You gave birth a week ago?"

Montgomery gave a braying laugh. "She looks amazing, doesn't she? We wanted her to get her figure back as soon as possible."

The smile froze on my face. I tried to ignore him. "How are you healing up?"

"I am fine."

"Did you have a natural birth?" Juliette drained her wine. "All my births were natural. No epidural, no gas, no nothing. Anything less just isn't childbirth, am I right, Susan? Oh, sorry. You wouldn't know."

"I had gas for the pain," Ming whispered. "So much pain. And then an episiotomy, as the baby's head was too large."

"I got the doctor to put in an extra stitch." Montgomery winked down the table. "The husband stitch. Best invention since breast implants." He threw his head back and laughed like a donkey.

I laughed along, louder than everyone else. "How embarrassing for you, Monty. Imagine telling the whole table that you have a tiny penis!"

Delia spat out her wine. The Saxby twins burst into hysterical giggles. Montgomery went purple and mouthed like a goldfish for thirty seconds. "I don't— I have— My penis is perfectly proportioned, thank you very much."

"Well, whip it out. Let's take a look."

He reared back, horrified.

"We need to know if you need surgery, Monty," I said patiently. "I mean, we all know you made your wives get breast implants."

"That's different!"

"Is it?" I took a leisurely sip of wine.

Out of the corner of my eye, I noticed Donovan suddenly stiffen. He was still watching me, but his eyes flicked left, out the window, just for a second. In the gaps of silence between the Saxby sisters' giggles, I thought I heard a reedy, high-pitched cry coming from outside. It sounded like a bird shriek. Or... a child's scream.

Donovan rose, unfolding his massive frame from the table as elegantly as a panther getting up to stretch. He tossed his napkin on the table. "Excuse me for a moment." He met my eyes, a silent order. *Stay here.*

I nodded, and he strode out of the room.

The second he was gone, Juliette leaned over the table. "Where did you find him, Sue?"

"He found me, actually." I took another small sip of wine. "But it's none of your business, Jules."

Her eyes narrowed. "Come on, now. This can't be a real date. Someone like him would never go for someone like you. You got lucky with Vincent because you trapped him while you were young and already high-up on the corporate ladder. Now you're old and poor, and, from what I hear, you're living in a shoebox and working at some shitty call center."

I shook my head, exasperated. "How is this polite dinner conversation? Seriously, Juliette, in what universe do you think it is okay to talk to someone like this?"

She sniffed and refilled her wine glass. "I'm just being honest. Honesty is virtue, Sue. The truth is important. That's the problem with most people these days." She put on a baby voice. "They're always wowwied about hurting their poor widdle feewings." She snorted. "It's bred a generation of weaklings who can't handle the truth."

"Honesty without compassion is just cruelty," I told her. "And we all know that with you, Juliette, the cruelty is the point."

"You can't talk." She snorted. "You just literally dogwalked Monty. He's not going to be able to open his mouth for fear of being humiliated for the rest of the night."

I took a sip of my wine. "He was being a misogynist. I just flipped the script on him, that's all. He learned something today."

"And I'm just being honest! It's a *virtue*," she said, tossing her ponytail fussily. "I want you to tell me the truth."

"You don't want the truth. You just like to hurt people."

"Bullshit. I just can't stand fake people."

"Oh, really?" I let my eyes drift to my right, where her best friend Dan Raine, with his fake tan, was tossing his fake hair, and smiling with almost all of his fake teeth, dazzling the Saxby sisters with a fake story about his vacation with an A-list celebrity.

Gladioli walked back to the table to clear the main course plates, paused, and rolled her eyes. All the plates were stacked around Donovan's spot. All of them were empty. Somehow he'd managed to steal everyone's lasagna and eat it without anyone noticing. Muttering under her breath, Gladioli removed the empty plates, and returned with three enormous plates of tiramisu.

It smelled divine. One plate went in front of the professor. She studied me carefully, then placed the other two in Donovan's empty spot.

Juliette scowled at me, ignoring Gladioli completely. "Look, we all know that your little 'date' is not what it looks like. If he is a real prince—"

"He is," the Professor stopped talking to the Admiral for one second to chime in.

"Then just tell us the truth," Juliette went on. "He's gay, and you're his beard while he's visiting San Francisco for business. Or you came into some cash, so you thought you'd pay him to pretend to be your date, so we'd all be dazzled by your new boyfriend, and let you back into our social circle. Just tell us, Susan." She smiled widely, a nasty smile. "We all know that a man like that would never go for a woman like you. Especially not now. You're used goods. Rejected stock."

Everything she was saying was true. I knew it. It shouldn't hurt—God knows I'd managed to withstand her barbs so far, but for some reason, her stating the truth penetrated the armor I'd wrapped around myself. I shrugged lightly. "Maybe it's my magical vagina."

"Your dried-up vagina, you mean. You've got to be almost ten years older than him, to start with."

"I think he's older than he looks."

Juliette wasn't giving up. "Have you got dirt on him? Is that it? Did you bribe or blackmail him to come to this dinner so you could try and muscle your way back into the social scene?" She curled her lip. "It's not going to work. The second you see Vincent, you'll go crazy again. They'll cart you back to the mental hospital and leave you there." She grinned, tossed her ponytail, and waited for me to respond.

I couldn't. The flash of memory smashed into me, plunging me back into the horrors of the past.

It was my biggest fear—the nightmare that plagued me every time I fell asleep. I felt the blood drain from my cheeks. My heart thudded in my chest, knocking against my ribs painfully, jerking as if it was suddenly trying to escape.

My biggest fear was to be stuck in that place again, with no hope of ever getting out. Trapped in a beige prison with linoleum floors and no door handles. The constant screaming of patients, day and night, shouting obscenities, recounting real-life trauma, true horror stories. The terrible thoughts that escaped my fuzzy, drugged-up head, spikes of desperate panic, not knowing what was real and what was a hallucination. Heavyset women with terrible hair who stood with their arms crossed, watching me use the toilet, every single time. Bespectacled men with buck teeth asking me again and again about my deepest secrets, my most personal thoughts.

No chance of ever getting out. It was the fourth circle of hell.

I swallowed. Juliette grinned at me, delighted with what she'd done.

The door opened, and Donovan stalked back in. He saw my face, and his eyes iced over. "I grow impatient, Ahdeannowyn."

"Fair enough." The professor let out a long sigh. "I think that will do it, anyway. Come with me."

CHAPTER
NINETEEN

The professor led us to his study, Bonbon leading the way, swinging his massive butt ahead of us. "I don't understand why we had to go through all this rigmarole," I said, my voice still a little shaky. Juliette's barbs had hit me hard. I spent a good amount of energy trying to forget the year I spent in the psychiatric hospital.

The idea of ever going back felt like torture. I curled my hands into fists to keep them from shaking.

Donovan glanced down, picked up my hand, and uncurled it again. Just then, I noticed a sharp tear in his shirt sleeve. "What is that?"

He grimaced. "Banwyn. They are swarming outside. Eryk and Nate were battling a dozen at the gates. Cress, at the rear of the manor house, was nearly overwhelmed. I had to step in."

"Oh, no? Is she okay?"

"No."

I gaped at him. "She's not? Donovan—"

"I had to help her. Cress is a warrior of legend. The fact that I had to intervene is a mortal insult to her." His grimace deepened. "She will sulk for days."

"Oh. Well... uh... nobody was watching, though, right?"

"No. Of course not."

"So just don't tell anyone. Nobody needs to know."

"Her pride is wounded," he muttered. "She will be impossible to live with for the next decade, at least."

A pang of jealousy thrummed in my heart, adding to the sad cacophony caused by the already-plucked-and-vibrating strings of anxiety, grief, and depression inside me.

Mentally, I picked up the whole pathetic guitar and smashed it on the ground. I couldn't be jealous of Cress. It was a waste of emotion. It was as pointless as a slug being jealous of a butterfly. Donovan's protective-date act was exactly that. Just an act.

"Don't worry about the banwyn. They cannot enter my Domicile." The professor skipped alongside us with an enthusiasm at odds with his elderly appearance. "My security is top-notch."

"Well, that's fantastic for you, Professor, but all your guests will have to leave at some point tonight."

"Er." He shrugged. "They're in no danger. The banwyn feed on fear and terror. My guests this evening are all so self-absorbed and conceited, I doubt they'd even show up on a banwyn radar."

"There are darker creatures out there who may seek to harm you, Ahdeannowyn."

"I know. Your brother's assassins are far away right now, Your Highness. I have it on good authority that he has sent them to the Lower World to source more stones—because he sees them as easier pickings, even though their powers are weaker—while he attempts to corrupt more fae in the Upper World."

Donovan nodded. "We have the same information."

"And now you know why I brought the stone here. We saw the chess pieces moving. Some of our people started toying with the idea that one ruler for all the Upper Realm might not be such a bad thing."

"It is if that ruler is Connor," Donovan muttered darkly.

"Well, yes, that's my point. Elonn fae are so open to new information, we can sometimes be easily corrupted. Your brother is very persuasive. One supreme ruler for all the creatures in the Upper World could create stability and harmony between warring realms." He glanced at Donovan, a little nervously. "You know as well as I do that your kingdom is more powerful than any other realm in the Upper World, so the Queen already assumes that mantle. So, it's not much of a stretch to entertain the idea of making it official."

"We do not rule the other realms in the Upper World." Donovan's voice was ice-cold.

"Not officially, no. But no one would ever be stupid enough to go to war with you. Your superiority is unparalleled. If you wanted to, you could unite the whole Upper Realm under your banner."

"Subjugate them, you mean."

"And *that's* where you're different from your brother." The professor threw him a sad smile. "The Devourer has whispered in many ears, promising favors and boons and an era of peace and harmony the likes of which we've never experienced." The old man huffed out a sigh. "But I know that he wouldn't stop at the Upper World. He will devour all the stones he can get his hands on and rule all Three Worlds as an overpowered tyrant."

"I will stop him," Donovan said quietly.

I couldn't bear the sadness I heard in his tone. "How long is this damned hallway, Professor?" I couldn't see the end of it. It was so far away, it just kind of faded off into the distance.

"Oh. Sorry. I needed to stretch my legs. Gladioli's

tiramisu is incredible, but it seems to settle in me like a rock." He waved his cane, and suddenly, the end of the hallway zoomed closer. "My office is just up to the right. We can talk there."

It still felt like half a mile away. Donovan was back in brooding-mode, so I jumped in with some questions. "If your realm's spark stone is in danger, why didn't you come to me and have me close it straight away?"

"Susan, my dear. We Elonn fae are scribes. We are the keepers of knowledge. We seek every piece of information so that we can divine the truth, and our magic helps prod us in the right direction. But truth, like time, isn't linear. Since only the now exists, we must base truth on our past experiences."

I repeated his words in my head several times. "So, you had to make sure I went through certain experiences before you could accurately predict what would happen to your spark stone?"

"Well... yes. For example, I heard about your little run-in with the sea witch." For a second, he looked horrified. "If you had been made aware of the existence of the merpeople before that, you wouldn't have gone anywhere near her. *Nobody* is brave enough to go near her," he added, shaking his head. "That hag will eat any living thing she comes across. But not only did you blithely have a nice chat with the most terrifying creature in the Middle World, you got her to teach you how to access your magic, and how to close the stones. It was a perfect sequence of events that led us here, and I'm confident now that you won't blow the scribe stone up instead of closing it."

"I also taught her about the patriarchy," I added faintly.

"That too. I'm sure we'll all benefit from the most powerful monster in all the Middle World knowing about the patriarchy." He sounded a touch sarcastic.

We finally entered his office—a sumptuous, cozy room with a vaulted ceiling, exposed wooden beams, arched windows, bookshelves lining two of the walls, a roaring fire in a massive hearth, cozy scarlet padded armchairs, and low tables strewn with knickknacks. Donovan took up his usual spot at the window, staring out and glowering broodily.

The professor picked up a plastic bucket and placed it on the lush Persian rug in front of his desk. "Bonbon. Come on."

The massive rottweiler trotted over.

Professor Owen pointed into the bucket. "Please?"

Bonbon grunted and shook his head.

"It will be fine. Come on, I'll give you a treat."

"Grrr." The dog shook his head. A huge glob of drool spattered.

"No, not a milk bone, you silly sausage. I saved you some of Gladioli's tiramisu." He pulled a massive leftover container out of his waistcoat. My eyes bulged as it expanded from the tiny pocket.

Bonbon's tail started wagging, and his mouth split open into a wide grin.

"He can't eat that," I said faintly. "There's at least three things in that dessert that are poisonous to dogs."

"It's either this, or a litter of fresh-born kittens, Susan," the professor said merrily. "He's a hellhound. Tiramisu or kittens. You decide."

"Erm. I guess he can eat it."

He nodded towards the bucket. "Go on, Bonbon. Cough it up."

The hound bent his head, and hacked, coughed, hacked again, and spat up a huge, glittery blue object. It clattered into the bucket.

"Good boy." He reached in and picked up the stone.

A low chime rang through the room, a strange, otherworldly vibration, almost like a song with no sound and no words. Goosebumps rose on my skin. I shivered as the magic punched through me. The stone was spellbinding, a whole realm's worth of magical curiosity and inquisition.

The professor held the glittering clear blue crystal in his hand. It was as big as his head, with a million facets reflecting the light back in an almost eerie way—not quite a rainbow but a dazzling prism of color from outside the spectrum. "This is the scribe stone, Susan."

"Really?" My voice sounded breathless. The atmosphere was too intense. I had to bring it down a little. "I assumed it was one of Bonbon's chew toys."

"The stone of the Elonn fae gives and takes," he said, ignoring me. "It gives us the power to know the truth. Truth is a journey, so we give knowledge as payment. Before you hold the stone, you need to speak your truth."

"I— I—" My heart hammered wildly. "You want me to tell... the truth?"

He nodded. "It is part of the journey. Your journey, Susan. You can't go any further until you speak it."

Suddenly, I understood. A jolt of terror rushed through me.

I couldn't do it. I didn't want to. I'd lost so much already. My memories were all I had left.

Donovan appeared next to me, moving so fast I didn't see. Or maybe I was so scared, my vision had tunneled. He reached out and put his hand on my shoulder.

I felt him grounding me. Holding me to the earth, holding me in place.

I swallowed. "What truth do you need?"

"Start from the start," the professor said, his voice soft, compassionate. "Tell me when it began."

CHAPTER TWENTY

"I've always been so sure of myself," I whispered. My lips felt numb. "So certain of how life works. And I was always so good with people, right from the start. I was student body president in elementary school, middle school and high school. Susan Moore, the leader, the manager—it was always my reputation. If there was a group project, I was in charge, because when I was in charge, everyone was happy.

"It wasn't about being bossy, though. You can't impose your will on people and expect them to be happy. I just always knew how to arrange things, so everyone got what they wanted. Even my dad, who drifted in and out of my life like a leaf blowing through the revolving doors of a hotel lobby..." I hesitated and took a deep breath. My chest felt too tight.

Donovan and the Professor waited patiently.

After a moment, I went on. "I accept people for who they are, and I understand them—that's the key to good management. Back then, life felt like a breeze. I started climbing the corporate ladder, and I found it easy. Find out what people want and give it to them. And if you can't, then gently nudge them in another direction. Manage expectations. It was easy. Then... then I met Vincent."

My breath hitched. "It was like meeting a shooting star as it blazed across the sky. He was unpredictable, blindingly handsome, dazzlingly talented. And... And I lost my mind. He loved me so much; all common sense went out the window. I felt like we were twin flames. Soulmates. Me, the practical level-headed manager, him, the haphazard, volatile artist."

I smiled sadly. "I managed to get an insane mortgage so I could buy Bayview Cottage—it's one of the oldest houses in the whole city, and it was always my dream to live in a slice of history. Vincent moved in with me, and we got married right there in the front garden, overlooking the water. Vincent wanted to have kids straight away, but he also knew that I needed to cement myself as an executive, so we put it off for a couple of years. Then, we put it off again, because my salary by that time was enormous, and we needed the money for the mortgage and for Vincent's studio. His parents had cut him off when we got married. I thought it was romantic that he married me anyway. It showed how much he loved me."

My vision wobbled; I blinked back the tears. "Nobody knew that he was disinherited. Vincent said he was embarrassed, so I didn't tell anyone. Everyone assumed that he was the rich one in our relationship because his parents are so wealthy, but the truth is, he came to me with nothing. I don't know why, but his parents always hated me." I pressed my lips together. "I assumed it was because they're very conservative, and the idea of their only son marrying a career girl was embarrassing for them. I didn't want Vincent to be emasculated any further, so I kept it a secret."

The professor stepped closer to me. The scribe stone shone brighter. Some of the pressure on my chest eased as the words spilled out of me. "When I turned thirty-eight, I was vice president of my company. Only one step away from senior vice president, but I knew my time was running out. I went off the pill, expecting to fall pregnant quickly, because my life had been so easy so far. But..." I shook my head sadly. "Nothing happened. Two years went by, and I got my period every month like clockwork."

My throat tightened. "I went to a doctor, then a specialist, then a fertility expert. All of them told me that nothing was wrong. Vincent got checked, but nothing was wrong with him, either. All the time, I had to smile and nod when anyone asked me if we were having kids. The questions got more invasive. People went from being curious to downright rude. *When are you having kids, Susan?* turned into *When will you give Vincent a child?* I felt like a defective vending machine."

My vision shimmered, as my eyes filled with tears again. Desperately, I blinked them back. Oh, God, I was going to cry. "These days, there are so many influential women speaking out about their choice to be child free. And I respect them so damn much." My voice hitched. "But... but that wasn't me. I always wanted to have kids. I wanted to be pregnant; I wanted to feel life growing inside me. The wanting became like a desperation. It nagged at me like a thorn in my side I couldn't tug free." I smiled sadly. "Vincent told me to relax. He was always telling me to relax. I was forty by then. When people asked me about kids—and they asked constantly—I didn't say I didn't want them, because I don't like lying."

"Good," the professor murmured.

"I always said we were trying. But as time went on, they'd tell me I better hurry. I better hurry because I'll be all dried up soon. Forty was *old*." I paused and licked my lips. "The whispers started behind my back, then grew louder and louder. If we missed out on kids, it would be my fault, because I'd focused too hard on my career. I couldn't give Vincent what he, as a man, deserved." I buried my face in my hands. "I loved him so much, and I wanted to give him children. I wanted to have a family. But every month..." I shook my head sadly. "Nothing. He said it was okay, relax, it will happen. But then, the hot flashes started."

I took a breath. It was too shallow. I tried again. "They'd spring up out of nowhere, an insane, burning heat in the pit of my belly, and with it came..." I shook my head, trying to put it into words. "A buildup of energy. It was so intense, it felt like boiling lava, but it was stuck, and it felt overwhelming, like if I didn't get it out, I was going to explode. I couldn't get it out, though. I saw a doctor, who of course told me it was early-onset menopause, even though my bloodwork didn't agree with that diagnosis. That's what it was," I said, shrugging listlessly. "Hot flashes. Menopause. I'd missed my window. I couldn't have kids."

I took another moment before I could go on. "Little things started to happen when the heat struck me. I broke a priceless vase, but I didn't remember even touching it. I was riding in a taxi with the most obnoxious driver one day, and the windows suddenly blew out. The driver accused me of smashing them. He sued, and I was so scared that I was going crazy, I settled straight away. Vincent sent me back to the doctor, who told me that sometimes menopausal women went through rage episodes. He gave me drugs. I took them, but I didn't feel like myself anymore.

"One day, when Vincent had a residency at Allwins Gallery, I went down to surprise him for lunch. On my way in, through the window I saw a girl—one of the curators—she leaned in and nuzzled him like a cat. The heat boiled in me, and the ceramic sculpture next to him just... exploded. The girl screamed and ran away. Vincent looked at me and asked me why I'd destroyed the beautiful sculpture. But I didn't. I didn't touch it. He said he saw me throw a rock at it. I didn't remember. I was so angry at that moment, I felt like I'd blacked out. But Vincent said I threw a rock, and Vincent never lied to me. So, that was it. I was going crazy." I shrugged listlessly. "My menopause was making me crazy. It became a fact of life. I was going through menopause, and it was making me crazy.

"Another year limped on, and more things happened. I heard noises—doors opening and closing when nobody else should be home. Muffled screams came from his studio, but when I'd check on him, he'd tell me I was hearing things. My clothes and makeup would go missing. Seraphina would show up wearing my jewelry and swear blindly that it had always been hers, and Vincent would back her up. Both of them would stare at me, looking almost scared. Then later, Vincent would cry and tell me he loved me so much, and he just wanted me to get better." Nausea lurched up in my gut; I swallowed it down. "He always wanted me to go away to a retreat or something, to go on a cruise to help settle my hormones. As long as I kept my job, though."

My hands started shaking. "Finally, one day, I was so on-edge at work, I faked a migraine and went home early. I found Seraphina and Vincent naked in my bed. She was on top of him, screaming. I realized I'd heard that scream *so* many times before." I squeezed my eyes shut. Tears poured down my cheeks. "After that, I don't know what happened. The force of emotion was so strong, I blacked out. But I still heard the screams."

I wiped my face with my hands; they came away wet. "The next moment, I'm in handcuffs, tossed into a little cell, because apparently I went crazy and tried to kill my husband. He told the police that he was all alone, in the bedroom, and I snapped in perimenopause-induced rage and went on a rampage, smashing the bricks of my beautiful old house with a sledgehammer, throwing them at him, tearing down our paintings, destroying sculptures and priceless art. Vincent went to the hospital. He had a concussion from a brick that had hit his head, and he needed stitches." I took a shaky breath. "And Seraphina was never there. Two of his other interns gave statements to say that she was with them, downtown, having lunch, when I attacked. I had hallucinated. *Again*."

The professor nodded. "They were having an affair."

I nodded. My heart broke all over again. It was so obvious now that I was forced to say it all out loud. "Yes. He'd been lying to me. He'd been using me from the beginning. Vincent's parents hadn't wanted him to be an artist, so he found me, and I financed his whole dream. I introduced him to the rich assholes I had to deal with as a stockbroker, and they bought his work. He got on the art scene. Everyone loved him."

It was a while before I could go on. "So yes, Vincent cheated on me. He and Seraphina had been sleeping together for years, using my menopause as an excuse to fuck with my head. People throw the word 'gaslighting' around so much, but when it happens to you, you don't know it's happening. Which I guess is the whole point." I chuckled bitterly. "I spent years having Vincent tell me that I was going crazy. Doctors confirmed it. My body told me I was going crazy. I accepted it. I was crazy old Susan. I saw things that weren't there. I had hallucinations. I got violent. I was dangerous." I fell silent. The last part was true. I was dangerous.

After a moment, the Professor moved closer. "Then what happened? After your magic exploded?"

"Vincent's parents stepped in. They were horrified that

I'd tried to kill their only son. They pushed for me to be put away for good. At the trial, I was drugged up so badly that the judge declared me not guilty by reason of insanity. Vincent filed for divorce, and I was so incapacitated that I couldn't fight for anything. He got the house, all the money. And alimony, too. Because he'd never earned much money, he was entitled to half of everything I would make from then on. Not that anyone expected me to make any money," I added bitterly. "I was told that I probably wouldn't ever get out of the psychiatric hospital. I was on a cocktail of antipsychotics and mood stabilizers, and in the moments I felt even vaguely lucid, I was horrified that I'd tried to kill Vincent, the love of my life. It was hell," I whispered. "It felt like I'd gone to hell."

"But you got out."

The ghost of a smile touched my lips. "A regular patient at the hospital was an anorexic; she taught me how to hide my meds in my cheek. I did it on a whim, but after a few days, I felt a little better. My head was clearer, so I kept doing it. Then, my regular treating doctor went on vacation, and the doctor who filled in for him—also on a whim, apparently—decided to run more bloodwork and do more tests. He found I was much better and recommended me for conditional release. So, I got out. I stayed at a halfway house for three months." I swallowed another lump in my throat. "That was more hell. More screaming, more fights. I swore I'd claw my way out, so I kept climbing."

Professor Owen reached out and handed me the scribe stone. It vibrated underneath my fingertips "Now you know the truth."

I nodded sadly. "I know I'm not crazy. I never was. Even without all the power I felt coursing through me. I know what I saw. Vincent and Seraphina had been having an affair. They told everyone they got together after I went to jail, of course. She was comforting him, one thing led to another..." I shrugged. "And now she's pregnant with his child. Living in my house. Sleeping in my bed. Vincent kept all my things, but he traded me in for a younger, prettier version who could give him what he wanted." I took a deep breath. Good God, the truth *hurt*. It was less painful to just think that I'd gone crazy.

I had to say it out loud. "The truth is that Vincent never loved me. He is like a child who manipulates the people who love him to get exactly what he wants. And that's it. I loved him, and he used me."

Suddenly, the stone buzzed beneath my fingertips. A pulse of energy punched through me.

My feet went numb. I felt like I was floating. "This is how my great love story ends," I whispered. "With me finally realizing the truth. It was never a love story to start with."

Donovan squeezed my shoulder gently. "Close the stone, Chosen."

I held it and concentrated. *Protect yourself. Sleep.*

It was easier than the last time. I felt the atoms in the stone move, solidifying, burying its magic and power deep inside. The giant sapphire darkened; the lights dimmed.

I held it out again. "It's done." My voice was toneless. I felt empty. Hollow.

The professor took the stone without looking at it. His eyes shone with unshed tears. "The pain will fade, Susan."

I nodded, swallowing back a sob.

There was a yak sound in the corner, and Bonbon puked tiramisu all over the carpet.

CHAPTER

TWENTY-ONE

I felt empty as we walked down the driveway of the Professor's house. Wrung out, like a wet towel before it was hung up to dry. Donovan walked beside me, close, but not touching. He seemed to sense how delicate I felt, as if I would bruise if someone even bumped me.

My phone buzzed. I checked the screen. Unknown number. I answered. "Hello?"

"Susie Bean? Is that you, darlin'?"

I stammered for a moment. *"Dad?"*

"Too right it is. How are you, little bean? It's been a while."

Donovan, walking slowly next to me, raised an eyebrow. I grimaced at him. "Too long, Dad. It's been too long. I guess you got my message." I'd made a flurry of calls to both my mother and my father as soon as I realized that Donovan and his company weren't hallucinations, but neither of them had answered. My mother was on a spiritual journey somewhere in Cambodia. I had no idea where my dad was.

"What message?"

"I left a voicemail for you."

"You know me, darl. Can't keep a phone on me to save my own life. What was the message about?"

"Er... where are you?"

"Still in Perth. We're heading down the mines right now, in fact. Thought I better give you a quick call before I lose cell reception."

"I had something to ask you, but now might not be a good time." Not if he was on a bus filled with other miners.

"Now or never, Susie Bean," my dad said cheerfully. "Once we get to the Pilbangabanga, we're going to lose reception."

I glanced at Donovan and realized he had tensed. No longer walking with me, he'd shifted into a new gait, stalking, eyes flashing, poised to strike, listening carefully.

"I wanted to ask you about your heritage," I said into the phone, dropping my voice to a whisper.

Dad hesitated. The phone line crackled. "Oh."

A high, reedy cry echoed through the night. The air around me prickled.

"Chosen." Donovan put his hand on my arm, stopping me in my tracks. Every line in his body was taut and vibrating with tension. We were just inside the warded gates; the odd blue glow of the ward shimmered in front of me. "Stay here."

I shifted uncomfortably, not wanting him to leave me, but I needed to speak to my dad right now. It might be months before I got hold of him again. *Okay*, I mouthed.

Donovan flexed his huge shoulders, shrugging off his jacket, and pulled an enormous sword out of nowhere. His eyes glinted emerald in the dim light. He froze for one moment, listening carefully, then stalked forward, out of the gates, past the ward, into the dark, leafy street outside.

"Okay, love," my dad finally said. "What did you want to know?"

A sudden urge to throw a tantrum poked at me. "Were you ever going to tell me that you're not exactly human?"

He chuckled nervously. "I did, love, I did. You remember what your mum used to call me? A devil, an imp, a wicked little pixie, a leprechaun, a yowie, a little bloodsucking vampire."

"I thought most of them were cute nicknames," I hissed. "I didn't know you were being serious. How was I to know that she was listing your *ancestors?*"

"Well..." he hesitated. "Your mum didn't want you dwelling on it all, so she never wanted to talk about it. She's a little mix of things as well, just like me. Mostly from the Upper World, though, so she was always a little embarrassed about falling for a handsome rogue like me."

I slapped myself in the forehead with my palm. Now I knew where I got my penchant for falling for untrustworthy heartbreakers. My own mother had done the same thing.

"Your mum was already uncomfortable about being a mix. Her granny and grandad were mixes, too, but they were a bit snobbier about it. Me, I couldn't give two shits."

"So, it's all true, then? I'm a mix of every humanoid species in all three of the Worlds?"

"Huh. I suppose you are, little bean. I'd have to get the ol' family tree out to take a look, but I think that on my side, we've got most of the Lower World and a good chunk of the Middle covered. Your mum is a mix of the Upper World, and some of the Middle. And don't be fooled—her great-great-great grandmother was part succubus, so she's got some of the Lower in her as well."

I sighed. "Didn't either of you think this would be important information at any point? I'm not human, dad."

"One part is human. Maybe one-twenty-six-hundredth of you is human. But... little bean." Dad's voice suddenly turned so tender, it made me want to cry. "Neither of us wanted you to think that it mattered in any way, because in truth, it doesn't. Fair dinkum," he said firmly. "You're you, baby. You're the most perfect thing in all the universe. Me and your mum never wanted anyone to look down on you for being a mix, so we kept you in the dark in the first place. I mean, I never copped that kind of shit—well, I did, but I never really cared. But your mum did. That's why she spent so much effort making sure you lived normally, as a human. The truth is, your mixed heritage is a good thing, not a bad thing. You got the best of all of us, Susie. You could negotiate a ceasefire in the Middle East *and* drink a Russian miner under the table."

A shout echoed over the gates. I flinched. A strange pattering sound followed it, almost like a thousand fat raindrops had started hitting the pavement.

No, not raindrops. They were footsteps. Hundreds of tiny footsteps. Children, running somewhere. Lots of children. And they were swarming. My heart started hammering. "Dad. Do you know what a banwyn is?"

"Sure do, love. Nasty little fuckers. My great-great-great-great granddad was a quarter banwyn." He let out a snort. "Good thing we're never invited to their realm for the holidays, because they eat their own when—"

The line cut out. "Dad?"

In the silence, I could hear grunts and smacks through the thick hedge to my left. The sounds of a fight. A clang of metal on blacktop. A sword dropped? A dagger?

"—then you have to scrub that shit out before it sticks. If you don't, it's worse than Gorilla Glue. There's nothing that will shift—"

Cress's voice, shouting a battle cry, came from my right,

then, the telltale zing and crash of blades clashing. There was a battle going on just outside the gates, just around the corner, hidden by the thick hedge that surrounded the manor house property line. I stood, frozen, my phone to my ear.

A kid ran past the gate, moving too fast for me to really focus on. Then, another. Another. Little kids. I caught a flash of one running closer to the gate. Five or six years old, flaxen-haired, wearing adorable school uniforms. The banwyn swarm was running.

"—sure that you hit them in the right place, or they explode and make a damn mess. Anyway, darl," he said cheerfully. "We're coming up on the Pilbangabanga now. Before you go, just remember, and this is really important. Don't—" His voice cut out.

"Dad? Dad?"

The phone beeped. Connection lost.

A chill ran through me. Goosebumps rose on my skin, and I shivered. The temperature was dropping; it wasn't an emotional response. My breath came out in clouds of vapor.

A low gravelly voice cut through the silence, colder than the grave, vibrating with a preternatural timbre. "Heir. Get out of our way or perish."

Donovan's voice was just as cold. "The scribe stone is already closed. You are wasting your time here, Agarthon."

I edged closer to the gate and slowly, heart thudding wildly, moved to the left so I could see out into the street.

Donovan stood there, poised in a half-crouch, with his sword held out in front of him, glinting silver in the dim light. He rolled his shoulders and shifted on his feet like a dancer, graceful but deadly.

Eryk and Nate flanked him. Eryk held two jeweled daggers in his hands, his reptilian battle leathers had visible cuts and tears on the trousers, glimpses of a sticky-tar substance splattered the bare skin. Nate's enormous muscles bulged, his arms outstretched, hands clawed and shimmering with an eerie blue glow.

To the right, Cress was in a warrior pose, a low crouch, a dagger in her fist, eyes blazing with fury. One of her sleeves was torn completely, her silky tan skin splattered with blood and dotted with what looked like tiny bite marks.

Horror gripped me. While I'd been eating bruschetta and drinking four-hundred-dollar bottles of pinot noir, they'd been fighting for their lives out here, trying to protect me.

Cress was injured.

"No," I mumbled, my lips numb.

A huge man—at least seven feet tall, his wide, enormous frame encased almost completely in pitch-black armor that seemed to swallow all the light—stepped into my line of sight. A helmet covered his head completely, sharp-looking spikes jutting out in a ring on the top, like a sinister crown. His footsteps clanged on the blacktop like the toll of a funeral bell. He walked two more steps forward, the rainfall-like pattering sound accompanied him. A crowd stepped with him, shadowing him.

Banwyn. Hundreds of them, surrounding the terrifying big armor-plated man in the middle of the street. A hundred little kids in neat, clean school uniforms—gray woolen shirts and knee-length trousers, crisp bright-white shirts, yellow and black striped ties—stood silently, blank-faced, wide-eyed, their dead-straight flaxen hair shining in the dim light

I'd never seen anything so damned scary in my life. At first glance, they might look like little kids, but I could never mistake these things for human children. They were horrifying. They stood too still. Their hair was too thick, too straight. Their uniforms were too clean. Their eyes were unmistakably alien, shimmering with an eerie light and glowing with a desperate hunger and cruel intent.

The enormous, armored man stepped forward again and raised a dull iron-gray broadsword. "If the stone is closed, we will take her instead. The rightful King will have his prize, one way or another. Perhaps another experiment is in order."

Donovan growled. "Over my dead body."

He lifted the sword higher, moving into a fight stance. "So be it."

The banwyn rushed forward. Donovan charged, lifting his sword. I let out a squeak as the swarm streamed past Donovan, running towards the others, leaving him to the enormous armored man.

Cress whirled in a circle, cutting down banwyn as they charged at her, their teeth flashing. Bursts of flame exploded from Eryk's palms, cutting gaps in the swarm's charge.

"No," I whispered. I had to help.

I pulled the heat from my core and poured it through my limbs. "**Stop**."

Something zinged, then smacked me. I froze, unable to breathe. The fight raged on beyond the gate. Donovan and the terrifying man smashed into each other—whirling, striking, parrying. Nate roared a challenge, his hands sparking blue, and threw bright flashes into the swarm of banwyn, scattering them like cockroaches. But there were more. More and more…

The huge, armored man whirled his sword in a circle, stepped one foot forward and thrust; Donovan dodged it by a hair. The last-minute change of direction made him stumble back.

The man let out a cold laugh. It echoed within his

helmet. "Your skills are substandard, Heir. Your brother would be ashamed of such a poor showing."

"Then that fault lies with you, Agarthon," Donovan spat out icily. "Since it was you who taught me to fight." He spun away, moving like water, and slashed out, ducked, and hammered an elbow into the back of the man's knee, dropping him. "You were the one who abandoned my training. You were the one who listened to the poison my brother dripped in your ears. He persuaded you to stop teaching me because I'd be too tied up in bureaucracy to go into battle myself, so there was no point. He manipulated you into stopping my training, so that he would be the better fighter. And you fell for his lies."

Holy smokes. The armored man was Donovan's old teacher. Obviously Connor's, too. So, this was one of the Devourer's assassins.

"He is the rightful King," the man said coldly. "You are the pretender. He made me see the truth. He was born to rule."

"I care not for the crown," Donovan said, breathing deeply, massive chest heaving. "If my brother wanted it, he could have it—*if* he would shoulder the mantle of responsibility. But he will not. I care for the safety and prosperity of my people; he only wants to dominate them."

I unfroze and heaved in a breath, sucking the air into my lungs desperately. Goddamnit, I'd tried to use my siren power, and it had obviously backfired against the ward. Donovan and his old teacher were fighting again. Swords flashed, and punches connected with sickening thuds. A wave of exhaustion crashed into me, almost knocking me off my feet.

The banwyn were still swarming. More poured into the dark street, their little feet pattering on the pavement like a million cockroaches. A thick circle of them surrounded Eryk and Nate, darting in, biting the air, retreating. Cress was moving so fast I could barely see her.

There were too many. I gritted my teeth. I couldn't help them from inside the ward. I had to get out there.

I held my breath and stepped through the ward to the other side.

CHAPTER
TWENTY-TWO

The sound of battle grew louder outside the gates, as if I'd just removed earplugs from my ears. Donovan let out a grunt and fell to one knee. The assassin Agarthon lifted his sword, ready to strike him, but Donovan sprang back effortlessly, rolling away. Agarthon moved with him, swinging with vicious force.

I had to stop him. Heat pooled in my belly. I stoked it, fanning the flames, and the fire grew. With enormous effort, I focused, and released it, letting it spill out to my limbs, my hands, down my legs, up and up into my chest. I took two steps forward, fixed the armored man in my sights and focused the power in my throat. "**Stop.**"

The sword stopped an inch before Donovan's neck. Agarthon's hands shook. Donovan whirled away. "Chosen! No! Get back!" On the backswing, he struck at the assassin's armor with the pommel, throwing him back.

He hit the pavement with a clang. Donovan wasted no time, ripping his sword out of his grasp. Holding a sword in each hand now, Donovan kicked off Agarthon's helmet roughly. "Get back behind the ward, now!"

I caught a glimpse of the assassin's face and saw only

scarred, pitted, shining white skin. His eyes were hooded pits, his mouth a lipless slash. *Oh shit.*

A pack of banwyn broke away from the circles around Eryk and Nate, and scampered towards me, eyes wide open, sharp teeth bared, their little feet making that awful cockroach noise. A little banwyn, her hair in pigtails, ran the fastest, leading the pack. She darted towards me, gnashing her sharp teeth.

Panic overwhelmed me. Without thinking, I shoved my arms out in front of me as if I was trying to stop the swarm with my bare hands. The heat surged.

Eeeeeeeee.

The banwyn launched into the air, flipping backwards head over heels as if she'd been tossed carelessly by a giant, letting out a high-pitched shriek as she sailed into the distance, past the massive cedars, over the row of houses opposite me, disappearing into the next street over.

Whoa.

Three more banwyn scuttled towards me. I pushed again, letting the warmth surge out my palms. Two of them suddenly jerked high into the air, spinning wildly like rogue tennis balls, disappearing into the darkness of the houses beyond the street.

The other one exploded. A dark-oily sludge popped where the banwyn had been, splashing on the pavement.

Oops.

The assassin—unfrozen now, swordless, helmetless, and back on his feet—bellowed an order in a thick oily foreign tongue. The banwyn kept coming. A half-dozen broke away from Cress and charged me. I kicked off my stilettos and moved into my tennis stance, bouncing lightly on my feet, and smacked at them frantically as if they were balls, sending them all flying back over the houses on the right. One, two, three, one dozen, two dozen... They all sailed into the air, until the swarm thinned, and I could see the others again.

They had rallied. Eryk's fireballs gathered pace, and Nate threw more magic spells, popping the banwyn into oily sludge where they stood.

"Don't toss them, you fool," Cress growled at me, slamming her black dagger into another banwyn's chest, then ducking to slash at a little one, crawling like a cockroach near her feet. "Kill them! You have to destroy them, or they will come back!"

I couldn't. Blowing up that banwyn made me feel sick. They were like water balloons filled with tar; I couldn't bring myself to pop them. Even smacking them into the air like this felt... wrong. They were monsters, yes, vicious little beasts, cockroaches, but instead of eating cupcake crumbs under your sofa at night, they fed on panic and fear.

Their diet wasn't their fault. And we were winning. There was no panic or fear to be had here. The scarred giant had commanded them to attack, but now, flung several streets back, his influence had dimmed.

Cress was wrong; they weren't coming back. The swarm thinned. One darted away, down the street. Another followed, little feet pattering, followed by a third, a forth.

The scarred man bellowed a command. The swarm rallied, falling back together, coming straight for me, but fell apart quickly as I stepped forward and threw another half-dozen into the next street over. Several surrounding Eryk and Nate scuttled away, disappearing into the darkness.

Donovan, now with two swords in his hands, came at the scarred giant, dancing forward, muscles bulging, blades flashing. The giant blocked a hammering blow with his armored wrist, then used his gauntlet to catch the next strike.

He pulled Donovan close. "This isn't over," he snarled in his face. "You will never stop the rightful king." He shoved Donovan back and turned in a circle. A huge black shadow morphed around him, swallowing him completely, spinning around and around like a black tornado.

Then, it disappeared.

The street fell quiet. The assassin was gone.

CHAPTER
TWENTY-THREE

Fatigue hit me like a train. My legs shook. I willed them to keep me upright, while the edges of my vision grew foggy.

A beautiful low, sexy voice drifted over to me. "Chosen?"

Hmm. A dream. Ooh, not a dream. I blinked, and Donovan's face came into focus. He had a small cut in his eyebrow and a scratch near his collarbone. It only made him look more blisteringly handsome, more dangerous.

The exhaustion surged through me again, and I wobbled on my bare feet. Strong, warm hands steadied me.

"I'm okay," I mumbled. "Who was that guy, anyway?"

Fuck it. My dress was already ruined. Cecil would kill me for getting banwyn sludge on it, so it wouldn't matter if I scratched the fabric up by sitting on the ground. I slumped into a squat, then eased myself back to sit on the curb, and shivered. It was warmer now that the scarred giant had disappeared, but it was still midnight in September, and I was only wearing a silk gown.

"Agarthon nyr o Xayddovan." Donovan sat next to me, letting out a low grunt of pain. "He was one of my old tutors. I never liked him much, even though I didn't understand why for the longest time."

"Well, if it makes you feel any better, I don't like him much either."

Donovan let out an odd huff. A laugh? Maybe. "He always favored my brother, who was more ruthless, more merciless. I was fine with that. We are different people. For me, it wasn't about winning at all costs."

I nodded slowly. "Sometimes, it costs you much more than it's worth to win a little fight."

"Exactly. That's why Agarthon is so scarred. He will not stop fighting, even when he's disfigured. The smart thing to do when you're badly injured in sparring would be to call a halt and treat your wounds. Agarthon never stopped. In time, I came to realize that for him, there was nothing outside the battle. For Agarthon, everything was black and white. You and your opponent. A winner and a loser. Nobody was equal, and only strength mattered." He looked down at his hands. "I think duty and honor matter more."

I gave him a wry smile. "That's a nice speech. But I can read between the lines. Even though your brother was more ruthless, I'm sure you beat him during sparring anyway."

The corner of his lip curled up, very slightly. "Most of the time, yes."

I promised myself I would replay the fight between him and Agarthon in my head before I went to sleep. Now that I knew he was fine, I could appreciate it more. He was glorious, a war song come to life—an avenging angel with a sword in each hand, emerald eyes flashing, dark hair whirling. It was probably the sexiest thing I'd ever seen in my life.

Suddenly, Cress stood in front of us. Even with her sleeve torn off her battle leathers and little bite marks all over her skin, she looked extraordinarily beautiful. Her raven-black hair danced in the breeze. "Donovan. We need to move. The banwyn will be regrouping somewhere. Agarthon might call in the other two as reinforcements." A flicker of fear drifted in her eyes. "If that happens, we will not beat them back so easily, especially with the Chosen depleted like she is now." Did I imagine her sneering down at me? No. God, it would be so much easier to hate Cress if she was more of a bitch. "We need to hunt down the rest of the banwyn in this area now," she said firmly.

A wave of empathy stirred me. "You can't. They can't help what they are, Cress. It's like getting mad at a t-rex for being a carnivore."

She stared down at me. "If we do not cull them now, the banwyn will find desperate, panicked humans to feed on. Vagrants, prostitutes, runaways."

Pre-med students. Army veterans. Literally everyone was desperate and panicked these days. A general state of constant anxiety had seeped into our collective consciousness and made itself right at home.

"Go on. Kill the little fuckers, then," I muttered.

Donovan nodded. He seemed as tired as I was. "You're right, Cress. If we put a dent in their army, they will be more reluctant to come for her. We must go."

The hollow, exhausted feeling inside of me expanded, and I yawned.

"We need to get you back to Violet House," he murmured. "Call your carriage."

"I can't."

"Why not?"

"I don't have any money left on my credit card, Donovan. The app won't book me a ride. I've reached my limit. That little ride with Amir wiped me out."

He stared at me for a moment. "You have no gold?"

"No, Donovan. I have no gold right now. My gold stash is gone."

He shook his head, bewildered. "I will give you—"

"I don't want you to give me anything." Oh, damn, I was going to cry. The whole night had wiped me out. I was too raw, too exhausted. Tired, sad, *pathetically* jealous. "Look," I said. "You have to go. I'm smart enough to know when I'm not needed. Let me go home, recharge my batteries, and we'll save someone else's realm tomorrow, okay? I can walk to a stop and jump on the light rail." It wasn't that far. As long as I didn't step on any broken glass in my bare feet, I should be okay.

He stared at me, hard, his eyes almost boring into me, as if trying to see the inside of my brain. Then, he turned. "Nate."

The combat mage bounced over. While the battle had drained the rest of us, Nate seemed more invigorated than usual.

"Call Cecil," Donovan ordered. "Tell him to find a mortal carriage and bring it here to pick up the Chosen."

Nate nodded, stepped back, whirled his hands in a circle, gathering up a blue flame in his palms, then clapped them together. Stretching them out, he created a circle of solid blackness and stuck his head into it.

His head disappeared. Almost immediately, he pulled it back out. "He's on his way."

Donovan nodded.

Cress huddled up with the three of them, and they began discussing plans for sweeping up the scattered banwyn before they reformed. I tuned them out. I was just too tired.

What felt like thirty seconds later, a sleek golden sports car roared up the street. It screeched to a halt right in front of me.

The door raised up. Cecil sat in the driver's seat. I glanced down. He was wearing glittery platform heels strapped to his back hooves so he could reach the gas pedals.

"Your carriage awaits, my lady." He leaned forward, his eyes narrowing as he looked me over. Then, his eyes bulged. "What the hell have you done to that gown, Chosen? Are you sitting on a curb in watered silk? And... and is that... banwyn goo?"

I got to my feet, groaning. "Yup. It is." At least Cecil was predictable.

He threw back his head and let out a heartbreaking whinny of distress. "Do you know how hard it is to get out?"

"So I hear." God, I was sore. I bent backwards, stretching out my spine, and limped towards the car.

"That was *couture*," he howled. "The silkworms were boiled in gold leaf tea! The hem was hand-stitched by Albanian orphans! It's ruined. Ruined! I might as well use it as a rag to clean the toilet." He glared at me for a while. "Get in. I will shout at you some more while we're driving home."

Donovan broke away from his huddle with his company and tapped on Cecil's window. "Straight back to Violet House."

"Oh, no, I thought we'd stop for cocktails downtown," he said sarcastically. "She's covered in dirt and banwyn blood, Your Highness. I'm hardly going to parade her out in public."

Donovan's face grew stony. "A simple 'yes' will suffice, Cecil."

"Yes, my liege. My most high highness. I'll take her straight home."

I climbed into the sports car. Cecil lowered the door and hit the gas. "Did you have a nice night?"

"No."

"Ooh." He glanced at me and raised an eyebrow. "You're a Debbie Downer this evening."

"It's been a long night, Cecil."

The city streets whizzed by. Cecil weaved the sports car in and out of traffic, missing bumpers by inches. We drove stupidly fast over the hills. At one point we became airborne. The sports car sent up sparks as we hit the pavement on the other side.

I couldn't bring myself to care. I was too tired. Burnt out. Wrung dry. "This is a one-way street, Cecil."

"So?"

"You're going the wrong way."

He snorted. "Maybe I'm the only one who is going the *right* way. Maybe everyone else is going the wrong way." Horns blared. Cecil spun the wheel wildly, turning a corner.

"Did Violet House grow the car?" That might be why he was treating it like a toy he could throw away when he was done playing with it.

"Nope," he said shortly, brushing the edges of a tramcar as he slid around a corner. "Violet is a Domicile. Not a... er... Ve-hick-a-cile. She can't grow a car like this."

I frowned. "Where did you get it, then?"

"I stole it."

"You *stole* it?"

"Relax," he snorted. "No one will know. I threw a glamor on it before I drove it away. Nobody will recognize it."

"Oh. So, it's not actually a gold Lamborghini?"

"No. It's a black Lambo. The gold goes better with my coloring." He spun the wheel wildly, drifting. I held on for dear life as we skidded sideways for several hundred feet.

"Home!" he announced. Suddenly, he peered through the windshield. "Ooh. Who is *that?*"

Slowly, I turned and saw him standing in front of my building. My heart, already thumping so wearily, gave up and stopped.

Cecil jerked in his seat. "Chosen?" He nudged me. "Bitch, say something. You've gone white."

"That's Vincent," I said. "That's my ex-husband."

CHAPTER
TWENTY-FOUR

I'd waited for this day for years. Dreaded it and longed for it at the same time.

I hadn't seen him since my trial. Two years.

"Okay, what are we doing here?" Cecil asked. "A quick goring? I can stab him in both kidneys at the same time if I strain myself. That will do the trick if you don't want to get your hands dirty. I'd prefer not, though. I did my back at yoga last week, so it would be helpful if you had a gun on you somewhere…"

It felt like I was looking at a photo of another time. Vincent looked as gorgeous as he'd always been. Some men got better looking with age, and Vincent was one of them. His hair, dark-blond and tousled in a way you couldn't replicate, hung thick and tangled around his face. His body was still lithe, lightly muscled, with barely any fat because he often got lost in his work and forgot to eat. Only faint laugh-lines in the corner of his eyes indicated his age.

"I could back up this Lambo and ram him into the wall. Although, it would make more of a mess," Cecil went on. "Violet's bones are in the earth now, though, so she might be able to swallow him. If not, we could dissolve his body in lye in the bathtub. He'd be gone in a week."

I barely heard him. I was too busy trying to see Vincent, trying to recognize him with my new eyes. He looked the same... but he was different. He wore the same clothes as usual, ripped light-blue jeans stained with paint and a plain white t-shirt—also so perfectly paint-stained it looked deliberate, like a thousand-dollar shirt you might find in a boutique. He leaned against the entryway of my building, gazing up at the sky with his piercing blue eyes. A beautiful man, lost in the beauty of the stars.

You couldn't see the stars, though. The city had far too much light pollution.

Was it all an act? Was everything about him an act?

I knew what he'd done to me now. I'd acknowledged the truth. I should have wanted to kill him, but I didn't.

I didn't feel anything at all.

"Okay, girlfriend. Give me a second. I'm coming with you." Cecil whinnied and bristled in the bucket seat. A sprinkle of glitter sparked in the air, surrounding him, raining like sparks of fireworks, slowly disappearing into nothingness.

A large goldendoodle sat on the seat next to me. Cecil, now a giant dog, grinned widely. His teeth were very sharp. "How's that?"

I hit the button to open my door, and it lifted slowly. "Fine." I didn't care what he looked like. I didn't care what Vincent thought about anything.

Well, maybe I did a little. I had automatically put my high heels back on, after all. I got out of the car and walked towards him slowly. He didn't look at me as I approached; he'd even completely ignored the gold Lamborghini screeching to a halt at the curb in front of the building, because that's the kind of guy Vincent was. He just leaned against the wall, head tilted up, looking at the stars, lost in thought.

It looked like a performance. Good grief, it was like I had new eyeballs, and they were showing me things that had always been there. Vincent looked like an actor in a stage performance, playing a handsome, enigmatic artist. Just waiting. Too cool to be looking at his phone because real life was much more interesting.

What an ass.

The performance wobbled a little when he finally turned towards the clicking of my high heels coming towards him. His eyes widened when he saw me; blood-red silk dress split to thigh-high, swishing dramatically out behind me, the gold Lamborghini in the background.

"Susan." He stood up straighter, then, with almost visible effort, forced himself to relax back against the wall again.

I stopped in front of him. Old feelings smacked into me like moths against a lampshade, trying to get through to burn themselves on the burning bulb. I loved this man so much. And he'd destroyed me.

It took me a moment to get a hold of myself. "What are you doing here, Vincent?"

"I came to see you." His lips curved up—a slow, sexy smile. "I *wanted* to see you."

I swallowed. "Why?"

He stared at me for a long time. I'd forgotten how much his eyes glittered. Vincent had a way of looking at someone so soulfully, so intensely, you almost stopped breathing.

A quiet little growl came from behind me. "Grr. Grr. Grrrepugnantlittlewanker."

Vincent frowned and leaned sideways a little. "You got a new dog."

Cecil's interruption broke the spell. It reminded me that Vincent hadn't answered my question. Realization smacked into me. Vincent never answered questions he didn't like. He would just stare soulfully or with unbearable hurt in his eyes, until you got uncomfortable and changed the subject. I clenched my jaw. "What are you doing here, Vincent?"

He turned back to me. Yep, there it was. The carefully constructed look of hurt. Brows furrowed, eyes hooded, mouth open very slightly.

A surge of heat boiled in my belly. This man had *destroyed* me.

No. He didn't destroy me. He tried to. He wanted me out of the way. He was a kid who had gotten tired of his personal candy store, so he'd burnt it down, and gone and gotten himself another one.

And I'd risen like a phoenix from the flames.

I eyeballed him, keeping my face blank. "Well? Are you going to stand there and stare at me all night, or are you going to answer my question? What are you doing here?"

A flash of anger flared in Vincent's eyes. He carefully disguised it and threw me a slow, sexy smile. "Like I said, I wanted to see you." His gaze drifted down from my face, taking in the shimmering skin on my collarbones, the tops of my breasts peeking out of the top of the corset of the blood-red dress, the silk draping over my curves perfectly, down to my bare leg, exposed by the split. "You're looking good, Susie. Real good."

"You've seen me. You can go now."

He leaned back against the wall, sexy and defiant. "It's been too long, Sue. I've missed you."

As the words left his mouth, something strange pricked inside of me. It was subtle, like static electricity running under my skin. I frowned. "What did you say?"

He stared at me again, the slow smile back. He was

trying to reel me in harder than a sports angler with a blue marlin on a line. "I said I missed you."

My skin zinged again. It felt... wrong. Like something inside of me was physically reacting to his words.

A realization hit me. A lie. Vincent was lying. He didn't miss me at all.

My mouth dropped open. I'd never thought to check if the scribe stone gifted me any magic, but here it was. I could actually feel the lie in Vincent's words.

"Vincent... why are you *really* here?"

He tossed his hair back lightly. "I wanted to check on you."

No buzz. Apparently, that was true.

"Why?"

He frowned. "What?"

I'd thrown him off guard. "Why did you want to check on me?"

"I still care about you, Susan," he said soulfully. No buzz. That was true, too. "I want to make sure you are okay."

Buzz. Mother fucker. He cared about me, but he didn't want to make sure I was okay? What the hell did that mean? "What is it that you care about, Vincent?"

He shifted on his feet uncomfortably. "I... uh... Susie, I've always cared about your life. I care about what is going on with you right now."

"Oh." I nodded slowly. "I just figured it out. Your lawyer told you I'd bought this building, right? And you care about where I suddenly got the money from to get it?"

His mask was slipping. The soulful gaze turned suspicious. "So, it's true. You did buy this building."

"Yep."

He nodded. A light of triumph flared in his eyes. He really thought he was going to get his hands on it.

"Feel free to let your lawyers know," I said breezily.

He held out his hands in a pleading gesture. "Susie... I don't want to take anything more from you," he said mournfully. *Buzz*. "I don't want anything else from you." *Buzz*. "But my lawyer is furious. You cannot hide assets. It is illegal." He stared at me urgently. "I'm thinking only of you." *Buzz*. "You are still on parole. You could go back to jail."

I threw my head back and laughed. This was crazy. "I never hid anything from you, Vincent."

"But... but how...?"

I shrugged. "Not that it's any of your business, but I've... ah... upskilled recently, and I am currently employed by a... a wealthy company. They have offered me a very generous remuneration package."

Fury simmered in his eyes.

I smiled. "You gave up your golden goose, Vincent."

His features arranged into a careful expression of hurt and outrage—mouth slightly open, brow furrowed, shoulders drooping. "I never thought of you as a golden goose, Suzie."

Buzz.

"Liar." I laughed out loud, almost giddy. "You're a liar, Vincent. You used me. You've been using me for our whole marriage, and you're *still* trying to use me."

I took a step closer to him, fury burning just under my skin. "I gave you everything. My heart and my soul. I loved you more than anything in this world," I bit out through clenched teeth. "And it was all a lie. For our entire relationship, you were just with me to get what you wanted. And the *second* I couldn't give you one thing that you wanted, you fucked me over and left me for a sappy, skinny ginger bitch. She's a terrible artist, too," I added, rubbing it in. "A shitty cook. An awful hostess. Bart tells me you don't hold dinner parties at Bayview anymore. You might want to work on that; your patrons all liked to be entertained. Your sales will dry up."

"Well." His jaw clenched once. "At least she could give me the one thing that you couldn't."

"Ouch. Well, funnily enough, we could have had kids. You didn't want to try IVF."

He reached out and grabbed me by the shoulders, his face tortured. "I didn't want you to go through any more pain, Susan!" *Buzz.* "You were tearing yourself apart, trying all sorts of fertility treatments. I just didn't want you to be disappointed, again!" *Buzz.*

"Liar." I grinned in his face. "What's the real reason?"

He reared back. "What?"

"What's the real reason you didn't want to try IVF? Come on, Vincent. There's something you're not telling me."

His eyes narrowed. I'd never seen him looking so angry before. "It's invasive."

"I've already established that you didn't care about me. So this must be about you. You would find it invasive. But IVF isn't invasive for men..."

Suddenly, it hit me. "Vincent. You did go and get your sperm count checked, didn't you?"

"Of course I did."

BUZZ.

I gasped. "You're fucking kidding me. You never did, did you? You let me go through all those treatments... you let me visit doctor after doctor. You blamed *me!* You let everyone else blame me! You stayed quiet while people whispered behind their hands. I listened to you tell people that you didn't care that I was infertile! It was *you* all along!"

Cecil growled behind me again.

"It was not *me*." His tone was cold. "It had to be you. Seraphina is pregnant."

"Well, you might want to think about a paternity test, then."

His eyes flared wide in true, genuine shock. I laughed. "That didn't occur to you, did it? You didn't think that a girl who would happily sleep with a married man and carry on an affair for years with the hope of one day prizing him free might actually cheat herself once she had him? Ha!"

He hadn't thought of that. His fists clenched. "She wouldn't do that. Seraphina is innocent. She's virtuous."

I cackled like a hen. "Oh, this is priceless. That girl lied to my face for years, stole my things, and slept with my husband. If you really believe she's virtuous after you watched her do all that, then she's playing you harder than a coked-up executive on a squash court. Whose idea was it to frame me as a crazy lady who had a breakdown?"

"You *are* a crazy lady who had a breakdown," he growled. "You tried to kill me."

No buzz. He was telling the truth. He thought I really did try to kill him. Of course, I didn't mean to—my magic exploded out of me and tore the whole room apart. But he'd gotten hurt badly, and it was my fault.

A sharp stab of guilt plunged into my heart, throwing me off balance. When I opened my mouth next, it came out in a soft whine. "You were cheating on me, Vincent. It's no excuse for what happened, but I caught you in bed with Seraphina. Both of you lied about that, and it made me look crazy. Two years, Vince. It was hell. I lost *everything*."

"I didn't mean for all that to happen," he muttered, looking away. No buzz zinged over my skin. That was the truth, too.

"Maybe you didn't. But you let it happen. I gave you

everything, Vincent." I smiled at him sadly. "You threw me away like garbage. I hope Seraphina is worth it."

He stared at me, inhaling angrily through his nose. I could almost see the thoughts buzzing in his brain. For the first time he wondered if he'd made a horrible mistake. The ex-wife he'd thrown away was standing in front of him, wearing couture, framed by a building she owned and a gold Lamborghini, looking better, richer, and more valuable than ever before.

He was furious. The mask was gone. This is the real Vincent I was looking at now.

"Of course she's worth it. She's giving me what I *always* wanted. A family. My legacy. There's nothing more important than family, Susan," he spat out through clenched teeth. "Fuck all the rest of it. You know what? You're just jealous. You can make fun of Seraphina all you want, but she's young, and she's beautiful, and she's pregnant with my child. *You* couldn't do that. You're old and dried up—Ouch! Ahhh! What the hell?"

Cecil had bounced forward and sank his teeth into Vincent's leg. "Grrr. Arr." He bit him again. "Arrr. *Arr*ogant asshole."

"He bit me!" Vincent hissed, outraged. "Susan, your fucking dog bit me!" He smacked Cecil away, and Cecil bounded back in and bit him on the other leg. "Ow! You little—" Vincent kicked out, but Cecil dodged him and ducked down into a play-bow, before bounding forward, sinking his teeth into Vincent's shin, and gnawing at his leg. "Get him off me!"

"Grrr. Grrr... yip! Yip! Yyyylittle prick!"

I took a couple of steps back. "He doesn't seem to like you much, does he?"

"I swear—ouch! Susan... owww!" Vincent dropped into a crouch, trying to swat at Cecil before he ducked in to bite again. "Call your dog off right now. I will have this fucking thing *destroyed* just like I—"

I went cold. "Just like what? Just like what, Vincent?"

He glared.

A wave of pure anguish washed through me. It took me a whole thirty seconds before I could speak, and when I did, the lump in my throat almost choked me. "Rusty didn't run away, did he?"

Cecil lunged. Vince waved his arms frantically. "He did!"

Buzz.

Oh, God. That's why the woman in the shelter was confused. She told me specifically that Rusty hadn't come in as a rescue, and that he'd been put down some time ago.

"It's true," I whispered. "You took Rusty in to get put down, because you couldn't be bothered looking after him when I went to jail."

"No, Susan." *Buzz.* "I would never do that!" *Buzz.* "Now, please call off your dog. I'm bleeding, for Christ's sake!"

He was. His light blue jeans were stained dark with his blood.

I shrugged. "He's not my dog, Vincent." I turned away. I couldn't even look at him anymore. "Of all the things you've done to me, this feels like the thing that might kill me. My sweet Rusty," I whispered. "He never hurt anyone. And he loved you."

"It's not my fault! He started peeing on the rugs, and Seraphina is allergic... Ow! You little... Call this damn animal off now, Susan!"

"I told you, he's not my dog. I don't own him, Vince. You can threaten me all you like, but it won't get you anywhere this time." Tears flooded my eyes, but I didn't want him to see me cry, so I walked towards the buzzer and hit the thumbpad. The door clicked open. "Don't come back, Vincent. I don't want to see you ever again."

"Ouch! You bitch! You fucking old hag— Ahh! I swear to God, Susan, I'm going to get my lawyers out here so fast, and they're gonna—Ow! You little... My lawyers are going to take this building, and your new salary, and everything else! I'm going to— Ahhh! My balls!"

CHAPTER
TWENTY-FIVE

Violet House had made me my own private elevator. I saw it as soon as I walked inside the atrium—beautiful scarlet and gold embossed doors with an old-fashioned bronze birdcage around it. It had one button, a security thumbpad. I smiled sadly. I'd just been thinking about how much I desperately needed some solitude, and my House had given me the peace I needed.

"Thanks, Violet," I whispered. The birdcage gates slid aside, and the doors opened. I entered and pressed the single button. Penthouse.

Above the door, two lights flashed, one after the other. Guest Quarters. Main Suite. Guest Quarters. Main Suite.

Violet House was asking me if I wanted to check on Audrina. "Is she okay? I thought she'd probably be asleep by now." It was well past midnight.

The Main Suite light clicked on and stayed on. Okay, Audrina was fine, and Violet wanted me to get some rest. I'd check in with Audrina tomorrow and make a plan to deal with her horrible mother.

The elevator dinged, and the doors slid open. I pushed

the birdcage gate aside and stepped directly into my beautiful drawing room.

My heart gave a stutter.

Donovan was there, by the window, looking out. He'd changed out of his beautiful dinner jacket and trousers and was back in his princely fae attire—tight black leather pants with a loose black shirt.

"You're okay," I exhaled. I hadn't realized it, but the fear niggled at me like a thorn stuck in my foot. It still did, in fact. For some reason, I was still worried about him. But he was here, and he was safe.

The rest of his company would be fine, too. Donovan wouldn't be here if they weren't. They must be in their quarters, resting.

Donovan turned to face me and smiled. "I am."

I swallowed roughly. He'd left the buttons of his shirt undone, as if he'd thrown it on as an afterthought. I must have interrupted him getting changed. The glorious, hard muscles of his chest were on display.

He took a step closer to me. "I have been waiting for you, Chosen." The candlelight flickered, throwing the features of his blisteringly handsome face into greater contrast. Those cheekbones. That hard, masculine jaw. The curve of his lips as he smiled at me softly. Oh, God.

I felt... terrified. "Y- Y- You have?"

He nodded, walking closer, his footsteps slow and deliberate. "I wanted to talk with you before you retired for the evening." Dark emerald eyes bored into mine, devouring me.

"You did?" My voice squeaked. "About what?"

His eyes dropped to my collarbones. "The future. What will happen after all the spark stones are closed." He came closer still, and I caught a hint of his scent—dangerous, explosive like whiskey and fireworks.

"What..." I swallowed. My heart beat wildly, like it was trying to escape out of my chest. "What about the future?"

His beautiful lips curled up again. "We should discuss the prophecy."

"P–P–P–Prophecy?" My knees shook.

"Hmm." The low rumble of assent came from deep within his chest and vibrated through me. "You have a say in your own fate, Chosen, but you must be curious about the prophecy."

I remembered Donovan mentioning a prophecy once or twice before. The first time, in fact, he'd shouted so loud my ears hurt. *Damn the prophecy.*

"We can discuss it later," he said, his voice low, vibrating over my skin. "I am merely glad you are here, in that dress."

He was too close. Too close. My breath felt shallow. I was terrified.

"I find myself unable to concentrate on serious matters tonight." He raised his hand and put it on my shoulder, gently stroking my bare skin with his thumb. "You look like a rose in full bloom at twilight."

"You know..." My voice shook. I paused and swallowed.

"What is it, Chosen?" He leaned in.

"When Donovan told me about his brother..." I looked up and met his eye. "He never mentioned that you were twins."

Fire burned in his eyes, and his hand moved so fast I could barely see it, slamming up against my neck. His fist clenched around my throat just as I let the heat erupt. **"Sto–"**

Too late. I'd been too late. I let him get too close, and he'd choked the command out of me. It didn't work. He was still moving.

Connor's face twisted. His hand tightened on my neck,

and the other hand gripped me by my upper arm. He strode forward, slamming me against the wall. Massive fingers moved on my neck, up to my throat, a wordless threat—he could crush my windpipe with just a quick flex of his hands.

"Clever girl," Connor murmured, leaning close to inhale my perfume. "Not many can tell us apart. Of course, Donovan cannot impersonate me so easily." His lips tightened for a second. "Probably because he has never bothered to try, as far as I know. But I fooled our mother for years, whenever the mood struck me. And our father. And our sisters." He gave a low chuckle. "And all of Donovan's lady friends. He always got *so* cross about that."

The floorboards rumbled beneath my feet; Violet House was confused, terrified. Desperately, I tried to send her a message. *It's not Donovan! It's not him!*

She trembled, scared and unsure.

It was so obvious to me. It had been obvious the second Connor turned around and smiled at me.

Donovan didn't smile. And Donovan didn't look at me like I was a piece of meat he wanted to eat. Connor did, though. To him, I was an object to claim. A female to devour.

When Donovan looked at me, it was either in exasperation or confusion. Mostly, he stared at me in angry frustration. Occasionally, he looked at me... cautiously. Tenderly.

But this wasn't him, and I'd known it almost straight away.

"There's no point appealing to your Domicile," Connor said. "She is too confused. She is still a child, you know. She does not understand that Donovan and I aren't the same person, and she would never defy the Heir," he added, a touch of sarcasm in his tone.

Connor was going to kill me. His hand was too tight on

my throat already; I couldn't get any air. Desperately, I stomped my foot on the floorboards. *Come on, Violet.*

He rolled his eyes slightly. "There is no help coming for you now, Chosen. My brother and his company are still out there killing my banwyn and searching for my assassins. And that ridiculous duocorn of yours is currently chasing a bloodied man towards the harbor." His gaze settled on my trembling lips. They must be turning blue.

"I arranged it all so we would have some privacy to speak candidly. I was hoping that I would be able to persuade you to see things my way. We could do away with all this foolishness of you running around this Middle World, closing all the spark stones. I could have saved you so much trouble," he sighed, and leaned back slightly. "You could have chosen me. The prophecy allowed for the possibility, you know."

I gritted my teeth. Never. Never in a million years.

"But," he sighed. "Thanks to the otherwise useless magic of the eoinn spark stone, I see your loyalty has already been solidified in favor of my brother. Trying to persuade you otherwise would be a waste of"—his hand squeezed; I let out a gurgled cry—"oxygen." He chuckled, watching me choke. He enjoyed my pain.

Desperately, I pulled at the heat in my belly. I needed to do something. Anything...

"And it's a shame," Connor went on silkily. "I am right, of course. My family lacks both ambition and vision. It is so disappointing that they cannot see it. We have conquered our realm, and we already rule the whole Upper World by default of military might and the fact of our higher status in the evolutionary chain. But for some reason, my family seems reluctant to take those next steps." He tilted his head, regarding me thoughtfully. "I am the only one brave enough to speak the truth out loud—the only one with the strength of will to do something about it. I don't think anyone truly understands how precarious the balance between all the realms is. We need to take our rightful place as rulers of all the Worlds, or our whole universe could devolve into chaos."

Desperately, I kicked out with my legs, trying to knee him in the balls, but he pushed his massive body up against me, holding me firmly against the wall.

God, he was so big, so strong. I couldn't move an inch.

"Don't fight me," he murmured. "I mean, you can. It won't do any good. You should know that I am already far too powerful. I have devoured a dozen spark stones already. And I will have them all."

Violet twitched beneath my feet. I could feel her shaking, terrified. Connor's hand tightened. The edges of my vision blurred.

I felt his breath on my cheek. "It's a shame it had to come to this, Chosen, but the prophecy is clear. I didn't want Donovan to die, but it can't be helped. Only one of us can rule, after all. No, no. Don't be sad," he whispered, his lips against my skin. "Don't be scared. My brother will follow you into the afterlife shortly."

No. Donovan couldn't die.

The heat flared inside of me, erupting like a volcano, and streamed into every inch of my body. I held back nothing. I exploded, blasting everything I could and letting all the pain and fear and anger shake the atoms of the room.

Connor flew back away from me, landing in a crouch. "You whore," he growled. "How dare—"

Desperately I shoved out with my magic. I had no control. I didn't know what I was doing, I had no idea what I was feeling, what I was gripping with my raw magic, what I was doing. All I knew was that I had to get Connor away from me. I pushed. His feet slid backwards on the floorboards. His eyes flashed.

I took a breath; my throat felt raw, powerless. Only a croak came out. A wave of exhaustion crashed into me. I was already burned out. I had barely anything left.

Connor straightened up, glaring at me. "You are a fool," he spat out. "You have no idea what you're—"

"Chosen!" The shout came from outside, in the hallway. Donovan?

"Violet, let me in!" Donovan roared.

My house shook uncontrollably; floorboards groaning, walls cracking. She was too scared. And I was too tired to stand any longer. I sank to the ground, soothing her with my hands. *It's okay, Violet. It's okay.*

Connor stomped back towards me in only two steps, yanking me back up by my hair. I tried to scream but nothing came out. My throat was on fire; my legs refused to obey me. I had no strength left. Connor wrapped his arm around my neck and held me up.

Donovan's voice in the hallway turned grim. "I will apologize for this later, Violet."

Bang.

The door exploded. My house flinched, and I felt her whimper.

Donovan strode in—an avenging angel, Lucifer fallen from heaven, sword drawn, murder in his eyes. "Let her go."

Connor laughed. "You changed your mind, brother? I thought you wouldn't care. You wish to keep her after all? You were always so adamant that you would not be a slave to fate."

"Let her go, Connor," Donovan growled, stalking closer, his knuckles white on the sword. "This is between you and me."

"No. She is already tied to you now, brother. In fact, it is a pleasant surprise. I don't need to kill both of you to get you out of my way. I only need to kill one, and—"

I turned my head and sank my teeth into his bicep, biting as hard as I could.

Connor screamed and shook me off. I fell to the floor and rolled away, hugging the floorboards. I tried to comfort my terrified House. *See, Violet?* I silently begged her. *There's two of them.*

Magic pulsed through the room as the brothers clashed, and a sound like a clap of thunder almost deafened me. Donovan roared, padding forwards on powerful legs, delivering crushing blows, thrusting, blocking, turning to miss the sword strikes by mere inches. Connor glided back and forth like he was boneless and lashed out in lightning-fast strikes.

Watch them. I patted the floor gently. I could barely see what was happening myself, my vision was blurring in and out. *See how different they are? It's like watching a python and a panther doing battle.*

Violet House shook, groaning softly. I understood her. She didn't know which one was the bad guy; it wasn't obvious to her. One of them had held me by the throat, but she wasn't sure if it was just an aggressive cuddle or not. And the other one had blown up her door.

Swords clashed again; the strike sent both stumbling back. Both blades were cracked down to the hilt, destroyed. Donovan tossed his aside carelessly, his face stony. Connor snarled and threw his broken sword hard against the wall. It caught the edge of the window; a pane of glass shattered.

Donovan wouldn't do that, Violet. He only broke your door so he could get in.

They fought hand-to-hand now; I wished my eyes could follow. Violent smacks, thuds, punches. Donovan's lip was cut, a smear of blood across his cheek.

I swallowed. It felt like I was trying to choke down a hot coal. "You can do it, Violet," I whispered. "I trust you."

I felt her shiver underneath me. Just then, Connor let out a terrible snarl, his words vibrating with dark magic—a curse left his lips. A flash of green light flared in the dark room. Donovan stumbled back, a ragged line of scarlet ripped across his chest.

I screamed. "Donovan!"

Connor flexed both arms. Daggers appeared in his palms, pitch-black, glinting malevolently, and he stomped towards his brother.

Violet shivered and moved. The floorboards rose up before the evil twin like a wave, and he slid backwards down the incline. His mouth twisted; he bounded upwards, daggers raised for the killing blow.

Go on, I begged her.

The broken window melted away like it was plastic exposed to a flame; a huge hole appeared in the wall, and Violet House flexed her floorboards with a sharp push. One board snapped free, shooting upwards, it smacked Connor right in the face. He stumbled back and righted himself easily, but the floorboards carried him, moving underneath his feet, pushing him out the open window.

He gave a scream of pure rage as he fell.

EPILOGUE

Cecil wouldn't stop crying. Balled-up tissues were scattered all over the kitchen floor, gathering in messy piles like tumbleweed against the designer furniture. He clomped towards me, still on his two hind legs, holding the little cup of espresso between his hooves. A stream of boogers poured from his snout. It was a good thing that Bart had taken Audrina out to get ice cream, or else she'd be wondering where the sad ghost noises were coming from.

Audrina needed cheering up. I made her reach out to her mother, Jessica, by email, first thing in the morning to let her know she was safe, and she'd contact her soon.

She got a message back almost immediately, but it wasn't from her mother. It was from Jessica's lawyer, who demanded Audrina go home immediately, or there would be horrific consequences. We had no idea what those consequences would be, but judging by the fact that she'd activated her lawyers, I assumed Audrina would be disinherited and buried in lawsuits the second she turned eighteen.

Jessica had already brought out the big guns, and we

hadn't even started the battle yet. If she caught wind that Audrina was in the building next door, hiding out with me, a recently released psychiatric patient... I'd be in deep shit.

I wasn't worried. Not yet, anyway. But Audrina was distraught.

Just like everyone else around here.

"Here's your cof-of-of-of-fee," Cecil sobbed, holding the cup out to me. "Cho-oh-oh-oh-sen. Can I get you"—sniff—"anything el-hel-hel-se?"

"Cecil," I sighed. "Please sit down."

"No," he cried. "I am not worthy of sitting. If I must rest, I will lie down in the dirt, where I belong."

"We're on the fiftieth floor, Cecil. There's no dirt up here."

"I'll bury myself down in the basement like the worm I am!"

"For God's sa—" I huffed out a breath. "For the last time, it wasn't your fault!"

"I wasn't with you, Chosen. You got attacked in your own home by our worst enemy, and I wasn't there for you!"

"No. You were too busy protecting me in another way, Cecil. I'll always be grateful you stood up to Vincent for me."

The stranglehold my ex-husband had on my heart was gone. I could almost feel it physically. Vincent wasn't the man I loved. He never had been.

The man I loved didn't exist. Instead of mourning him like he was dead, I mourned the love that never was.

"That human?" Cecil sniffed and tossed his mane back dramatically. "He was not even worth the effort. I got carried away."

"You chased him, bleeding and crying, all the way into the bay. He had to get rescued by the marine unit."

Cecil's lips wobbled. "And I left you in your greatest time of need. Oh, I bring shame on my whole family!"

"I thought you hated your family."

"If I wanted to shame them, Chosen, I would have carpeted the bathroom, put a plastic laminate countertop in the kitchen, and painted a feature wall in primary colors in every room. I wouldn't ever do something so embarrassing like leaving my charge alone to get attacked by a mad tyrant!"

"I'm *fine*, Cecil."

I was fine now, anyway. I broke a habit of a lifetime and even tried to take the day off work, just so I could recover. Yvette approved it, urging me to rest, and come back fresh after the long weekend.

I only lasted two hours before I got fed up with all the brooding and dragged myself into the office.

And it was a good thing I did. Not only was I managing my own team, but I also had Ritchie's team to cover. Richie, apparently, had sent a curt text message to Yvette yesterday, resigning effective immediately. According to his office cronies, Richie had a family emergency.

In Alaska. He wouldn't be coming back. The promotion just had to be signed off by the executives, and it was mine.

Cecil sniffed back an escaping long dribble of snot. "Oh, I will never recover! Never!"

I swore under my breath. Donovan had been bad enough to have to deal with in the fallout of his brother's attack. If tortured brooding was an Olympic sport, Donovan would win every single medal. He also blamed himself for Connor attacking me.

At least he was quiet about it. Cecil was driving me crazy.

They all blamed themselves. Cress, Nate, and Eryk all

indulged in a little self-flagellation when they returned to Violet House and stumbled upon Donovan and me, bleeding all over each other on the floor of the drawing room. Luckily, the ragged cut on Donovan's chest was mostly healed by Nate's first-aid glowing hands. He'd healed my bruised neck, too, although my throat was still scratchy and sore.

Connor had disappeared. I'd been hoping we'd find him later, splattered like a goth watermelon on the sidewalk, but Cress reported seeing a bright flash of green light outside Violet House as they were running towards us. There was no trace of him anywhere, so they could only assume he'd opened a mini-pocket dimension and disappeared rather than do the convenient thing and fall to his death.

He was out there somewhere, planning his next move, his next attack. Deciding on his next target. The company was out there in the city, trying to find traces of him right now.

None of them were surprised Connor had fooled Violet House, though, and confused her enough she didn't know which twin was which. I found it odd, until Cress patiently explained that at one point or another, Connor had fooled all of them. Apparently he'd impersonated Donovan on a number of occasions with devastating consequences. None of them would elaborate any further.

I didn't understand it. Donovan and Connor felt like opposites to me. They didn't even look alike. Connor was just a man. Donovan was...

He was the full moon on a dark night. He was gravity, holding me to the earth. He was an avenging angel. A living god. My walking salvation.

"Oh, no," I moaned, slumping on the table.

"What have I done now?" Cecil wailed.

"It's not you." Dread settled in my belly. This was the worst thing that could possibly happen. "It's me."

I was falling in love with Donovan.

The front door slammed open, and Bart rushed in, his face pale, shaking from head to toe.

I leapt to my feet. "Bart! What is it?"

He stared at me, his eyes wide. "They've taken her. They *took* her, Susan. They thought she was you!"

Audrina. Oh, God, no.

"Who, Bart?" I demanded. "Who took her?"

He swallowed roughly. "The berserkers."

TO BE CONTINUED

Printed in Great Britain
by Amazon